FOR LOVE OF JACK LONDON

FOR LOVE OF JACK LONDON

His Life with Jennie Prentiss— a True Love Story

EUGENE P. LASARTEMAY
AND
MARY RUDGE

VANTAGE PRESS
New York • Los Angeles

Some minor characters or conversations in this book are composites, fictionalized versions, or archetypal representation of real people or ideas.

Published by Vantage Press, Inc.
516 West 34th Street, New York, New York 10001

Manufactured in the United States of America
ISBN: 0-533-08838-0

Library of Congress Catalog Card No.: 89-90494

1   2   3   4   5   6   7   8   9   0

To Ruth Hackett Lasartemay, who through her constant urging and assistance inspired her husband, Eugene Lasartemay, to center his years of research since 1966 on the life of one Mrs. Jennie Prentiss, a black woman known by relatives, friends, and acquaintances to have been the foster mother of Jack London.

Appreciation is expressed to the many wonderful people, some mentioned in these pages, as well as others too numerous to mention, whom the authors have known or met while gathering information for this manuscript and those whom Mr. Lasartemay met through his work as originator and first president of the East Bay Negro Historical Society and Library Museum, now established at the Golden Gate Branch of the Oakland Public Library—a life's work he shared with his beloved wife.

The greatest and strangest of all novels is life itself.

PREFACE

We hope, in this book, to show how a black woman, in kindness, loved and raised to adolescence a boy of the white race.

Jennie Prentiss, a black person, born the daughter of slaves, was married to Alonzo Thomas Prentiss, a son of a slave owner and one of his slaves. Alonzo's mother was very fair. She was consequently taken for white in the white community. Alonzo kept his lips sealed on the subject of race. Jennie also never mentioned the subject of her husband's race, due to the shocks he had received in his life in this very area. Racial problems had severed his career with the army, had created many personal conflicts in his life, and had stood in the way of his employment. Alonzo Prentiss lived the life of a white man, not always by choice.

Jack London knew of the situation. He too kept it concealed. Throughout his life his actions and attitudes indicated how delicate the subject of racism was to him. He learned early in life how hard it was to live as a black. He learned kindness and later in his adult life acknowledged through his own acts of kindness just what he had received from the special interracial relationship he had with Jennie Prentiss.

This story gives witness to knowledge, outside the scope of previous researchers and writers, that members of the black community have shared about this heritage and how the interaction of closely intertwined lives shaped human destiny and had an effect on American literature.

The true story of the relationship of Mrs. Jennie Prentiss to Jack London has never been published. It is in order to honor and give credit to a stalwart black woman, proud of her race, and to acknowledge her contribution to the life of Jack London, one of America's most renowned authors, that we tell this story.

Jennie Prentiss nursed Jack from her own breast and raised him into teenage years, instilling many qualities into his character. Jack London recognized Mrs. Jennie Prentiss, throughout his life, as his second mother.

Jack London was first introduced to religion in the Sunday school of the First African Methodist Episcopal Church located on 15th Street, near Market Street, in Oakland, California, where Jennie Prentiss was an active member of the church's Mother's Charity Club. She remained a member of the club and church until her death. Though originally a Baptist, registered on the rolls of the Berean Baptist Church of Chicago, she worshiped and served her faith as a Methodist, as there were no established black Baptist churches in Oakland at this time. One of Jack London's sizable charitable contributions was to this place of Jennie Prentiss's worship, made in 1915.

Although it is well known that in his adult life London became a socialist, the writer is certain that when the reader has finished this story of Jennie Prentiss and Jack London, he/she will more easily understand why this exceptionally fine man became a socialist, why as a boy he became an author, and, as certainly, why this strange but very special story of Jennie Prentiss and Jack London has never been written until now.

ACKNOWLEDGMENTS

Certain conversations and characters in this book are composites and prototypes. All are symbolic of real people who interacted with members of the Prentiss and London families. Those thus presented as factionalized versions or archetypal representation of real people are: Caroline, Sally Mulcahey, Mary Foley, Mr. and Mrs. Baker, the English couple, Mr. and Mrs. Roanoke, some of the characters in chapters 2, 4, and 10, some of the characters in chapter 11, the men in the bar in chapter 16, and the storekeepers in Alameda. All others have been documented and researched by the authors, and some also, where reference is made, by authors of other published books on Jack London.

Acknowledgment is given that chapter 26 is composed of information from Alameda's first newspaper, the *Argus* and the *Encinal*, compiled by Melody Decena for *Alameda Heritage Days Souvenir Album, 1978*, and edited by Mary Rudge, published by Mary Rudge and committee; Alan J. McKean, Melody Decena, Alice Grace Chalip, Brent Ryder, for City of Alameda Heritage Days. The poem introducing chapter 32 is part of a poem by Mary Rudge published in *To Build a Fire*, the Oakland anthology edited by Floyd Salas and published in 1976 by Mark Ross, GRT Printing (then California Syllabus), 1494 MacArthur Boulevard, Oakland. Descriptions of early Oakland in chapter 35 were inspired in part by the historical photo collection of the Oakland Free Public Library. From the article "Reverend George Washington Woodbey: Early Twentieth Century California Black Socialist," by Philip S. Foner, professor of history at Lincoln University, published in the *Journal of Negro History* in April 1976, was derived information and quotations for the development of Chapter 43. Information on the Forty-ninth Infantry in chapter 3 is based on Civil War documentation, "Ohio in the War."

In coauthoring this book, Mary Rudge stated she "read every other book available to me on and or by Jack London, researched materials in the Oakland, Berkeley, Alameda, San Francisco libraries, the Jack London material at Bancroft Library, University of California, Berkeley, made trips to Glen Ellen, the Valley of the Moon, the House of Happy Walls, created by Chairman London, the Jack London museum and ruins of Wolf House, and Carmel and Monterey searching for Jack London memorabilia. Thanks are due to numerous persons in all of these areas, with special thanks to Robert Martens of Star Rover Press (based in a historic house Jack London once occupied in Oakland), James Sisson (deceased), Harriet Ziskin, Maureen Hartmann, and Helen Malkerson, all of which live in Oakland; Jesse Beagle of Berkeley, my grandmother Mary Lucretia Roberts Moss Millar Stafford of Louisiana and Texas and uncle John Eaton Millar of Louisiana, Texas, California, and Mississippi (both deceased), who from my childhood shared with me personal reminiscences about plantation life, slavery, the Civil War, the experiences of Irish people, and other social history of which they knew or were a part; Louis L'Amour, who visited my school in Oklahoma and validated for me the joy and purpose of being a writer, which enhanced and changed my life, though he never knew and would have been surprised to know and be thanked; and my late father, Glen Seymour Woods, who introduced me as a child to the works of Jack London and created my lifelong interest in Jack London's life, which I pursued upon coming to Jack London's own inspirational epicenter, Oakland, and the island, Alameda, where I live in a hundred-year-old house across from the once site of the Kohlmoos Hotel that became Anderson's Co-ed Academy, where Jack London prepared for the university and where I formerly lived in a housing project on land adjoining the ruins of the Clarke Pottery and Tile Works and acreage farmed by John London. Jack London's history permeates this area.

The following sources were used by Eugene Lasartemay: Mrs. Joan London Miller (now deceased), Jack London's daughter; Mrs. Esther Jones Lee (now deceased), for whom Jennie Prentiss acted as midwife; Mrs. Ione Wright (now deceased), playmate of Jack London; Mr. Maynard Wilds, (now deceased), son of Jennie's close friend; Mr. Irving Shepard (now deceased), son of Eliza London Shepard and Executive, after Eliza's death, of Jack London's estate; Mr. Russ Kingman, former director of Jack London Square, Oakland, California; the Oakland Free Public Library; the city directories of Oakland, San Francisco, and Alameda; Oakland and Alameda Unified School Districts; the Oakland Public Schools Microfilm Section; the Oakland Public Schools Guidance Department; Fouché-Hudson Funeral Home; the Albert Brown Mortuary; East Bay Contra Costa Title Company; the *Alameda Recorder*; the State of California Vital Statistics Department; the Alameda Historical Society; Mountain View Cemetery, Oakland, California; Napa State Hospital; General Services Administration, Washington, D.C.; the State Library and Archives, Nashville, Tennessee; the State Library of Ohio, Columbus; Mothers' Charity Club (with assistance of the East Bay Negro Historical Society, Inc.); Miss Theo Bruce, Flora Disard-Bruce's daughter; Ms. Ruth Bridges Stoval, Moriah Bridges's granddaughter; Mrs. Genevieve Thomas; Ms. Elizabeth Fisher Gordon; wife of the late Hon. Walter A. Gordon, and Mrs. Dorothy L. Akers, Lucy Ann Dewson's niece.

INTRODUCTION

This novel is intended to tell the human saga of the courageous Prentiss family and their friends, who helped shape the mind, character, and destiny of one of America's foremost writers, Jack London, in his formative years, especially of Jennie Prentiss who was bonded to him for life by their love. It is to acknowledge the contribution of persons of the Negro race in the shaping of a person great in American literature. It is to praise and honor and include the love and contribution of other races, as well as of this special black family and their extended community, in the life of Jack London. And it is to stand as a tribute to the many writers who have written masterful works, based on what they could document. It is for this reason that the research of Eugene Lasartemay, encompassing more than twenty years of his own lifetime, has special importance for all writers. Andrew Sinclair, another chronicler of Jack London, states of his own two years' research: "A biographer is entirely dependent upon the testimony he can find."[1] Eugene Lasartemay had access to previously untapped resources, the rich, vital perceptions of an interconnected black community, that enabled this book to reveal previously unpublished truths.

Jack London himself wrote: "I have lived twenty-five years of repression . . . There are Poseurs. I am the most successful of them all . . ." in a letter to Anna Strunsky. Beginning with a partially untrue biography he concocted for his first publishers, even from the first instances of his life at school, when he bypassed his own home to protect himself from peer ridicule and shaming of his extended family, Jack knew his vulnerability. Responding to a publisher's insistence that he present a good face for his readers, he realized he must create a fictional Jack London.

This persona, vivid as any character he imagined, received additional embellishment from both Flora and his widow, Charmain, through the years. Jack also rewrote himself, giving heroic attributes as needed. But his goal, to achieve a humane existence for mankind, remained constant though his self-image and his means to his goal changed.

In a letter written just before his death Jack wanted to make a last method for his purpose clear: ". . . I am trying to do what the Chinese have done for forty centuries . . ." He was rebuilding land, restoring the quality of the earth.

xiii

Our purpose here is to work that fertile, protean material that comprises the earthly life of Jack London, regenerating, acknowledging others that have "worked the land," and having the hope that because we have written he will be a more understood human; our purpose is to restore the man, sharing new knowledge on the depth of his humanity. Although he claimed to have given twenty-five years, which he called "the flower of my life," to moving and changing the world through social action and considered that under socialism no race problems could exist and that it would mean a fulfillment of religion's precepts as a plan for feeding the world's hungry, he, according to Andrew Sinclair, could give up one plan for a better one. His interest later turned toward a new knowledge presented by psychology for understanding and changing the nature of man, creator of social plans. He could thus profess to believe: "The remedy for social ills did not lie in the faiths of the jangling sects, but only in the individual's nobility of action and love of mankind."

Remembering himself as the child who hungered for meat, starving on failing farms because of human failure, remembering he was exploited in factories with work that brought too little earnings to appease his hunger and those he struggled to feed and that he sacrificed the poetry he dreamed of writing to turn himself into a writing machine for the selling, to financially care for those depending on him, he wanted at last to produce a farm model to serve people as he had described them and their needs, in his model of compassion, *People of the Abyss*.

He was demonstrating his concern for the earth and for feeding the world's people through what could be brought forth from the earth. He was showing this love by demonstrating what could be done through human vision, just as he proved he could support others by his ideas in writing, the product of his own mind. That he went to death with this love and concern intact is a significant statement on his nobility of action and love of mankind. Something of him lives on, so we write.

Our voices tell that religion and its purposes were an underlying motif throughout the life and times of Jack London, just as spiritualism and its possibilities were an influence on Flora. Then emergence of Psychology as a natural science relevant to the world's human evolution captured the imagination of Jack London. He died before a body of his work expressed it. But had his life not suddenly ended he may well eventually have written such a book, as his was a constantly evolving mind.

After his death there were some who claimed Jack London wrote through them or spoke to them. Sir Arthur Conan Doyle, a spiritualist, corresponded with some of these claimants, stating his belief that if any writer could evolve beyond the barrier of death to continue as a creative literary force, Jack London, because of his strength and endurance as a writer, would be the one.

The spirit in which this book is written speaks to the provocative question: Why Jack London, that you should be concerned now with his life? Almost as interesting as: Who are you that you should be concerned? Valid questions.

There are some good ideas that are an answer for almost everything, including these questions. These relevant ideas are present here, as taken from a book by Stewart Edward White (1873–1946) who, as Jack London did, authored many short stories and books, much writing. They sometimes had similar themes. I believe these two writers knew and influenced each other well.

These are from *The Betty Book*, now out of print but available in the Bancroft Library, University of California, Berkeley, and these statements are not here in sequential order. Read the book for the context in which they are used there, and further development of the author's own thought, which continues in a subsequent book, *The Unobstructed Universe*. I chose only what is a relevant voice to the writing of this book and its content. Here is what is important:

There is a terrible responsibility for entering this consciousness, and that is to do more than your share to make up for accumulated wrongness. Be a sympathetic workman in clearing up the debris of folly, stupidity, misunderstanding.

We evolve by the assimilation of experience.

For this evolving we are responsible not only to ourselves and neighbor but to all that make up our world of belief, through the perspective of time.

Bountifulness makes it possible, as surely and accurately as the human heart exists, to pass on what we have received.

What you are emanates, transmuted into an available earth source. This is the secret of religion.

Any progress or work has its accidents and failures. What compensations and faults there are and how they are made good is the issue.

Your spiritual instinct prompts your questioning of seemingly random impulses.

This includes the grafts from life to life of those handicapped, who die young, who have unexplained lives; the grafts mean some crossed growth, to a purpose.

A world run as it is demonstrates individual responsibility.

Choose inspiration, whether in the gifts of the dead or the living.

MARY RUDGE

We go through book after book on the life of Jack London and we find writers that speak of the mysterious Jack, the alcoholic Jack, or the racist Jack. For this reason the true life story of Jack's early boyhood should come to light. To look into those years of his life is to learn of his playmates and, in adult life, his friends, his girlfriend, his companions on his trip to the Klondike, Alaska, and, back again in California, to understand his continuing love and devotion to his foster mother, Jennie Prentiss, and her family.

That I have tried to make this material available to all writers in the past by encouraging collectors of Jack London memorabilia to look to this information and by trying to have material displayed in public museums to bring this material to light is a matter of record.

I have included in the appendix letters that I have written, to have Jennie Prentiss recognized for her contribution to the life of Jack London, as well as a speech which I presented on numerous occasions. My presentation was attended by and complimented by certain family and friends of Jack London and supporters of the memory of Jack London. Not once were any of the facts ever contradicted by anyone. In fact, some family members, in support of what I said publicly, gave me whatever documenting evidence they could so I could continue making this public. It has culminated in this book.

I have personally felt that Jennie Prentiss was discriminated against by those who have minimized her importance to Jack London because she was a member of the black race, and it is to right this wrong to her that this book must be shared. If these facts have not been included before in publications, it is because of the separateness still existing between black and white communities so that previous writers did not seek out knowledge and opinions and material that members of the black community possess and give validity to, which are presented here. It is to right this wrong done to the black members of our world who could make contribution to the publication of material about the life of Jennie Prentiss and Jack London that this story is now made public and this book published, as well as to present to the world this further information about Jack London, an American writer known and loved all over the world.

EUGENE LASARTEMAY

Note

1. Andrew Sinclair, *Jack: Biography of Jack London* (New York: Washington Square Press, Inc., 1983).

FOR LOVE OF JACK LONDON

CHAPTER 1

Some of the fellows from the Saturday-afternoon sandlot baseball teams were sprawled informally in the rough bleachers and on the sun-warmed grass, sweat towels around their necks, sarsparillas and root beers from the push-stand man who routinely came through the park in their hands. Good-natured sports, they recognized each others' strengths in a sporting game, which would be the last play for some of them who, within a week, would be gone to the deadly serious game of war.

" 'A house divided cannot stand,' " Larry repeated to himself the suddenly popular catch phrase that almost everyone was saying. His mind was full of thoughts that had been coming so fast he didn't know when his mind had ever thrown him so many fast ones!

Those Southerners seceding from the Union got to be stopped from weakening the country, he thought. *Must be some stupid, ignorant country people, who can't see what they are doing, selfish people thinking only of their personal fortune, putting their economical gain ahead of their nation's good, making a civil war!*

I don't know so much about the slave issue—haven't studied it—but secession is the thing. We got to fight. Those Southerners don't understand about being a team. What it is about is just having the right spirit!

The boys from Tiffin, Ohio can show them, learn them a thing or two about unity, strength.

Haven't the papers just pictured one of them political leaders taking a bundle of sticks and showing how one by one they could be broken but held together no power could break them? This has got to be a united nation.

We can't let the South break off and endanger the strength of a growing country, can't let them get away with that now.

Look at Alonzo there now; he's a good player, outstanding! A real teammate, a natural leader, somewhat on the strong, silent type, nevertheless popular, impressive already joined up to be a part of this cause that is greater than one individual's concern. Well, hell, if Alonzo can leave a wife and little kids to join up so can some of the others. We know how to play the game.

Of course, Ruth's family is well fixed. Her old man will look after her and the kids, and Alonzo's parents will be glad to help, too, no question.

But look at me. I got no sweetheart even. Naturally I'll go, and Joe. His dad can spare him from the foundry, and Bud, sure, we'll all go!

I'm the best pitcher around here. I got a good eye and a steady hand. That's going to make me a good soldier.

1

CHAPTER 2

He never thought about black women, why should he? Or about black men either. His mother was mulatto, but she was very fair skinned and was taken for white, and his father was white. Alonzo was fair skinned and his features were Caucasian. The race of his family, and his own, was never questioned.

The friends he played with and went to school with, and his associates throughout adult life had all been white, so it was natural that he married a white girl, Ruth A. McConnell, with whom he had no reason to consider how life could be different from that which he had always known in Tiffin, Ohio.

Tiffin, located approximately forty-five miles south of Toledo, was a quiet yet fast-growing city in 1818, the year Alonzo Thomas Prentiss was born. It had nicely laid out tree lined streets, a bank, commercial buildings, and even an opera house. Alonzo had never received, in Tiffin, any shock to his senses.

He had become a popular man about town, a great athlete, wonderful dancer, and a community leader, quiet but inspiring of confidence. He could have said he was typical of the young adult men of his city. Alonzo was twenty-two years of age when he married Ruth and twenty-four when their first son, Thomas Wilson, was born. A second son, Lyman Edwin, was born in 1847, and then a daughter, Ruth Edna, in 1856. Alonzo was interested in his family and busy with building his carpentry business.

Feelings that divided the white people to make them fight against each other, that divided brother from brother and city from city, were building in the North and in the South, but Alonzo was not yet involved. He had not felt the divisions of race.

In 1850, a thirty-nine-year-old housewife and mother, the little known daughter of a noted preacher, Lyman Beecher, with sisters and brothers already active as reformers, ministers, and speakers for many social and moral causes, had an unusual religious experience that led her to an act that changed the country. The idea came to her in church, as she received communion, that she had a mission, moral and political, to compose a story about a black saint struggling to survive under the soul-destroying conditions of slavery.

Harriet Beecher Stowe was mourning a child who had died the previous year. She felt an urgent personal need to give a child a voice in what she would write to speak for all children, black and white. This would be a message of family love for all humanity. She saw slavery as the dissolver of family life, destroyer of childhood, and corrupter of society. The pulpits were not open to women, but she could write.

From her home in Maine, this plain, serious small woman, Harriet Beecher Stowe, began what became a serialized novel that intensified antislavery sentiment throughout the North, awakened a new empathy in many sympathetic Southerners, and even focused the attention of other countries on slavery as a serious issue for all in the future.

First as a series in the National Era, then published in book form, March 20, 1852, within three months her work *Uncle Tom's Cabin* was selling ten thousand copies a week.

Charles Dickens and George Eliot in England and Leo Tolstoy in Russia acclaimed Harriet. Elizabeth Barrett Browning became numbered among her friends. She was read fervently throughout the North and South. Strong humanitarians of the North had been declaring human enslavement intolerable. Abolitionists had been demanding emancipation. Now, this novel, a passionate narrative of the dreadful horrors of slavery, reached people on this subject as nothing had before and captured their emotions. Abraham Lincoln would greet Harriet Beecher Stowe in 1863 pronouncing that she was "the little lady who made this big war."

Cities such as Cincinnati and others became major crossroads of racial tension. There was hardly a place that was unaffected. Young men of Tiffin, urged by their mothers and wives, stirred themselves to fight. War, as a means of achieving social justice for enslaved people was inevitable.

The Southerners would not be able to change the basis of their economy. Since 1820, cotton grown on plantations chiefly through the labor of slaves supported the South. Some plantations, to offset the expense of importing and subduing slaves brought across the waters, had turned themselves into breeding factories, raising slaves as merchandise. Many people protested later that if through human creativity the invention and promotion of machines that did the work of laborers, as proved by the cotton gin, had only come in time, slavery would have been made unnecessary.

Although neither North nor South was prepared militarily to fight each other, war was declared. Most Southerners owned guns and horses as part of their way of life throughout these rural states, so the South was better equipped, as these were the tools and weapons of war.

The Forty-ninth Ohio was organized at Tiffin, in Seneca County, under special authority from the secretary of war, Simone Cameron. Among the volunteers, along with his high-spirited friends, was Alonzo T. Prentiss. He received the commission of first lieutenant.

3

CHAPTER 3

On September 10, 1861, the Forty-ninth Ohio Volunteers started from Camp Noble, near Tiffin, and went to Camp Dennison. They received their equipment on September 21 and moved to Louisville, Kentucky, arriving on September 22. They reported to Brig. Gen. Robert Anderson, who had assumed command of that place. They were the first organized regiment to enter Kentucky.

The months ahead held for them withering and destructive fire, constant skirmishing, foraging expeditions in advance of the national forces, and severe campaigns in which they suffered greatly only for the capture of one or two guns. It was a time of dangerous maneuvers and hard fighting under mortar and rifle fire, of suffering severely in long marches with rations exhausted, clothing worn and torn, a time when many were without shoes, leaving a trail of bloody footmarks as their regiment struggled on toward their next challenge.

They fought at Dalton, Pesaca, Dallas, Kenesaw Mountain, Chattahoochie River, Atlanta, Jonesboro, and Lovejoy Station and the battle of Franklin and Nashville.

Of the 1,552 men who were privates, 616 were discharged as a result of severe wounds, 167 died of hardship and disease, 127 were killed in battle, 71 were mortally wounded, and 7 perished in prison at Andersonville and Danville.

And of the 440 men from Seneca County, one young officer was discharged because it was discovered that he was black and he could not serve in a white regiment.

But on the day they were first received in Louisville, at the start of the regiment's heroic career, there was cheering and martial music to welcome them. They arrived on two boats that had been lashed together to form one huge shipment of eager young men. Only military headquarters knew the regiment had come from Ohio. The people of Louisville hurrahed them as Kentucky's own and gave them enthusiastic greeting as the Kentucky regimental band performed on the wharf.

They marched in best military order through the main streets to the hotel where General Anderson was quartered. The general appeared on the balcony with a welcoming speech to which Col. Wm. H. Gibson responded. The people of Louisville followed the regiment in a spontaneous gala parade and celebrated them with patriotic fervor.

That evening they were celebrated again with a magnificent dinner at the Louisville Hotel for all the regiment, and afterward they were transported in cars to Lebanon Junction and the Home Guards. The next morning their duties began with the arduous work of crossing Rolling Fork by wading the river and marching to Elizabethtown, to camp on Muldraugh's Hill. They remained camped there until October 10, then moved to Nolin Creek and finally on to Camp Nevin.

After subsequent organization of the Second Division of the Army of Ohio, the Nineteenth was assigned to the Sixth Brigade, Gen. R. W. Johnson commanding. On December 10, they were fighting on the bank of the Green River, driving the Rebels across the river and claiming the town of Munfordsville, where they established Camp Wood, which they named for the Hon. George Wood, who lived in Munfordsville.

On December 17, the national pickets from the Thirty-second Indiana Infantry on the south side of Green River were attacked by Hinman's Arkansas Brigade and Terry's Texas Rangers. The Forty-ninth troops forded the river and came to their aid, followed by the Thirty-ninth Indiana. Colonel Terry, one of the Rebel commanders, was killed in battle and the enemy repulsed.

From December 17 to February 14th, the regiment lay in camp, perfecting itself in drill and discipline. On February 14, 1862, under orders, they left camp and moved to Bowling Green.

But 1st Lt. Alonzo T. Prentiss of the Forty-ninth Ohio Volunteers did not move with his regiment. On February 15, 1862, he was in Nashville, Tennessee, under circumstances that would change his life. There had been much talk against him.

CHAPTER 4

"Come on, Skelly! He's as white as you are! You know him!"

Skelly's arm went up, rigid as a gun stock, stopped short of a blow. "Look out, you! Ernest, you want to start a personal war right here in this Civil War with that tongue!" Skelly glowered and turned gruffly.

Will took the next charge. "I ain't fighting side by side with no darky either. I ain't having no nigger officer over me!"

Ernest spoke quick again, easy-talking like always. "We already did that. We fought with him. We took his orders. He looks white. All this time we thought he was, and you know we liked him. He had the hardships, the scrubby food, what there was of it, the drilling and marching, just like us. He was friends with them that died, just like us. How could things change because of what his ancestors were?"

"It's the law!" Will said. "One drop of black blood makes a person black!"

5

"And one drop of white blood can't make a person white! You're saying black is stronger than white?" Ernest tried to make it light but serious.

"You know one drop of ink in the water can make it darker. All those drops of clear water can't clear up ink," said Will. "One drop of pollution in the well pollutes the whole well. Can't nobody keep it quiet what color is in them; it will come out some way, maybe in their child's face."

"So you don't want your sister . . ." Ernest stopped abruptly, knowing he was accelerating the verbal battle. "I mean, see here, this war, what we've been fighting for, is about the colored being treated different from whites, the injustice of it."

"No. You're wrong about that! It's about not selling human beings as slaves. It's not about them being the same as me." Skelly took up the fight again.

"Equal but separate!" Will shot back.

"We don't agree why we're fighting. Save it for the Yanks! We don't have to fight about who gets rank and who gets out. We should want every good man with us when we fight. We need all the bodies we can get between us and death! Who gets out, for whatever reason, is lucky. That's my last shot!" Ernest left the field.

First Lt. Alonzo Thomas Prentiss was dispatched to Nashville to answer charges on his true identity. All had gone well for him in the military, so no one knew for certain whether it was jealousy over rank or some other reason, but tongues had begun to wag. Investigation disclosed the facts of his racial identity. It was decided he could not be transferred to a black regiment because his appearance was totally white. First Lieutenant Prentiss was prompted to resign from military service.

The results of the review board are registered, showing Special Order #36, Headquarters of the Army Adjutant General's Office, Washington, D.C., which state:

> The following officers, having been adversely reported on by the Board of Examiners: and the President of the United States, having approved the report of the Board, are discharged from the service, to take effect at the dates opposite their respective names:
> 1st Lieutenant Alonzo T. Prentiss, 49th Ohio Volunteers
> February 15, 1862
> By command of Major General McClellan

Alonzo, discharged from military service and confronted with the exposure of his racial background, decided to remain in Tennessee.

6

Faced with having to start a new life as a member of the black race, Alonzo did not want this to destroy the relationships his parents and other family members had in Tiffin. He did not want to go back where he had had so many happy memories to find this must change. He determined to remain in Tennessee. Ruth, his wife, decided to join her husband with their children and set up housekeeping in Nashville.

With so many men still away or damaged by war, it was possible for an able-bodied man to find good work, especially with the skill of a carpenter. Alonzo and Ruth knew that life would be more difficult, with the attitude of society still to be surmounted, but they remembered their happiness and thought they would still be happy.

The war was not yet over. Alonzo could learn swiftly—was learning firsthand—reasons why the war must be won by the North and attitudes toward blacks changed. He was personally, emotionally affected by the customs and the many unwritten as well as written laws having to do with the black race. He had never realized a state of life where his ability to function freely would be so affected.

Not only did this include how he could speak to other people and how they would speak to him, his social relationships with people, but his right to own property, and if he could be served in restaurants or shops or make business contracts, and these could even affect his marriage with a white woman. Ruth also was affected by the attitude of white people toward her relationship with Alonzo, now a black man. She felt she would not be able to move freely in white society or feel at one with the blacks. They did not accept her, and there seemed to be no place for her and Alonzo's children.

Because of war's turmoil many of the rules of the old system of the South were not intact. People's lives had been disrupted and changed by the years in which their concern had been survival during the privations of war. The structure of the plantations was being broken throughout the South by raids of soldiers, and the plantation owners had already lost power and suffered, as others did, through war's devastation. But enough of those Southern attitudes remained in the minds of people, both black and white, in the community around them to give Ruth and Alonzo a clear look at a world unlike any they could have imagined.

CHAPTER 5

In 1832, just thirty-one years before Pres. Abraham Lincoln severed the chains of involuntary servitude in the United States, on a small slave plantation near Nashville, Tennessee, owned by John Parker and his associates, James West and T. M. Isbell, a child was born and named Daphna Virginia by her white owners. She was born the daughter of slaves and was separated from her parents when she was just a child. She had no remembrance of receiving parental love and care. Being of the Parker plantation, she became known as Jennie Parker. She was kept on the Parker plantation when her parents were sold to other slave owners. For some unknown reason, her owner had her cared for, and when she was old enough to work it was in the "Big House."

The Big House was stately, with pillars in front, painted white, and only a few feet away in back were the cabins for the slaves who worked the acres of cotton.

Very early in life, Jennie was taught the chores of the Big House. As she looked back on her life, she considered herself fortunate to have had what was then the privilege of play and, more important, play with the plantation owners' children, because it was through their games that she was able to teach herself to read and write. Playing school and teacher, using the blue book spellers, with pictures of spellings, was fun.

Jennie was tall, modestly sedate, and intelligent. She had the proud air and bearing of the well born, and when she became a free woman whenever she was seen she was dressed handsomely. These distinguishing characteristics indicated that she had spent nearly all of the first thirty-one years of her life in the Big House of the Parker plantation in association with a mistress who, though exacting in demands, was gracious.

Jennie learned to read and write, most often forbidden to people in her condition. She also learned to keep her own counsel. She spoke of nothing that could jeopardize her personal interests or the interests of those close to her, a trait that continued to be useful in her future.

With a rare sense of herself as a unique and special person, Jennie also had a pride in herself as a person of race, which stayed with her all of her life. When war to free her people was won, she internalized the fact that because of her importance and the importance of her people this war had been fought. The strong impression made by the signing of the Emancipation Proclamation came at a time in her life when this would lead to her mature independence. She knew her inner strength. She left the Parker plantation as a free woman of thirty-three years of age. She took her first paying job as housekeeper for Ruth and Alonzo Prentiss.

Jennie dropped the name Daphna Virginia and chose never to use it again. She never mentioned the reason why. We can assume that she felt she was leaving her past when emancipation was won. Coming into the employment of Alonzo and Ruth gave Jennie an economic base for her freedom.

And she was on the verge of a romance that was going to last for her lifetime, but she did not know it yet.

CHAPTER 6

Jennie had worked for Alonzo and Ruth for over a year as their house-keeper. She was more than competent in the art of creating a pleasant home atmosphere with industry and thrift.

Alonzo had come to respect her, to admire her, attracted by her beauty and manner as well as her competence, her way with children and her energy and strength. In her graceful decorum she was equal to any lady he had ever met. He was impressed that so many diverse qualities could be in one person.

He was intrigued by her presence as a woman of the black race, the first he had ever known with pride in her dark skin. Knowing himself now as a black, with society's label on his white face, for his inheritance of race from a grandparent he had never known, he was filled with a great curious sense of longing for an identity with Jennie Parker. He was drawn to her in sympathy as a kindred sufferer of the injustices he saw all round him in Nashville, which were directed against the large number of blacks who were trying to learn what their newly given free-dom would mean for them. The infectious interest in change, hope in hearts of the blacks, was sweeping through the city. Jennie was filled with an excitement about what this would mean for her, though she did not put it into words.

In time, all his ideas about Jennie culminated in Alonzo feeling that the right name for these emotions was love. But he held that thought to himself.

Ruth did not know herself how she felt about the morality of being married to a black whom she had had to stop believing was white. In her lack of social conditioning about such a thing, and having no one close to her with whom she could talk about it, it began to prey on her mind. She had never known anyone else in such a situation. At times the idea became intolerable. She was growing more frightened, fretful, irritable, and intolerant. She would think, *But this is really Alonzo, whom I love!* and then wonder if she really knew him!

She began to fantasize that their marriage was not legal, that black and white could not be allowed to marry. Wasn't her husband now legally a black man? Hadn't she married under a false assumption, and didn't this annul their vows?

The army had made an issue of this very thing! They had claimed Alonzo's army contract was not valid and he had had to leave the service because of public opinion and emotions involved and, yes, the law.

She let her worries and frustrations, anxieties and nervousness, about their circumstances spoil their love. She could not make a new start in Nashville and could not make friends or social contracts because she was afraid of what others might say about her husband's race. She became obsessed with what people would do to her for being married to a black man if she went on the street to a store or even to church, and so she became reclusive.

The shock of seeing how black people had lived and been treated in the South made it impossible to indentify with them. She could not stand for such things to happen to her, she knew.

Ruth now saw her own relationship with Alonzo was based on something other than their melding together as husband and wife, something other than their childhood attraction for each other. It had never been, for them, "we two, out of all the world," she thought, but had much to do with their position in the community, how the parents of each had felt about them both, their mutual friends, and what they had experienced growing up in the same town with the growing respect and support of other people.

Alone, Ruth felt deprived of family, neighborhood, familiar home, and warm and loving friends with memories and daily events to talk over and share. That community was her need and her real love. Alonzo and her love for him was only a part of that kind of security. Now she wondered if she really loved him. Perhaps she did not love him enough for the suffering she saw ahead.

She wanted to return to their remembered world of the past. She did not want to stay and brave a new and changed relationship. A relationship of black and white—she knew no approval for this sort of thing. Ruth felt that everywhere were whispers about her husband's race and about her. She felt their past, established in Ohio, would hold true, their family and friends would be loyal and accept them in the old way. But Alonzo had suffered people changing against him and did not share confidence in their world going on as it had before.

Then again, she thought, *it's all over! Nothing is going to go on as it was, and our happiness is gone.* She knew fate had been extremely unkind to her.

More, she believed she saw love for her husband growing in the glances of their servant girl, Jennie.

Jennie, over a decade younger than Ruth and Alonzo, had a past strange to them, having been raised in the home of whites, living among whites only to serve them, taught strictly by them, sheltered and limited in social relationships. There were taboos about the association between whites and blacks, between house servants and field hands. The white people who made the rules made sure Jennie, like other people of her race, learned that.

Could she be allowing herself to fall in love with Alonzo because she knew he was black like herself?

Jennie had lived many years with love unexpressed, kept in the Big House with the servants' rooms apart from the master's family and apart from the field workers, too. She had never been allowed to know the field hands. The other servants in the Big House were seemingly ancient women and men, old when Jennie was born.

She had to feel love for some human creature. She thought some of the white people around her sometimes were worthy of love. She knew she would never be allowed to express this. She thought the field workers could be loved. Yet she was kept apart from them. They went to their work before dawn, sweltered in the hot sun, and returned after dusk, drained of strength. She saw from the upper windows, the light on their muscular bodies and on the deep purple-blacks and shining ebonies and various other shades of their skin.

She knew white people could choose to breed their slaves, without love, and could choose someone for her in this way. She knew she was a slave, subject to sale and degradation. Her parents had been sold before she knew them. She heard only that her mother had been brought from North Carolina and sold away again, she did not know where, and her father was unknown.

Still, she had been selected by the people of the Big House to be protected from the fate common to slaves. She had been secure in the fondness for her of the children of that family whom she was raised to serve but who had played with her when they were young, gave her childish confidences, and turned to her for their needs. She had been secure in the moral training given by the stern yet gracious mistress who read the Bible with the master to the family on Sunday. This mistress had a high regard for religious marriage.

Yet no religious marriage was proposed for the black girl in the Big House. As she grew to adulthood, the child, Daphna Virginia, felt somehow she must love someone or perish, though she had no one. White people would not love her in return.

But now, and her heart sang when she was near him. Alonzo Prentiss, with his white face, she knew was black.

11

Jennie, this beautiful black woman who had lived all her life among whites as a house companion and servant, did not herself see how vulnerable she was to a man who, though he looked white, was accessible to her because he was black. But he was married. Or was he?

CHAPTER 7

"You never fought for me," said Ruth. "You didn't have to fight a war for me. Don't forget it was me you left to go fight for her!"

"I didn't know her." Alonzo knew Ruth was being unreasonable. She had been furious for days, for a month. She just wanted to fight him now. "I fought for what was right."

"For people like her!" said Ruth. "And now I'm bitter. At her, because she's of the people you would have given your life for. I want you to give your life to me, to me and the children, from now on. Promise!" she cried, grabbing at his wrists, pulling him to her.

Alonzo took both her hands and held her away from him so he could look at her steadily. "People like her," said Alonzo, "yes, people like me. I'm like her."

"Oh, but we never thought about that. Oh, why do you remind me? Why does it matter? I told you I don't care about things like that." She was crying again. She cried all the time now, every day, and she would continue to get angrier now. She only wanted to fight again. "When we never knew, we never cared. Black! White! The whole world saying it makes a difference to people's love. And people hating and having wars over it. It's just the whole world's crazy!"

"I'm crazy, too, then, Ruth; it makes a difference to me. After a person's been through what I've been through, it makes a difference. I found out I'm a different person. I want to know what different person it is that I am."

"And you love somebody different, is that what it means? And what of our children? They're white and when we lived in Ohio you were white, too. I don't care what the army said or what anybody says, and if you are not white and the whole world says it, then I don't care what the world says. I want to go back like it was, back to Ohio. No one there will say our children are not white."

"Don't you care what I feel, Ruth? I don't want to have to be put in a category, but if I am, by others, I want to learn as much about what that means as I can. It has changed me."

"Oh, I'm too mixed up. You're not the same man I married. You don't love me the same! What of the children? They'll have a better chance growing up like we did in Tiffin. They're just what they are and you're their father and I'm their mother and we ought to stand by them and by each other and raise them together and keep on loving each other."

"If I could, Ruth, if I *could!*" Alonzo's cry was anguished. "People can't make themselves go on loving. I love you, but I . . . love Jennie, too, and now I've said it—I do! I didn't want to say it, or think it. I wanted to go on loving just you. But that was another life, Ruth. When I was some other way, back in Tiffin, Ohio. That was just a dream. You've got a right to hate me or leave me or—"

"Leave you! No, I want to leave *with* you! I want us to go right now back to how we were, away from this place and from that person who is breaking my heart."

"Don't blame her. Jennie's not to blame that love is so strong and so unforeseen it hits people like lightning cracks open trees. One strong, brilliant flare and you're bursting open with fire—"

"Burn then!" She was crying now and flinging things out of the drawers and closets onto the bed. She was dragging at the old travel chest and the suitcases she had traveled with from dream to nightmare, from Tiffin to Tennessee.

She cried for hours and put things haphazardly into the cases and chest. There was a steamer trunk that she couldn't move, and she filled it, too. It was all she could do for hours, going to the children's room and through other rooms, for hours going back and forth, the children prattling and playing and bringing toys to throw into the big box and saying, "Mommy, mommy." It was a new game, going. She had made up her mind that she was already gone to where she couldn't be hurt anymore. Yet she was still packing things and still crying until the children, confused, crawled on the bed and stared at her. And slept. And she would never come back, and he would never come to her and the children. She knew. And she would get over it, but she didn't know how. And it all had something to do with how black people and white people were separated, and why this should ever be she would never, never understand.

Alonzo found Jennie out in the field where the trees shadow hid her. She had run out of the house when the screaming started like that. He put his hand to her breast and his mouth to her mouth, but she pulled back.

"I can't help it," she said. "They were so strict. The way I was brought up, there was so much I couldn't do—and I can't do this." Tears came in wet strands down her face, but she strengthened herself against them. "And I'm a person that doesn't cry about what I can't have, and there's been enough of that." She gave a turned-down smile and broke away from him. "I work in the house where your wife and children live, and you're not a free man, and this is not what I can do."

"You're a free woman," Alonzo said. "I fought in the war that made you free, both of us free, and I guess I have some scars to prove it. It was worth it. You're magnificent. I love you, Jennie. I never knew such love. I love you."

"I will have scars on my heart if I can't prove to you how much I love you. But there's a war going on now, too, and it is in my whole body—and I'm fighting it. I love you. And it's just going to kill me to go, but I've got to leave your house now."

"No, you're wrong," he said. "It's Ruth who is leaving. She's taking the children and going to Ohio. I've refused to go with her. She doesn't believe we are, or should be, married anymore. She is going to claim the marriage invalid, have it annulled or get a divorce. I don't know what people can do in a case like this. I've lost," he said, "and I've won!"

He came closer to her in the shadows. "I've won the freedom to love you."

With both arms he pulled her body close against his. "Tell me I've won this," he said.

CHAPTER 8

That August, 1865, Ruth Prentiss and her three children went back to Tiffin, Ohio, leaving Alonzo with the housegirl, Jennie.

In the city of Nashville, throughout the year 1866, Alonzo Prentiss was courting Jennie, believing that soon he would be legally free to marry her.

Jennie had been brought up with a Baptist morality and her own never expressed but passionate desire to love and be loved. Marriage was more than a bond, Jennie thought; it was a blessing.

Alonzo was monogamous by nature, he believed of himself, and Jennie was intrinsically loyal. No two people could be more devoted to each other; so they each thought. They hoped to have children, to cherish them, and in this way to do good in the world by their children. They did not want to have servants. Work was their domain and each excelled in his or her own industriousness. Through their love and their own work their fortunes, they decided, could rise like the phoenix from ashes. They would achieve great happiness. Such was their vision as they planned their marriage.

War, the great leveler, had made men equal in poverty, equal in death. Old men of Nashville had died of disease and deprivation, many of them, and many young men had died far from their city, their homes, in numerous war battles.

There remained in Nashville, among other struggling businesses, a general store of sorts for those survivors who could afford the few sparse tools and commodities offered for sale. Appearing among the more urgently needed items were furnishings and other belongings salvaged by their owners or whoever remained to claim them—things from homes gutted and burned or dug up from their burial places in old trunks, from behind barns, or from under bushes in the woods and brought hopefully in trade for more essential items. There were not so many purchasers for these pieces of silver, fine linen, and now impractical ball-gowns and top hats. The need was for goods basic to survival. Sometimes people came in just to gaze at remnants of the past, as to a museum, and perhaps to quietly weep. Others sometimes came to look and dream of what could be theirs in a mysterious future and of how they could rebuild their lives.

It had been a long walk to the store and she would walk back, too, so Jennie could not come very often. She stood in the shadowy recesses of the store and waited, not because she must, but for her special reason. She waited until the three white patrons put down their money and left, the man with a small container of flour and some lengths of rope and the two women, one buying one spool of thread.

Then Caroline, the store owner's wife, was alone with Jennie in the store and they swiftly embraced. Caroline's moth-pale frail face, with skin so white and thin it had a quality of translucence in the store's interior dimness, had a radiant smile for Jennie. Under a duster, she wore a dress familiar to Jennie, a once-fashionable full-skirted dress embellished with tatting at throat and wrist. Jennie herself had many times heated the iron and pressed and pressed those voluminous skirts when it had been a favorite day dress of Caroline's older sisters. Caroline had come sometimes for long stays with her parents and brothers and sisters, of whom she was the youngest, on the Parker plantation where Jennie had been raised.

Caroline's life had been one of being callously ignored by those pretty older sisters who talked of curls and petticoats and had big-sister secrets, excluding a too much younger sister. She felt teased and negated, as if older brothers and sisters had conspired not only to be bigger, better, and more beautiful, but to have all the value and the power. In some families it is that way, as if some people have a pecking order like farm chickens. The parents, caught up in their adult world, had a blind spot in that they never saw the sensitive little sister cruelly teased, ignored, and excluded from companionship. There were no words a child close to the pain of emotional death could speak on her own behalf.

Rarely in the South, but sometimes it did happen, between two people race did not matter. Their spirits would meet and they would know each other and transcend the reality of the prejudice around them.

Jennie would steal away from house chores to seek out Caroline alone in a window seat or where she had hidden herself behind a bedroom cupboard door or forlorn in an old rocker on the wisteria-covered veranda with a rag doll and corn-husk doll snuggled close to comfort her in her solitude. Jennie responded to the unspoken need by telling her stories, hoping to bring a smile to her, and would walk with her down to see the horses, a calf, or a certain flower, point out shapes she saw in the clouds, weave grasses into little doll baskets for the corn-husk babies, put new corn-tassel hair or caps of catalpa flowers on the smallest doll's head, and serve play cups of make-believe tea in acorn caps stirred with twigs, imaginary feasts on leaf plates.

And Jennie, herself a child who had to grow old before the age of ten and at twelve could work ten hours a day, would have a few more hours of brief childhood. When Jennie was ten, Caroline was seven. They would see each other from year to year, Jennie each time giving sharing and laughter and a presence that to Caroline made life's terrors seem bearable. Caroline felt a strength and concern in Jennie that she knew was on the side of life.

Caroline's brothers came back from their hunting with dead rabbits, pheasants, and quail, soft things and beautiful, all dead, heads dangling, blood-spotted, blank-eyed. There were times chickens' heads were cut off. Headless, the chickens ran in circles while the boys whooped and laughed. The pigs were gutted and skinned and strung by their back feet. Even the calf was butchered.

So in all the long spaces of time until she came back again to Jennie Caroline had no soulmate.

It was only to Jennie that Caroline could say that her life held fears, that she saw herself as one of those mute creatures. As she grew older and more verbal, she would say to Jennie (and only to Jennie) how she disagreed with the ideas of her family, how wrong they were to support the Rebels, to perpetuate their own dominance over lives of people held as slaves, treated like the animal creatures whose lives were held as nothing. She saw that in the system of the South women such as she

16

would remain voiceless. She said once to Jennie that she was afraid to grow up to marry because most men believed women to be another possession to be worked and used. In this way, white women were raised to be owned and enslaved. She said, "To love my family whose ideas and behavior, toward me as toward others, I have hated, is this the test of my true religion? To pray and say, 'Forgive them what they do; they know not what they do,' is to love my own enemy?" Caroline knew there must be other white people who searched out the answers to such questions and knew better how to act. After all, there was a war involving such people, fighting against the ideas of people like her family, but Caroline did not know how to join them.

She could see that Jennie's life called for a greater endurance than her own. She admired and loved Jennie because Jennie did not bear a grudge against her for being white but acted, whenever she could, as her true friend. Caroline knew they were bonded. It was not a secret pact, no cutting of thumbs and pressing blood to blood, but a bond of the spirit. There were times Caroline cried in Jennie's arms against the cruel world of her older brothers and sisters where great wrongs were ignored. She did not understand why Jennie, with more reason, did not cry.

But as Caroline grew older she learned there were men who made a difference—one, at least, for her. It was as if a door had opened and she could see that all along a feast had been in progress, the glasses with claret and burgundy in the candle flame, the gleaming china piled with chicken and yams and succulent desserts waiting on the sideboard, the glitter of silver, mouths smiling, opening and closing to taste and laughter. None of these material things was what she wanted; they were only symbols of the feast of love she felt for Benton. He had come to Nashville as a Union soldier and returned to marry Caroline. They opened the store.

Caroline was freed by marriage from her repressive family. Jennie was free by the president's proclamation. This much the war had done for them both. Jennie and Caroline could come to each other's arms now as loving sisters and as equals.

"Jennie, I'm so glad you're here. You look all in a glow! Tell me why you look so happy!" Caroline said.

And Jennie told Caroline that she and Alonzo had arranged their marriage date.

"Oh, I'm so glad, truly glad for you, Jennie, that you've found your true love. I want to come to your wedding as your friend and family, your sister. And here is my gift now. We were going to sell it, like everything," she admitted, "from my once home. But it is yours for the feast of love!" She folded into Jennie's dark hands with the amber palms a tablecloth, lacy, soft, ivory white, delicately designed. "Maybe it could make your bridal veil. Or whatever you want.

"Oh, Jennie, that Mr. Prentiss is just so lucky, so blessed. And he must know by now what a wonderful person you are and how you have the special gift to make gladness! Oh, Jennie, live happily ever after!"

CHAPTER 9

When Alonzo recieved his service discharge, he still had the benefits due a hero of the war and the friendship of men who had been in the army and shared the comraderie of soldiers. The result of his trial had been changed to allow his resignation with honor. When he arranged his wedding with Jennie, it was a military wedding. They were married by an army officer in March 1867.

Jennie's very dark complexion was in contrast to the ivory white of her dress and the ruffle that crossed her breast. The soft lace covering her thick hair waved and scalloped along her high cheekbones, her full and sensual lips. Her eyes' dark depths reflected the glow of the candle lit for the ceremony. Alonzo, though very serious, had an almost ecstatic smile. His complexion was, by contrast, almost as white as the bridal gown. It was unusual in those times for two people from such a wide spectrum of color to vow to love each other until death.

Although Alonzo was not a particularly religious man, he was moved by what the preacher said the Scriptures gave as the marriage blessing:

> Your wife shall be like the fruitful vine on the walls of your house. Your children around your table like the olive shoots. . . .
>
> The man who loves his wife is loving a part of himself. No one ever hates his own body; he nourishes it and treats it with loving care . . . be joined and become one flesh . . .
> —Ephesians 5:22–23
> I pray that you may bear fruit in every good work as you advance in the knowledge of God. I pray that through his glorious power God will fill you with all strength to face the future with endurance, with fortitude, and with joyful gratitude to the Father, who has made us fit to wear the inheritance of saints . . .
> —Colossians 1:9–14

The mood and feeling compelled by the ceremony stayed with Alonzo and so moved him that much later, after the celebrating and when he and Jennie were alone, he took up the Bible himself and by candlelight read to Jennie something out of his memory that he had found again in that book, from the Song of Songs: " 'Let him kiss me with the kisses of his mouth, for thy love is better than wine . . . thy name is as ointment poured forth, therefore do the virgins love thee. Draw me, I will run after thee. The king hath brought me into his chambers, we will be glad and rejoice in thee, we will remember thy love more than wine: the upright love thee.

" 'I am black but comely, O ye daughters of Jerusalem, as the tents of Cedar, as the curtains of Solomon . . .' "

Jennie had heard portions of the Bible read to members of the Parker family by the master and mistress as she stood with the other house servants on their periphery every Sunday of her life. But she was astounded at the beauty and portent of these words, which she had never heard before.

Alonzo gave her this Bible, the first book she had ever received. She had told him she had a craving for a book of her own. From that time she read diligently.

Alonzo and Jennie settled themselves to live the life of blacks. By now many people knew their romantic story, and they made friends in the community.

Alonzo, at the age of forty-seven, had weathered as beautifully as seasoned wood. He had not begun to grow gray but looked young for his age and very handsome. His military conditioning and the physical work of a carpenter had kept him lean and made him strong-sinewed and muscular.

Jennie, at thirty-four, was a beautiful person with an intense gaze, high cheekbones, and full lips. Thirteen years younger than her husband, she also seemed younger than her biological years. For some women the midthirties brings a change of life; for Jennie it was the awakening of her sexual expression and fertility. For the next ten years she would be like the fruitful vine. Their firstborn, William G., was born in Nashville in the same year of their marriage.

Alonzo and Jennie felt rich and blessed by their marriage and the birth of their son. But the South continued to deteriorate into a drawn-out postwar poverty by which blacks were most affected. With the plantation system destroyed and no other economic base for the South, there were many people without direction. Homeless black people without work flooded every community. There was talk of a Reconstruction program, but it was disorganized, too long in coming. Entrepreneurs, carpetbaggers, and opportunists of all kinds came through cities such as Nashville, competing with each other, exploiting where they could.

Alonzo realized he would not be able to support a growing family under the poor conditions of the South, and Jennie and Alonzo felt they had no reason to stay in Nashville. They were concerned for their future.

Jennie felt toward Alonzo as the biblical Ruth to Naomi: "Whither thou goest I will go . . . thy people shall be my people."

Alonzo felt that as far as he was concerned, the only people he needed were Jennie, his son, and any other children that might come to them, and of these he planned to take very good care!

CHAPTER 10

"What do a white-looking man stay here for, taking the po' blacks' jobs?" George, as he talked, was feeling the huckleberry skin split between his tongue and his back tooth.

"Got no jobs. Got nothing to do but be dusting off the steps with the seat of our hand-me-downs!" Bill was talking around the grass stem held in the center of his full lower lip.

"The old masters sent off they white-looking offshoots to Europe, someplace I hear like that. France. Somewheres like that. They pass. We never saw those no more."

"Never hear of some white-looking people trying to say they's colored. Must be some government money coming to the South for colored."

"Hoo, there ain't nothing going to come here south of the Mason-Dixon line but what's worth nothing. Same as your Confederate money."

"It's like passing the jug from mouth to mouth. Well, the first mouth gets the big swig and the last mouth gets the least swallow. The money for the South goes from hand to hand and just purely sticks to them up there in Washington and on the way here. Comes to our hand, why, there ain't none."

"Sure, a few samples of the jug in Washington, a few swigs of it on the way here. I ain't had nary a sip of that jug in a passle of time! No job, no money. Nothing."

"Way I see it, that man has got some duty to go north and look white just enough to take away a job from some white man. Don't need no more hungry blacks down in Nashville, that's for sure!"

CHAPTER 11

In his search for a better future, Alonzo took his family to Chicago, Illinois. They had been given the name of a wealthy mulatto businessman there known to have been an active abolitionist, John G. Jones. Alonzo and Jennie rented a place to live on property Jones owned. He had been a conductor on the underground railway and continued to help people from the South to establish themselves in Illinois, to make connections for employment and find places to live.

In Chicago a daughter was born to Jennie and Alonzo in 1873. She was named Priscilla Anne.

Jennie joined the Berean Baptist Church and took Will to the Sunday school so he could make friends. This was her first chance to be part of a church community.

Mr. Jones took an interest in the Prentiss family. He pointed out to Alonzo that California, after the Gold Rush, was building. Alonzo, being a skilled carpenter, could very well make good. There had been much news about the completion of the new Transcontinental Railway and how it benefited the opening of the West. The trip itself would be an adventurous train ride, practical for traveling even with young children. Alonzo was encouraged to take his family to California. It was still a new frontier where a new society could be formed. It would be good for a growing family to become established in a part of the country still called the "virgin territory." Alonzo and Jennie talked it over, convincing themselves to go west!

Many people still arrived in San Francisco with "gold dust" in their eyes. Bonanza Street, the Barbary Coast, wild individualists, exotic characters, rugged frontiersmen, and immigrants of all kinds gave the city a flavor and color like no other. Although it was approximately thirty years since the discovery of gold, people still had "the dream." But most, like Alonzo, came to work in their craft or develop a business in the city. There was a great influx of migrating people, and San Francisco's population was increasing rapidly. Naturally, housing was needed. Alonzo learned at once that carpentry in San Francisco was a good business. His ability was an asset, as always. He knew he could make a better living in San Francisco than anyplace he had been. But there was a problem.

It was not, after all, as wide open a town as he had anticipated, particularly in business and the building trades. Forty-niners and the settlers that followed came from other parts of the country but brought their prejudices with them. Race was an issue in California because of the railroad and other building for which Chinese labor had been conscripted and used. Now these laborers needed other work. The newspapers were full of the "yellow peril" and the proposal for a Chinese Exclusion Act. Keeping the Chinese people from the labor force and from establishing themselves in the city in any way extended to a prejudice against other races. Californians had chosen to take the consensus agreed upon in other parts of the country that even one drop of Negro blood meant a person was black. Trades and professions barred their doors to blacks, too. To become known as a black meant Alonzo would not be able to get work as a carpenter in San Francisco.

But employment was open to Alonzo. He was accepted as white, for the people lacked evidence of his true identity as a member of the black race. It was ironic that though he had become intrigued with his heritage, united with Jennie, racial barriers penalized them. After all they had been through, here they were at the end of land. Beyond was the ocean, and they would not go back. They would do what they must to establish themselves in San Francisco; they knew they had to survive.

The subject of color was mute with Jennie. For economic reasons she aided her husband in his passing for white.

With Jennie being a conservative and thrifty housewife, they saved a great deal from Alonzo's earnings, and it was not long before they settled at 17 Priest Street, in the area now known as Nob Hill. They had a neat and comfortable home, a four-room redwood frame house with a nice garden area in the back. The family adjusted to their new way of life.

There would be a new society for their country someday; they were sure of it. There had been a war, but that was not enough. Something beyond war would be needed to bring this great change. Jennie thought always of the importance of their life together. What it meant to them both, Alonzo's white face and her black face side by side on the pillows, their lips meeting in kisses, their arms in passionate embrace. She pictured them walking through San Francisco streets, their hands clasped with their mutual pledge of love and support for each other. This would grow stronger as the years passed, she thought. *If there will be a new society, could it come through love such as ours?* This was her question and her answer!

In January 1876, Jennie was expecting another child.

CHAPTER 12

From a Southerner's Notebook, 1880

I remember as if I were still young in the South. Here the trees open like fans against the day's heat. Someone keeps clover bees and a blue hound, a 'possum hound. Every little leaf whirls in a circle. Corn, in close rows, flaunts its tassels over our heads. Our feet are careful in the stubble when the corn is cut, stalks sharp enough to penetrate flesh, like a thick knife. Corn husking time. Sunflowers against whitewashed wood, each petal like a bright piece cut into a quilt pattern. Aunts, cousins, friends, set up a quilting frame in the parlor, stay. Those saved and treasured scrap materials, remnants from worn coats, shirts, petticoats, skirts, cut into shapes for a design that has a name.

Starlight and Firefly, the 2 little black horses with white markings on their foreheads. Captain, the shining sorrel, Big Red, the blood bay. Their beautiful massed feathery tails and manes like hay in the field tossing in wind. Wagon load of yams. Outdoors, the iron tubs for washing clothes, making lye, cooking chickens.

Remember that old man that sat singing by the side of the road, out of his head, preaching sermons to dust-devils? The dark-skinned boy who whispered around that he could go North because someone had gone there who "had two children by my sister, going to look him up, get a start, send money to my mother." Oh, we weren't supposed to know such things. Once, black men came through, wandering through, looking for family that had been sold from one place to another, sold and sold again, probably dead now.

There were girls with names of sweetness. Whose very names were their treasure; Annie, Bess, Selma, Sarina, Pearl, Janna, Mellie, Melita, Summer, Blossom, Jasmine, and those who loved them, called them sugar, precious, taffy, dumpling, sugar-pie, sweet potato. Why do I remember them as beautiful, white girls and black, could it be they were all beautiful?

The home-boys. How they were called; Crawdad, Cotton, Bull, Bro'. And they were called Shanks, Slick, Dandy, Cream. White boys and black. Remember the men who owned stores, all white men, who ran the town, who died. Once they were young. Their names were Earl, Traver, Dalton, Johnny, Swain, Willits, Deacon. . . .

Letter from San Francisco, 1872

Dear Billy;

I am homesick for the hominy grits, the cornbread, and the pecan pie like mama cooks. And here the streets ain't paved with gold.

But there is something in the air. The sea wind comes past the furled sails of the boats at the wharf and brings me a taste of fresh day like nowhere else in all my travels. . . .

CHAPTER 13

In the past Jennie had helped to bring new life into the world by assisting in the delivery of others' babies as midwife. In the big city of San Francisco she planned to have, for the first time, not a midwife, but a doctor. Alonzo had found him, Dr. Hall. Jennie was preparing a layette of little shirts, gowns, and blankets and folding soft cloth diapers for the coming baby, due to arrive the next month by all calculation.

Now it was Christmas, their first in San Francisco, and this "surely was some sweet chile's birthday to celebrate, wasn't it?" Jennie told the children. It was their most prosperous year yet. She looked over the gifts for the children, with great pleasure that she and Alonzo had made these wonderful surprises. Each one was as magnificent as anything in San Francisco's great emporiums.

Alonzo had made wooden pull toys, a wagon with slat sides and wooden wheels, and for the three-year-old Priscilla Anne a polished wood horse with a hemp rope mane and tail. William G. was a strong, smart boy, going on ten years old, and already making things with hammer and nails, and he had helped Alonzo make the small dollhouse for his sister that the children would have fun making play furniture for in the years ahead. William's own presents were more on the practical side, including a warm, thick sweater to wear through San Francisco's fogs. Alonzo had also bought William some tools of his very own, just what he had been asking for, wanting to be the man his father was. Jennie planned a stocking filled for each child with walnuts, almonds, oranges, hard candies, and some strange nuts Alonzo had found for them in the Chinese district that Jennie didn't know the names of. And, marvel of marvels, there was a charming toy he had found, too, the likes of which she had never seen. It was a doll, like a marionette, on a string with a ring on it, and when the string was pulled the toy's arms and legs flew out as if the little man was jumping, and it was rightly called a jumping jack. This would be something for the whole family to enjoy. She smiled to think of the children's faces seeing this!

What surprises and wonders there were in San Francisco! True, it was Alonzo that made most of the discoveries and told about them, bringing home odd things to share. Jennie had more trouble adjusting to the climate, so cold compared to the South, and to walking hills that went straight up, especially in her pregnant condition. The baby was heavy and low between her pelvic bones, and there had been some spotting of blood. She was moving more slowly and her back ached, but she trusted her strong and vibrant body to do a good job with this birth. Her breasts were large and maternal now, her hips widening, and in all her fullness she had bloomed into a perfect receptacle for the baby.

But something went wrong. On January 12, 1876, Jennie sent urgently for the doctor. A daughter was delivered and it was stillborn.

The doctor that same day delivered a baby boy. His hands held both life and death in just the space of a few hours. He was immensely sad when he thought of the home where it was evident so much love and care had awaited the baby that was dead and saddened also when he thought what kind of life might be in store for the living boy. That child had been heralded into the world by newspaper reportings of scandal and violence. The name of his mother was already well known, Flora Wellman, listed on the birth certificate as the wife of W. H. Chaney, whom the newspapers had made equally notorious.

CHAPTER 14

Flora Wellman had been always willful and demanding as a child, with a young, ineffectual, undisciplining stepmother who, to please the child's doting father, humored and indulged her, more so since the dreadful typhoid had left her just alive, thinned out her hair and stunted her growth, and, some murmured compassionately, damaged the child's nervous system, poor high-strung little thing, or maybe, just a touch, her mind, poor flighty little thing.

The baby of the family, pitied as motherless, Flora willfully left home at an unheard of young age to live with first one married sister, then another, until having exhausted her sisters, she went off as a paid traveling companion for an older woman to another state. Not an unrespectable position, but unnecessary to a young lady from as wealthy a family as hers had been.

Nevertheless, she did not return home and no one was ever quite sure how, after that, she got all the way to San Francisco, where she was then known to have met and to have lived as "wife" to both a Mr. Smith and a Professor Chaney in the same boardinghouse in sequence and at one time, to the consternation of the other boarders, simultaneously. The outraged moral sensitivities of the other boarders brought complaints that forced her choice, and during the time she became pregnant she was considered the wife of Chaney.

Chaney at that point became defensive of himself, because of the quick succession of lovers in her past. The presence of Lee Smith was still a continued insinuation. She had been sewing for other men. The intimate process of taking their measurements, with her light hands and a tape measure traveling the length of their arms and shoulders and circumference of chest, Chaney assumed and charged, had led to other intimacies.

Now she was unable to liberate herself from the primal anger of the betrayed and abandoned, the unloved woman, ultimately alone. True, she had not really loved, but *wanted*. She would survive this blow to her ego, but no matter what she had done or was, she had wanted to be loved.

Abandoned, she was in anguish as if crucified. She would frequently spread out her arms in a great swoon. She broke out in giant hives. She would moan and roll on her bed for hours. She was sending shock after shock of her own emotion through the child in her uterus, the still-forming, embryonic child.

The woman's womb was the cause of it all. She was betrayed by sex and by the evolving human in the womb. Some chance connection of cells had burst into a new being that she would have to feed and clothe, babysit for years, and educate. It would take her time and freedom, and she was dreadfully imposed upon by this monster of creation. Now it was too late to have it removed. She had struggled and fought Chaney, too long seemingly for the baby's sake, and she had taken a public position that she could not give up. She had done this for Chaney, to get Chaney bound to her, and not for the child. She didn't love it. She didn't even know it. Its sex, the set of its face, all its characteristics were determined by random coupling of genes. What a horrible chance way to get stuck with a lifelong responsibility. How would she even support it? If it wasn't for the personal charity of the Chronicle reporter William H. Slocum and his friend Mrs. Amanda, who were also co-editors of *Common Sense*, for which Chaney had written articles, who offered to take her in until after her confinement, Flora would have to go to a charity ward.

If she lived to be a hundred, she thought she would not live long enough to express her overwhelming anger at Chaney and yes, too, at this now unwanted child, cause of shame and misery, cause of her suffering. She would have to endure the immense ordeal of labor. Maybe it would be the death of her. Many women died in childbirth, and she felt herself to be very frail.

In such a situation, with immense anxiety, who wouldn't drink? Yet no matter how much she drank, how strong the drink, her anger was stronger and more lasting. The drink wore away. The anger stayed, and she would have to drink more. Should it give her some commiseration that "these accidents of fortune went with the convictions of those in free love," as Mrs. Amanda said, and "free love must continue to be a buffer to the social shame and stigma of the deserted woman, of the unwed mother and her bastard." Easy for Mrs. Amanda to say; she had her man. Now what man was going to take and care for Flora and saddle himself with someone else's brat to support?

She loathed her misshapen figure with the enormous protruberance in front, she so tiny and bird-boned. There had been something minute and appealing in that little doll figure. Jealous ones who had their eyes on the professor, too, had said "too quaint" and "frivolous," but she knew they envied the tiny waist, the tiny feet.

Now she would be merely an object of comment about her ludicrous appearance, in her wig and spectacles, humped over, carrying the big, gross forthcoming creature that she couldn't love. Soon, she imagined, milk would be seeping from her breasts for it. She would have to stuff in rags or cotton padding that would go smelly and sour quickly in the heat. Her sisters had said it was painful to have a child nursing. When it began to grow teeth it would bite the breast. One had to get up in the night and lose sleep for babies, especially the colicky ones. The tender nipples chafe and get sore, and you know the baby is nothing but an appetite, a parasite, and what you give of yourself to it goes through it and out its raw behind that you must constantly sop and clean and wash cloths with which to diaper it. The thought made Flora sick to her stomach. She was sure she would have to vomit each time she had to do that. *And who will care for it besides you,* she thought, *or give you rest and peace so you can work, as you must, for your own shelter and food?*

She had never wanted little brothers or sisters. She was the little one, petted and indulged. She had never indulged anyone. Flora never put up with anything from her father or stepmother. It was they who were supposed to give eternal, ungrudging love, with no limits.

She bore a deep, malevolent grudge against Chaney that he did not give her this love. He had betrayed her love. Her resentment of Chaney was extended to the innocent child, cause of hard new knowledge and insight, catalyst of change.

CHAPTER 15

Flora was slow to recover from childbirth. The doctor soon knew the baby was starving, and would starve, as Flora could not make milk to nourish her child. Whether due to her nervous condition or other physical factors, there was just no milk, and the baby boy was unable to hold anything but breast milk. The doctor thought at once of Jennie, who was grieving for her dead child and in pain caused by swollen breasts in which the milk had already begun to flow and could not easily be stopped. He consulted with both Flora and Jennie, and it was agreed that the baby boy would be boarded out to Jennie, who would feed and care for the infant. Flora was not pulling herself together after her delivery at all, so this would be to her advantage, too, as she would have time to recover from her weakened condition, to realize that she had to live and to somehow find a way to care for the baby, as yet unnamed.

Jennie had the milk that the infant desperately needed. The child began to rally strength and to come back from a starvation-death. Moreover, he received love, for Jennie's was a warm and loving home. Little Will and Priscilla, who had expected a baby brother or sister, accepted the baby, and Alonzo, too, showed an interest in the welfare of the reddish wrinkled infant.

It was Jennie who decided to call the baby in her care Jackie. She stated years later to her friend, Mrs. Esther Jones Lee, that the little fellow was so squirmish and jumpy he reminded her of a jumping jack. Since the baby's mother was not ready to name the baby, Jennie continued to use the name Jackie. Young Jack loved his name so much that he would continue to choose to use it as an adult.

Flora continued on in a depression, and her behavior was still erratic. She was lost as to sense of direction after the turbulent emotional trauma she had suffered. She had turned to hard drink during the time of her pregnancy to block out mental pain. Now she continued to drink in secret.

CHAPTER 16

The men Alonzo met in the bar with whom he shared a few drinks, an occasional pastime, often led him to job contacts and offered knowledge about the developing city, the latest political gossip, and other news, as well as exchanges about what was going on in other places, shared by

28

newcomers to the city. Immigrants arriving from other parts of the country were attracted into the glittering bar scenes along the old Gold Coast as a first taste of San Francisco. Some stayed tight-lipped about themselves. Others, made garrulous by a few drinks, had plenty to share. Alonzo heard wild tales. From what he heard from men who arrived from other places, San Francisco was considered a real crossroads of culture, a world city, cosmopolitan and sophisticated, but decadent as no other.

Some primitive instinct was satisfied at the bar. A bar was like some ancient watering hole where men of the tribe bathed, wet their faces, drank, relieved themselves, exchanged knowledge and opinions, and found a unity in their maleness.

The man Alonzo was having a drink with tonight was from New Orleans, Louisiana. Mr. Beaumont had just arrived and was talking about "back home." He was telling how the favored future of young girls who were quadroons, octoroons, or mulattoes was decided in New Orleans. Knowing marriage to a white man was out of the question, these light-skinned beauties were raised with the hopes of becoming the mistress of one and were brought out to be seen and chosen at "Quadroon Balls." The man boasted he had such a mistress and had abandoned both mistress and wife to come to California. Oh, not abandoned completely, he hastily corrected himself. He planned to send some money back from time to time for sake of the children. "I might send for one of the boys when I get my business going," he added as a magnanimous gesture.

After all, thought Alonzo, *a son would be cheap help in his company*. But whether one of the sons by his wife or by his mistress the man did not say. The effusive fellow had already said how many hours he would work his help and for what pay. Alonzo kept his bitter comments to himself. What may have seemed good pay in the South was inadequate by San Francisco standards. *With that man's mentality, his self-conceit, either child would be the man's work slave, less than a son,* was Alonzo's private opinion. Alonzo could imagine the sufferings that man had left behind him—two families dependent on an occasional sending of miserly sums. How could they subsist? What must they do to live? Well, he was no better, he thought angrily. He had sent no money to his former family. It had been accepted that Ruth's father would have her and the children back at her family home, going on as they did when Alonzo had been off to war. She would have a substantial amount from the sale of the fine home she and Alonzo had together, or she could continue to rent it out for income. He fervently hoped she had married again soon, but with a pang realized it was not likely some other man would readily parent his children, their children. It would take a special man to take someone else's child to raise.

Alonzo had this guilt that he never acknowledged. There was no need to tell these white strangers, with whom he drank or passed the time, that he was not white, that he had a black wife and two children of color right here in San Francisco, a wife from whom he led a separate life at times, like tonight, white and separate. He met people and heard things that he did not share with Jennie. *Society has made us a house divided,* Alonzo thought. He felt uncomfortable, unclear about himself, somewhat bitter at times, now that he thought he was less than a hero. *It's society's fault that I deny my race. What is this race business that it should interfere with the capabilities of people, my ability to do business as myself.*

He wanted to bash the man from New Orleans, standing beside him, right in his smug white face. Yet Alonzo continued listening with a gruesome fascination. The men on either side of them also turned to listen and were seemingly ready to enter into conversation with the charming, smooth-talking Southerner. Words fell from his mouth, sickly sweet as the smell of magnolia petals. A few drinks in him made the unspeakable possible to say. For some reason he was now talking about voodoo, the secret practice of an old religion brought into southern culture by Negroes from Haiti, by which they controlled each other through fear. He had seen small burlap figures with stick pins, drenched with chicken blood, that could inspire death.

The man to his left got onto the subject of strange religions. He had come through Utah and was talking about multiple marriages among a cult of people who had been hounded into Utah from place after place by mob violence and would perhaps be driven from there, persecuted for beliefs that were "against the laws of the country and even, probably, against God and man. Heard some had been coming over the mountain range in wagon trains for years, right into California; maybe some were even in San Francisco. Better be on the lookout for something alien as this among you." No one else knew anything about this news.

Now the talk turned to a phenomenon that had gained a foothold right here in San Francisco. People were involved in spiritualism, holding seances, and practiced free love!

What Alonzo Prentiss knew or thought about this he kept to himself this evening. But he drew a little apart, as these remarks had hit a nerve. He was well aware of at least one person who had been involved in these practices, Flora Wellman, Chaney, as she was called, for her liason with the notorious Professor Chaney, who had suddenly left town some months before. Flora's child, assumed to be Chaney's bastard, was right now lying in Alonzo's wife Jennie's arms. The conversation at the bar was getting a little too close to home.

Alonzo's decision to withdraw was made easier by a feisty Irishman

30

who decided to move into the slight space that by now existed between Alonzo and the man from New Orleans. He had overheard most of the previous irreligious conversation and had a few words to get off his chest about these spiritualists and free-love supporters, one and the same, who he said "were starting San Francisco along the way of Sodom and Gomorrah. Mark my words! There will be fire and destruction such as no one has ever seen, and this city will quake and tremble and be devoured in flame!"

With humor and to lighten the evening, one of the men sprinkled salt over a hard-boiled egg and offered a taste of "Lot's wife" to the Irishman. A ribald laugh and some more hushed conversation issued from the man from New Orleans.

The Irishman looked at Alonzo, who was lost in his own thoughts, and not finding another ready opponent for a rousing argument or perhaps a good fight, moved on down the bar.

One man told the stranger from New Orleans a little more about the city he had come to. "Above us is Nob Hill. The 'nobs' live above the rabble of the Barbary Coast, and right up there a man named Kearny is going to take angry rallies of marchers to put fear into them, the rich."

It is amazing, thought Alonzo, *that I should stand here and so calmly listen. They have no idea where I live or how I got there or even what I am, as they pass judgment!*

The men went on talking about Broadway, the main drag of the old Gold Coast, with its carnival atmosphere. Women were there in suggestive dress to reveal the swelling breast, the turn of ankle under lifted ruffle. Inside certain places were women in even shorter skirts, with raised ruffles. A man could see black lace corsets and black net-stockinged, gartered legs. Persuasive rowdy barkers would entice you and practically pull you into open dens of iniquity. A few staged acts verged on the obscene. Gaudy, flamboyant men in flowing neckties, with diamond rings and stickpins, moustaches, and showy ways of dress, were there ready to gamble. Alonzo felt himself lured, too, by the man's talk. He felt he could really become two different people in San Francisco— one the devoted, serious husband, the other a sampler of the exotic. He thought of the shock after shock that had shaken him to his roots and almost ripped him asunder. He stared, silent and moody, into his drink. "A house divided cannot stand," was what he brooded on as other talk flowed on around him.

The War between the States was nothing compared to all the separateness of everything. Alonzo could find no way to put it together in his own mind—society's behavior. Those pious-mouthed, churchgoing hypocrites he had known in the army, some of them were among the

31

ones who had rejected him for his race and refused to serve with him once he became exposed, labeled as a "nigger."

San Francisco encompassed every character, type of person, and way of thinking, yet was also a city so limited in its acceptance of race, giving shock to Alonzo's individual being, what he was, a Negro with a white man's body. He could love more than one woman. Ruth once, now Jennie, and yes, he was humbled, ashamed, to admit it, but he had been unfaithful to Jennie, too, right here in San Francisco, but those occasions had nothing to do with love. They had something to do with acknowledgment, being accepted as a white man again, and the shock to his system of how he had been treated since he was black—the shock of who he was. There was such a thing as culture shock, too, when it came to a place like San Francisco. There were things he would never have thought about or even heard of anyplace else. He had thought Tiffin a big, fast-growing city, but it held no shock to the senses. It seemed to him that San Francisco gave opportunity for experience, sexual and otherwise, as no other place.

By now the number of men at the bar was thinning out. Even the man from New Orleans and the Irishman had each left the bar with chosen other male companions. Other parts of the street could offer wild tastes of fruits forbidden elsewhere, for men who had such appetites. Alonzo assumed the stranger to the city was gong to be initiated into exotic vices and lusts north of Market above Montgomery, for he had heard someone whisper, "Chinatown." He knew what was to be found, for he had been there himself: narrow, dark, even dangerous alleys, where through door crack or curtain, by oil lamp or candle flicker, were glimpses into rooms where as many as forty men crowded for the night on shelves from floor to ceiling. One out of every ten men in San Francisco was Chinese, brought as "Coolie slave labor," most now in desperation for work, willing to take the most menial job for the lowest pay just to survive. The opium from Hawaii came directly to Chinatown to enslave them in another way. The men from the bar, Alonzo surmised, would go straight to cheap-bought flesh, for there was unrestricted traffic in Chinese prostitutes. Four thousand young girls had been brought here to be sold, enslaved for life.

Alonzo felt a sudden overwhelming hunger and thirst. It was not what could be satisfied in a bar or in places he could imagine the others had gone. He had felt it before, when he joined flesh with Jennie. Now, strongly, the powerful realization came over him that he could only be satisfied with Jennie.

CHAPTER 17

Alonzo left the bar alone and decided to walk the long uphill blocks home, pulled along by his thoughts of Jennie.

In fact, it would be his last such night in a San Francisco bar. He had gotten something out of his system. This night was the turning point.

As he walked home he thought more about the direction his mind had been taking him over the past few months and where he was going from there. He tried to think clearly about Jennie. Jennie knew a lot about man's inhumanity, but she would be protected from knowing what he saw and heard around him in sections of the city where a woman like Jennie wouldn't be found and from what he did elsewhere that it would hurt her to know. Let her be protected from the earthquake he knew in his own mind that could rip them apart and shake the foundation of her love for him. Let her belief in his goodness and her religion continue to protect her.

Alonzo had come out of war without a religion. He had seen death, and when soldiers died it had given him no feel of immortality. He saw a man with half a face shot away as if war were a giant maggot that feasted there. As suddenly as this he was aware that maggots would devour the perfect body of that man, that human beauty, and found himself gagging and retching under a tree. He had gotten a good look at himself as a mortal, disintegrating, temporal being. Until his marriage with Jennie he had never again felt a striving for immortality. If he had any feel for religion now, this seemed centered in her. To feel at one with a religion, a community, was to focus on her and what she meant to him. She had some simple concepts about virtue and acts that were her biblical practices and truths.: "the greatest of these is charity" and "love one another as God so loved you." This form of simple religion he could manage, and that seemed to satisfy her that he was not without soul. In his dealings with others and his example for the children, she gave him her trust that he would be guided by these same values she held so dear and that motivated her whole life.

When Alonzo met Jennie he was a man grown into prime, already developed and set in certain ways. He knew his first grasp of things was visual, as a builder knows materials that can be measured—form and substance, texture and shape.

There was so much he could not express. Sometimes he thought if he could only have known Jennie when he was very much younger he would have been inspired to learn to put things into words. Perhaps he would have had to become a poet, his unexpressed feelings were so deep, so strong.

Alonzo remembered the first time he had touched Jennie's hair. It shocked him, so unexpected, a texture of hair unlike anything he had ever touched before. He had no previous awareness hair could ever feel like that, rough-bristled, wiry, causing almost a scrape of his hand like sandpaper. He became totally absorbed in a sensation through his hand that took over his body completely. A thrill of excitement had encompassed his entire nervous system. All of his senses were affected by her. He felt the same excitement through his eyes when he looked at her hair. She parted it and fixed it into designs. She had many ways of dividing and braiding or fastening it into arrangement of pattern, each section of hair, with a ribbon, a bead, a small bud or flower entwined. At other times she wound cloth around her head, like scarves that were twisted or tied into styles he had never seen a woman wear before. Material tucked into itself, folded, overlapped, knotted or crossed over, always clinging to the head in a way that defined and ornamented the beautiful oval shape of her head. Women of the South, and especially black women, Alonzo had noticed, wore their hair differently from the women in other parts of the country. No other women would wear sweet-smelling flowers in their hair that he recalled. He saw a vision of Jennie rising up from the abyss of the city, like a flowering plant blossoming just for him, as a plant grows out of decayed compost. She could keep him fresh from decay also, make him into a bursting pure bloom. Let other men go out rotting from the bar into the debauchery the city offered. It was as if two people in him had come face to face and integrated into one whole again. Jennie's sweet spirit was his sacrament, their children his redemption, their baby's death in some way his punishment. He would make it up to her, be now and for always only the person she knew and loved.

He thought of the other woman's child drinking from Jennie's breast—Jennie, giving life and love to another human being. He had to admire and love her the more. He felt his own head cradled in her arms, his mouth on her breast.

What had he been doing drinking in a bar, relatively alone, for he was not like those men around him who had no Jennie to return to? He affirmed to himself, again, a sort of litany, for she had begun a transformation in him and this must continue—their home, his church; her body, his worship; their children, his redemption; her love, his religion, her eyes, his altar candles.

He was hurrying home. Blood pounded in his veins, turbulent from his thoughts of love and from the hard uphill walk. He would love her tonight as if love were his sacrament. *This is my blood, my body, eat and drink.* He would take her in his arms and drink deep the kisses of her beautiful sweet wet mouth.

Out of the bar, he walked the long way home up the hill, and it was a clear night, with no fog, and in the direction in which he was going there seemed to be holy lights ahead of thousands of stars.

CHAPTER 18

Professor Chaney was long gone from her life, but Flora continued to dwell on their past, her mind overwhelmed by memory. From the time of Flora's pregnancy, when the newspaper reports sensationalized her situation, she continued in a turbulence of emotions. Flora wanted still to be considered the wife of W. H. Chaney, who had abandoned her during her pregnancy, and he had admittedly lived with her for a year from June 1874 to June 1875, during the time the child was conceived. But Chaney stubbornly rejected the child Flora carried and accused a tenant in the rooming house where they lived, Lee Smith, of being the father, while at the same time reminding Flora that they had lived together without the commitment of marriage and with complete sexual freedom and there were others he would not name publicly, who could have fathered the child. Whether she herself wanted a child was not the question. She had wanted her pregnancy to be an advantageous situation for compelling Chaney into a more permanent bond and was stubbornly intent on furthering their relationship in this way and willing to commit great desperate acts to force him into a marriage he did not want.

He would rather see her dead! This became terribly and dramatically evident to Flora when she put that to the test in several failed suicide attempts. Chaney remained unshaken to the end in his resolve to stay free of parenthood and legal marriage.

Flora, in making dramatic public appeals to win allies to her side in the attempt to force Chaney to do what she thought would be an honorable thing, may have been impressed with tales told her by Chaney himself. He had had a stint as a newspaper editor in a previous town and had experienced the power of the press.

In regard to Flora, Chaney took the way out he had taken many times before, including the time he clashed publicly with a priest. After he had his public say, regardless of the damage created, he got out of town.

Flora was left wounded and bloody, so to speak, on their personal and public battlefield. The child was just a casualty, victim of a lost war between two strong-willed, adamant people.

Chaney had advertised himself widely in San Francisco as a professor of astrology. Flora had been more than Chaney's personal companion; she had been his business associate, promoting his ideas, selling tickets at the door for his lectures, which ranged from astrology to occult phenomena. She conducted her own spiritualists meetings. She held seances, gave piano lessons, and had a clientele for whom she sewed. Professor Chaney accused her of being promiscuous.

Spiritualism, a growing fancy throughout San Francisco, had become a cult with hundreds of fervent devotees and leaders, among whom Flora was considered a very colorful and much talked about personage. Professor Chaney exerted a leverage on Flora to keep her interests broader than the spirit world. He remained unconvinced of the powers of the spirit world alone to guide destiny, but tried to persuade Flora to give credibility to other things, predominantly the influence of the stars. He also upheld the power of writing for publication to convince the public through the medium of the press. He had had a number of articles published in magazines and had written several tracts whose readership gave him valuable feedback for developing his ideas and which also impressed a considerable number of people.

When Chaney was a newspaper editor he had instigated a citywide crusade of anti-Catholic bigotry, until he went too far in provoking the actual act of the public tar and feathering of a priest, after which outrageous act public opinion turned against him, and in that backlash he himself had to leave town. Coming to San Francisco, he had formed an alliance with Flora. She was willing to join him in support and development of his career as an astrologer.

Neither the stars nor the spirits aided them in their misadventures with one another. Flora demanded Professor Chaney marry her and acknowledge the unborn child. He demanded that she get an abortion and thus rid herself of the child. Each asked of the other what the other was violently opposed to doing. Eventually the professor passionately wished Flora dead and she was desperate enough to attempt to oblige, putting a bullet wound in her own forehead.

At this point the young, sensation-geared *San Francisco Chronicle* reported as many gory details of Chaney and Flora's life together as could be ferreted out in the guise of reporting. Professor Chaney, furiously angry at Flora and feeling himself abused by the press, left San Francisco and the pregnant Flora. Her followers gave her what public support they could, attending the lectures and events she continued to hold. They continued to pay and to take up collections for her and pitied her condition. She had received a terrible emotional blow and drowned her fears and frustrations with strong drink. She and Chaney never communicated with each other again. It had been a pattern for each in the past to make a break and never go back. She had been a well-bred person from a fine home but had left when young, never to return. Her background was Welsh; the professor's was Irish. He had been a bond servant as a child who had more than once run away from cruel masters.

After being abandoned by Professor Chaney, Flora moved from the place they had lived in, between Mission and Valencia streets, on what was at that time called First Avenue and was taken in, until her child was born, by a writer, William Slocum, and his friend, Mrs. Amanda.

Flora, now alone, having given her baby over to Jennie to be fed and cared for, was moving inexorably into the realm of the spirit world, withdrawing from other realities. She hardly knew or cared that her child existed, except for occasional sudden and imperious demands that he be brought for a visit. But she could not, even then, relate to him with love. She developed no feeling for him, other than vexation. He served only to remind her of her anguish and failure.

In being a medium to the spirit world Flora had found an area in which she was in control. She could escape the daily pain of her problems of loneliness and the lack of a sound economic base for her life. The lure of the spirit world was very strong. She was enamored of the escape into power, to a position where people could see that the spirits would accept even her admonishments and surely could not make contact in this world except through her. She was not alone if there were a host of spirits at her beck and call. People who depended on her powers to make contact for them had to seek her out and pay money for her services, for her bringing words "from beyond." They had to respect that she was an unusual, gifted person. There were many benefits. She began to again hold seances on a regular basis, giving less time to seeking music students for piano lessons or a clientele for her sewing.

Though a good seamstress, she was slightly bizarre in the clothes she made herself up in, appropriate as a guide to the spirit world. To add to her mystique she wore a wig of black hair coiffed high with curls on top and sausage curls falling over one shoulder. Less than five feet tall, her growth having been stunted, she claimed, by childhood fever, she was, nevertheless, a compelling entity by force of her personality, sharp, erratic, verbal, with a penetrating gaze, for which she wold remove her spectacles. She would size up and quell any person she desired to dominate. But her powers failed her in compelling Chaney to her side. Only her ghosts remained. All else became as illusion of the mind and a remembrance of the wrong she had suffered.

CHAPTER 19

The memories pieced together—memories of people, some now very old and some who said things they knew, long ago, to others, and some who had died, memories collected from time and people and place as told by Jennie or by Alonzo or by others who knew them or things that the people who told saw with their own eyes, heard with their own ears. Most of this was, no matter how strange, very clear.

But of just one circumstance no one was very sure, and this was the part that had to do with whether Alonzo had known Flora before Jack came into Jennie's care and if he was, in fact, the one who found through Flora the doctor who was also Jennie's doctor or if Alonzo and Jennie were put in touch with Flora by the doctor. Some state that the doctor who delivered both infants brought the two mothers together. Some believed that Alonzo had known Flora for many months. Called in on carpentry work, he had met her. Some believed that he had had her make the shirts he wore, that he had first known Flora in a relationship unknown to Jennie, who did know that Flora, as a seamstress had made Alonzo shirts. Voices! They would never agree! One saying one thing, one now another.

The fact is that Alonzo wore shirts made by Flora and that Flora either began to or continued to make shirts for Alonzo in payment for the boarding of the baby boy Jennie called Jackie, whose first baby words were "Mama" for Jennie and "Papa" for Alonzo.

CHAPTER 20

The wealthy English couple whose child had died came to the United States on a drastically adventurous cruise to take their mind from their sorrows. But the woman's grief seemed to grow only more intense. At last, her husband, while they were in San Francisco, took her to Flora, well advertised as a medium who could do impossible things to bring peace of mind to people. Perhaps she could put the woman in touch with a spirit guide for information about what to do in their sorrow and for information about how their child was faring in the next world.

Lonely, and feeling in a certain mood after partaking in the seance, a strange event that had disturbed more than consoled them, the grieving couple invited another couple who had been there to join them in a nearby café, for they were sorely in need of afternoon tea. The English custom revived them somewhat, and they confided their deep sadness because of their child's death. The other couple, Mr. and Mrs. Baker, a little gossipy, told of Flora having a baby she was unable to care for and that she had let out, so the story was spread, to foster parents who lived not too far away. Flora was hard put to support her baby's board and care, so that day, out of pity, the Bakers had given to her rather generously.

The English couple were, in the course of the afternoon, encouraged to test out the idea that they might adopt this perhaps unwanted, certainly neglected, nearly abandoned child. For the child's mother was unmarried or at least had no visible husband or father for the little boy. It might be a blessing for all.

"Could we see him? Is he a healthy and handsome little chap?"

"Why, yes, you can be assured on that score. Flora has had the Negro woman who is wet nurse for the child bring him by for visits some rare afternoons when I and others have been there and that is how some of us are acquainted with the facts. One day, when my dear husband called for me, he kindly offered to take the nurse and child back home, so I can give you the address. Of course, newspapers had printed the beginnings of the dreadful story as to how Professor Chaney, the famed astrologer, quite well known here, left Flora. What a scandal! It is no reflection on the child," the woman hastened to add, "that the parents behaved badly. I understand they were both from fine families and that the child has good blood in him.

"But passion," she sighed, "can cause people to do wild, unaccountable things!"

Then she went on to add, "Perhaps Flora has become, after all, a little strange. Affected by her affair with Professor Chaney, who has seemingly abandoned her forever, she seems irritated and provoked by the infant's fretfulness in her presence. She seems to have no talent for showing love to her own child. She is given to nervousness, swooning, demands for attention herself. It seems she will hardly be able to raise the child alone. And after all, she has a living to make. She seeks customers for her sewing and her piano lessons, as well as her seances.

"A child could get pretty neglected, lost in such an atmosphere. I wouldn't say anything, except I have some intimate knowledge of that sordid affair which brought Flora to all this suffering. It doesn't mean she doesn't have the gift of contacting spirits and, I hasten to add, her skill is quite remarkable. It seems we must judge her by a different set of standards!"

The English couple thanked the woman for having spoken and

assured her they believed she had done so only in the child's best interests. They resolved to go to see Jennie the next day, having obtained her address. They wanted to see the child before approaching Flora with their plan. They could well afford to educate and raise the child in comfortable style and were wealthy enough to make it agreeable to Flora, they supposed.

Although the woman had not really said it, she had put it into the minds of the English couple that this might be a baby of "pure" English heritage, that the mother had become emotionally unstable to the point of never undertaking to raise the child herself, and that after all perhaps Flora could quite easily be proven to be an unfit mother.

The only time that anyone, including Alonzo, remembered that Jennie ever berated her husband was after the visit of this well-intentioned but blundering English couple to her home. She was so upset her voice carried and she could clearly be heard, after that couple's rather hurried departure, saying, "Oh, Alonzo, how could you let those people in here? Oh, this poor, dear baby!

"Don't ever let anyone on a cause like that come here to try to take this child from us. We have cared for him as our very own. We have given him his life. You know how I love him!"

From this time on Alonzo and Jennie expected no more shirts made by Flora for Alonzo or other contribution of payment for Jack's care. No pressure was ever put on Flora in any way, as Jennie suspected Flora had sent the couple because she was under financial stress. In fact, Jennie now saw that if they were to help Jack they would also have to further befriend and find ways to help Flora.

It had been an extremely unpleasant experience for Jennie to think someone might come along who could take Jackie out of her life, even far across an ocean! "If he is to be given up, it is we who deserve him," she said to Alonzo. "We have kept him alive!" The English couple had left quickly in consternation, for they soon realized their idea was but a misguided fantasy. The infant was only a few months old and not nearly ready to be weaned, and at any rate, both man and wife in that house had put up such a show of strength on behalf of little Jack that the English couple were convinced of their integrity as the child's devoted protectors.

"Why, they are well-to-do!" said the embarrassed Englishman to his wife. "Their home is tastefully furnished and so clean. We don't know the truth here. Suppose he is the father! I mean, he acted with a concern and affection toward that child, as if he were the real father."

"It was the woman that impressed me," said his wife. "The wife,

Jennie. She showed me she loved the baby as much as I loved our own little one. Oh, one mother can know another mother's love. She shows her love for that child."

"Were our faces red!" confessed the woman's husband. "She routed us out of there like a mother hen protecting her young. She treated us with compassion to our faces, yet as I came down the stairs I could hear her scolding her husband for letting us in. Oh, my dear, I know you had a dream, but this baby is not our concern. It is not for us. You can see it is nurtured and loved. It is well cared for there."

"I understand, my dearest. I am quite ready to go back to England. I never saw a white man married to a black woman and her nursing a white child. Strange things happen in America!"

Alonzo was exceedingly troubled at this confrontation.

How well he knew the English couple had been right. They said to Jennie what he could not say, that Flora was not a fit mother. The time would come when Jennie would have to turn Jack over to Flora, as she could claim the child by legal right. Though Alonzo held his tongue, he felt it would perhaps have been kinder to have allowed that sad but hopeful and gentle-appearing English couple to pursue the adoption of little Jackie.

As Jennie had known her own mother to have been sold away from her on the slave block, never to be seen again, and had lost one infant, it was going to hurt Jennie to lose again. Alonzo could understand how Jennie could not allow an ocean to separate her from Jackie. But it could hurt her worse to see the kind of treatment that Flora alone might give little Jack, if Flora continued on her present course. So much would depend now on Flora. Flora and her stability would become of increasing importance as the child grew.

Jennie had done more than give Jackie the milk of human kindness, done more than save his life; she had given him her heart. Flora, though she seemed not to love her baby, would keep a possessive hold on him. She might not have given up hope that someday Chaney would be persuaded to return again. Flora would still want this hold. Alonzo knew that because of the question of race, he and Jennie would never have a chance to adopt Jackie. What judge would see a mother so dark of skin for a child so blond and fair? And this is the final, dismal fact.

Oh, Jennie was wrong, thought Alonzo, to allow herself to love so deeply a child she could not claim. But Alonzo loved him, too, he admitted guiltily, and how could he, a logical, intelligent man, have allowed all this to happen?

CHAPTER 21

Jennie, in her delight in reading, gave encouragement to William from the first time he was able to bring a book home from school. Every word he learned to read meant a thrill of discovery. William and Priscilla were both impressed by their mother's excitement over their amazing ability to read words and share this with each other. William always wanted to bring books home when he discovered their importance to his mother, and he would be asked by Jennie to prove to her and to Priscilla all that he could read. Then Jennie, too, would read the same book aloud. She was proud that her son and daughter would have an education that was forbidden, in her childhood, to her.

Jack took in the flow of words along with the flow of mother's milk that nourished him for all his babyhood. Two things were intermingled, with his head against her heart: the rhythm of her pulse and the rhythm of her reading. She made a practice of reading her Bible aloud daily. She sang to the children and told them stories—not only of the way things looked growing in their seasons where the land was so beautiful, back in Tennessee, but even things as remembered and told to her by those seemingly ancient men and women who were the servants in the Big House and who remembered Africa, being brought from there into slavery, some in their own youth, some in their prime. Each knew something different about Africa, as a memory. They had been brought in slave markets at different times, had even been brought from different parts of Africa, and did not have a language, culture, customs, or tribe in common. But all could tell, in English with a southern dialect so thick no one outside of Nashville might have understood it, murmured remembrances to each other, at rare and stolen times. The child Jennie grew up knowing there were mysteries of other languages and other parts of the world and wishing she could learn more of them. Through this reading she was relearning how to pronounce all the words in William's schoolbooks more the way Alonzo, in Ohio, had learned to pronounce them. The history and geography books opened new ideas. The world and society as taught to little children in school, to her child, for Jennie were fascinating reading.

Jack, seated in her lap as she held the books, grabbed at books as at everything else, with his curious nature. The look and sound of words he assimilated as naturally as milk and breath. He never knew when or how he learned to read. Later, as an adult, he assumed he must have been born knowing. It was as if he was never taught, because in this preconscious awareness reading was always there for him. He learned

42

letters and words and how to read them without knowing he was learning.

Priscilla, too, learned to read almost by osmosis, so that when she started school her teachers considered her very precocious. She brought her own primers, speller, and arithmetic book home, and Jennie studied with her. William joined in. With baby Jack on Jennie's lap an integral part, they shared the learning process.

If such energy surrounding a child has a role in deciding what pattern that child's life takes, Jack was being gifted with the power of words and books. Alonzo would listen with approval at the more verbal members of his family expressing their pleasure in their learning activities. He too had a rich store of words and ideas in his head, though he was not as freely given to expression as the others. He was respected as the strong, silent type, and his praise and opinion were doubly more impressive to his family as they were to others who knew him. He taught by doing. William and little Priscilla, with Jack's hand in hers as he toddled after, would follow Alonzo to his work area and see him put arithmetic to good use by measuring and shaping with his tools smaller models of the things of the world that delighted them. The ships that sailed the bay before their eyes every day, in a beautiful view from Nob Hill, when the fog lifted, looking like miniatures in the distance, appeared as tiny sailboats made with Alonzo's hands and put to sail in the backyard washtub. It had amused Alonzo to humor Jennie's wanting an old southern-style outdoor tub when they lived in a rich man's house with a modern clawfoot tub in an indoor bathroom that had even a toilet with a pull-chain. There were built-in tin washtubs with running water in a room off the pantry and a clothesline reel that operated with a pulley across the backyard by his workshed. Here Alonzo let William help him fashion with his carpenter's tools little furnishings for Priscilla's dollhouse, a whatnot stand for Jennie, a spice rack, and a footstool. He liked to take the family on his day off to see, every few months or so, what work he did when he was away, the important building. He let them feel that building a house had honor and magnificence and meaning. A multiplicity of houses, one by one, progressed right up the precarious hills of San Francisco by sheer tenacity of the builders, architects' plans, the carpenters' talents. Curliques and shingles, hand-turned ornamental columns, bannisters, all abounded. Gingerbread, gabled windows, cornices, decorative eaves, turrets, and colorfully painted trim adorned these houses. There were Carpenters' Gothics, Queen Annes, and Stick Houses, costing three thousand dollars, seven thousand dollars, and even more to build. And the building went on.

Alonzo had steady work. He made sure each long and particular job, even the most tedious, was well done: doors fit in their frames;

43

window casements and window seats were exactly and neatly made; high ceilings, solid and stable, would hold ornate chandeliers for gas light or even the new incandescents, in rooms with French fireplaces that burned coal or had heavy-manteled, wide-open stone, brick, marble, or tile hearths for wood fires; gleaming oak floors and dark paneled rooms to hold furnishings brought for them into the harbor on sailing vessels, dangerously around the horn, across the isthmus, or shipped from the East on the railroad.

The weather was good enough almost year round for Alonzo to work, and redwood structures rose their frameworks against the sky into the sun or the fog. He could vision his firstborn, William, saying proudly to a child of his own, far in the future, "That's where my father worked. A fine carpenter, he helped to build this . . ." and that child could tell the next generation. The houses were built for the centuries.

Alonzo liked to take his family, too, on a carpenter's holiday down by the shipyards to see the wooden hulls in various stages of progress. Some seemed like imagined skeletal ribs of a beached whale; others were near completion, with stained woods gleaming. His family knew from him that it was a fine, strong pleasure to build a ship or a home, a great work.

CHAPTER 22

The "Nobs" were expected to be an exalted social class, high-quality, the lofty rich, San Francisco's nobility. In reality the neighborhood was a hodgepodge of people who kept to themselves, not a cheery, close community. No one knew each other too well or inquired into backgrounds or personalities. One wealthy, unapproachable man's wife was rumored to have been a Romanian princess, although other rumors were that she had been an erotic dancer and in one of the city's more remarkable bordellos. If there were neighbors who had won money heavily through gambling or gained it by dishonest means, it was never said. That would have lowered the quality of life on Nob Hill.

Jennie did not visit any of her neighbors, and they did not visit around among each other. With an accent that few of her neighbors had ever heard before, she was assumed to have come from some romantic place, like India or Egypt, the West Indies, or a South Seas island. Neighbors wanted to think that. It made the neighborhood more cosmopolitan, more exotic. Some of the Nob Hill residents may have at first thought of Jennie as the housekeeper for Alonzo. But eventually she was acknowledged for her neatness of place and person and her proud bearing, and they offered a nodding acquaintance in recognition and acceptance of her presence among them. Certainly no one dreamed that she had been a slave, property bought and sold, a Negro from a southern plantation, and that her husband, too, was black. They were an unusual family, with varying shades of skin. Priscilla had skin like café au lait with lots of cream and fluffy soft brown hair and tawny brown eyes with incredible lashes. William, the firstborn, was darker, with skin of a dusky glow, hair like his mother's, and midnight eyes. Alonzo was an ash-blond, hair bleached lighter by the sun and white skin suntanned golden bronze. He was as blue-eyed as little Jack, whose thick blond hair fell in waves over his forehead and who was considered by all who saw him with them to be part of the Prentiss family.

Jennie's life on Nob Hill was self-contained. So she had lived in the Big House, among but not a part of the white people around her. On Nob Hill, it was her choice, as she had been pregnant, had become a surrogate mother in nursing Jack, cared for the three children who had her constant interest, kept an immaculate house, and did her own extensive baking and good southern style cooking, plus trying out new things to cook that she learned about whenever she went to market, where people of diverse cultures sold their produce in a city-block-size area. She learned for the first time about Chinese foods, tasting bok choy, won ton soup, bird's nest soup, sizzling rice soup, long greens, and many other interesting things to eat, buying vegetables from the Chinese men with the "yeo-ho" poles over their shoulders, baskets balanced on each side, buying equally from Mexicans who cooked and served tamales and tortillas and refried beans at their open stands and Italians whose huge pots of garlicky spaghetti sent steamy fumes to mingle with the fresh-fish smell of the ocean breeze. She marveled at the mysterious shapes and qualities of ginseng roots and ginger and undecipherable other things for sale in the musty strong straw-smelling baskets and thin wooden boxes that crammed the sidewalks of the market. But whatever she tried, she always went back to cooking the way it was done in the South, and this is what her family felt was "home-cooking."

She relished the outings on which Alonzo took the family and would have liked to see more, all parts of this unique city. But she was always busy, with the three children and all the work she did by hand, washing, starching, mixing the bleaches or the blueing or the starch for the shirts, skirts, blouses, petticoats, sheets, and pillowcases and all the other things of their voluminous wardrobes. From dawn to dark she did the household necessities, the ironing, polishing of furniture, and braiding the rag rugs

45

as she had learned in the South. She was making them round and thick and colorful for the kitchen of their home. She trimmed the kerosene lamps in their wall fixtures and table stands. She encouraged the studies of William and Priscilla.

When she went to the market and shops she felt she would never have to go on one of those sailing ships to see other countries of the world—it had all been brought here to astound her. Even in one lifetime she would not see all that had been brought right into San Francisco.

She began attending the First Baptist Church in San Francisco, taking William and Priscilla to Sunday school and Jack to the Cradle Row. She socialized with people at church, but hardly had time to visit new friends in their homes or to entertain. She did not visit around the neighborhood. That was not her custom. Because of the select separateness of the "Nobs," their tacit agreement that anyone who lived on the hill was one of their own, the Prentiss family felt no prejudice directed against them there, no matter how isolated from the others each household might seem. The Nob Hill residents could lift their brows at the people below.

Jennie never wanted to be a snob. She never intended to again be part of a society separated by class or race. Those days were over, she thought, never to return, and could not touch her anymore. Alonzo had more skeptical views about the divisiveness in people and kept seeing new evidence all the time that reinforced his view that it was best to stay uninvolved with people and say nothing about your true situation or feelings.

Alonzo, in his own way, absorbed the essence of the city and enriched his mind, walking through neighborhoods created by people of many cultures in San Francisco. He wandered alone through the Italian sections of North Beach where the air seemed composed of coffee and garlic-thick bread. He watched old men playing bocce ball on the clay courts they had made, hearing the bells of churches mingled with chant of the Mass on early Sundays and, in conjunction, the raucous laugh of gulls that called to each other and circled him with a windy rush of wings. He passed through the shadows of black-clad, black-shawled women in little Italy into the narrow, crowded streets of Chinatown, where language, to his ears, was a new form of music.

Just as the rock seals' community below the pier where he saw these sea creatures at play or sunning themselves was a separate entity, so the immigrants, who had sailed past them, came into the city and separated their division by ethnic groups, developing each part of the city like some old world community to recreate what they had left behind. They repeated patterns that had sustained their grandparents, generations ago, in other parts of the globe. Russians, Irish, Germans, Polish, Jewish, Mexicans, Italians, and other groups, each wanted a part of the city as their own. Continuing traditions, customs, and, yes, the jealousies, angers, rivalries, ambitions, bad memories, fights over territories, and old attitudes that caused contentions, the neighborhoods were smaller versions of countries whose inhabitants still fought with each other over real and mythic histories.

Alonzo knew race prejudice was strongest when it came to employment, and he was hearing a great deal about men in San Francisco planning rebellions and uprisings for employment and against wage slavery. One leader was Dennis Kearney, whose Irish forebears gave him knowledge of an ancient history of bondage and rebellion. The Irish were among the first slaves. Even before the coming of Christ, the Milesians had held them in bondage. Vikings, Norsemen, and Icelanders all preyed upon Ireland, to take slaves from there for themselves. Later, the English took their lands, their employment, their rights, and persecuted them, the Irish poor, to make them more poor. The British, who wanted to claim all fertile land of the Catholic Irish, continued pushing that already starving population into a worse famine, to destroy them. The English poet Spenser, who received from Sir Walter Raleigh some of the forty thousand acres he had seized from the Irish, wrote that the Irish should not be allowed to settle their land or grow food or pasture cattle, but should be forced to eat each other. He wrote that this would clear the entire land of the Irish for the benefit of the English, their intention at the time.

Many Irish sold themselves into bondage to come from their famine-ridden country to the United States. Dennis Kearney, as an immigrant, had come, too, to escape economic persecution, in the forced mass exodus of the starving. He got it into his head to lead the poor and unemployed of San Francisco in demonstrations. He picked Nob Hill as the target for one of his more terrifying torchlight marches and demonstrations. He was already planning to incite the jobless to mob attacks on the Chinese to burn and loot their small stores. He intended to persecute them for the condition of being Chinese, because prejudice forced them to take jobs for less pay. He vowed to drive them into the bay. There were no means to free them from a pitiable condition.

Alonzo felt a furious frustration coming back on him, thinking of all this. He had fought one war where race and justice were factors. He excelled at his work because he gave it all his concentrated skill and dedication, yet he had suffered from the powers of bigotry directed against him. He had finally managed a home for his children and for his wife, who was surely one of the most loving, forgiving, and under-

47

standing of all women. Now couldn't he just be at peace with the world? Why would anything more have to happen?

He remembered the Irish man at the bar predicting the very ground would tremble, quake, open, and swallow up human evil. How precarious his peace seemed.

He was growing older. Certainly he could see the gray hairs coming in his loose curls and especially in the long sideburns. Maybe his life experiences had changed him, like the forehead wrinkle and the sun-squint wrinkles at the corner of the eyes and the deep-cut wry lines at each corner of the mouth. He was not at all that kid he had been in Ohio, that good fellow, the team player, a popular man about town, who thought he could be a hero and change the world with a war. It seemed like it was other people who brought trouble and change to his life. He liked Nob Hill, where it was "live and let live." If it wasn't for troublemakers like Kearney, with their misdirected cruelty, their prejudiced zeal, Alonzo could almost say this was the happiest time of his life and he would like to just go on like this.

What could happen next?

CHAPTER 23

Through this interlapping of their lives, Alonzo and Jennie became primary factors in the life and future of Flora Chaney. It was they who affected her destiny, not, as Flora would have surmised, the spirits on whom she relied.

Alonzo was working as a carpenter with an Englishman, named John London, who, having put his two motherless daughters into the Protestant orphan asylum on Haight Street, had to pay for their care. He had brought the girls, Eliza and Ida, to San Francisco after the death of his wife, seeking a climate for the recovery of his son, Charles, who nevertheless died soon after arrival.

John, like Alonzo, had been in the Union army. Alonzo had gotten out of the service with minor surface body scars from one skirmish and one deep psychological wound that was never to be healed. John, like many of the soldiers who had known hunger, privation, and exposure to the elements, had been partially wrecked physically by the war. He had become ill with typhus, which had spread through the army carried by lice and fleas, and was left with one lung. Once the typhus was in his blood, recurrent attacks, so debilitating they affected his working ability, would occur. When he was at his most physically fit he was a willing and steady worker, such as at the time he came to work with Alonzo.

John London was a lonely man who needed to love a woman. He found a young woman, Kate Castleton, an aspiring actress to whom he was attracted and who was attracted in turn by his handsome and easygoing charm. But she refused to become his wife and take on the mothering of his little girls. Putting freedom to pursue her career aspirations in light opera ahead of the bonds of marriage, she would not forsake the stage. Her friends had interests that made him feel an outsider. He was older than her set, and he wanted a home and family. John wanted to hang around with Alonzo. Alonzo was a good listener, and John desperately needed a friend to talk things over with. But Alonzo had found it expedient to keep his home life and his marriage to Jennie separate from his work and co-workers. He did not at first take John London into his home to meet his wife with her beautiful dark satin skin and lovely and gracious manner, although he knew John was yearning for a marriage and love and their love was an example. Alonzo was tempted to show Jennie off to John, her wonderful southern cooking and her sweet spirit. John looked as if he could use some stable meals and some sympathetic friends.

John admired everything he knew about Alonzo: his craftsmanship as a carpenter, his firm and responsible but good-natured leadership of his co-workers and crew. His physical strength, for his body moved easily as an athlete, muscles rippling as he carried out his work. His sense of style. He looked good in his clothes. John admired his shirts, and here was something Alonzo could do for John. The money would help Flora, too.

Alonzo took John to Flora to have some shirts made like his. What began inauspiciously enough with a commonplace, for John, who had admired Alonzo's shirts and wanted to get some for himself, suddenly took on another dimension. Flora's primary business was the spirit world, and she tried to draw out people to bring them into one of her seances, her main interest and source of income. She soon knew from John his current situation and feelings.

As John told Flora, he admired Alonzo because he had background, experience, knowledge of his trade, and outstanding skill. Without an outstanding skill in a specific trade, John had gone from job to job. Now he was working with Alonzo as a carpenter to get a grub stake together to rent land so he could farm, the work for which he was best suited. He thought it was good to get people back to the land and that people belonged on the land, where they could harvest wholesome food. It was deeply soul-satisfying, to bring food out of the earth, and he believed he would be a healthier person doing this. It was what he could do better than other things. He wanted to get his daughters out of the orphanage and back with him. He had good intentions, was willing to strive for his family, and had had devastating blows in the death of his wife and illness of his son. The desire to save his son from death after that serious illness caused him, on a doctor's advice, to bring the critically ill boy and two youngest daughters for a healthier climate in "sunny California." Landing in San Francisco's dampness and fog, unable to travel farther, Charles, his son, in a few short weeks was dead. John had the expense of burial for Charles. He had to seek employment and a place to live, with no one to care for Eliza and Ida. He could not simultaneously work and care for them and placed them in an orphans' home. Grief-stricken, he had found cheap lodgings, and employment and was just now returning to a renewal of life again, meeting people who could enjoy life, including his new young actress friend.

Flora intrigued John with the idea that voices from beyond often give direction for life and might have a special message for him. Perhaps he could hear his wife or his recently dead son speak to him from the grave. Perhaps he needed to assure himself that they had found each other across the vast amount of distance of country he had traveled and of time. Did he wonder if they were happy? This might console him, to know.

John's curiosity was aroused with the idea of the spirit world, something beyond his ken, and he went once to one of Flora's seances. The one experience satisfied his interest. He did not become a devotee of the seance, but he continued his interest in Flora, as she assured him they had a bond of feelings in common. Flora indicated she was suffering over being separated from her infant even as John suffered to get his daughters out of the orphanage and together with him.

Even the current illness John had was a bond, for Flora had suffered an illness so severe in her youth that she had lost hair so that it would no longer grow long and thick (one reason for her wearing a wig) and the illness had stunted her growth. The idea of a farm, fresh country air and milk, food for children, and room for them to run and play was appealing, she assured him. She hoped he would realize his goals, which he could always talk over with her, she said.

She told him of her terrible treatment by Professor Chaney and how he had outrageously commanded her to terminate her pregnancy or forfeit her relationship with him forever. She had been quite a heroine in her refusal when Chaney had demanded the life of the chld and insisted she endanger her own life by an abortion. These were things she would not ordinarily discuss with a gentleman, but as Mr. London had been a husband and father and she so needed an understanding male friend, she took the liberty of confiding, she said. She could see he was a generous-spirited man who would hold no judgment against her. John was not even aware her case had been publicized.

John was appalled at the behavior of Professor Chaney, who had wished to kill an unborn child. He had no sympathy with that attitude. That Flora had been miserably and unjustly abandoned he agreed. He assured her she could call on him if she needed a protector.

Then John at this time fell very ill with one of the recurrent fever bouts that flattened him temporarily, and this time Flora undertook to be his nurse. As John London lay ill in bed, a malaise of his mind concerning his little girls overcame him. If in one of these reccurrences of illness he should die, they would be abandoned to an orphanage forever. He had been foolishly enamored of the young actress. He saw now his mistake. Loneliness did lead a man into unsuitable choices. He thought more speculatively of Flora, who, for whatever reason, had also made a human mistake. She needed a man to make a living for her and to provide for her own baby, that John knew was being cared for by Alonzo and Jennie, special people who could give love to their own and to others' children. The Prentiss family would also be good to his own children, if he asked them. But no, though they were in middle age, they might still have others of their own, and the talk of the big depression that had swept across the country and now into California made everyone very serious. Anything could happen in the building trades.

Better to do what he had planned, get to a farm somewhere, back to the land, provide his children with a mother, and live for his children. This time he was going to make it. He felt a resurgence of strength. He tried to rise out of bed but, too weak, fell back, light-headed and gasping. Flora came quickly into the room and to his side, reaching a hand for his brow. The perfume of her body mixed with his heavy breathing. He grasped her hand and held it. "Listen," he said, "this is what we must do." Soon they were in each other's arms.

Flora went to the orphanage at John's request to tell the children their father had been too ill to come to see them and that she was his nurse. Now he was getting all better and they were going to be married, so she would be their new mother. Their father would be able to bring them out of the orphanage again.

The little girls were greatly disturbed by this news. Flora thought it was hearing their father had been ill, but it was more than that. They were confused and upset by all of this information. After Flora left, little Ida, who had fond thoughts of the pretty would-be actress their father had once brought to visit, wanted that storybook creature most strongly. She felt sure she could never have such a strange-looking person as Flora for a mother. That night she cried herself to sleep and then had awful dreams.

Eliza, more aware of the disappointments of the world, every day said to Ida they would do whatever they must. To be with their father was the important thing. She did not talk of her own dismay but comforted Ida, and so the little girls waited out the days until they could again see their father and know from him what they must do.

For the rest of her life Eliza looked back on the orphanage as the one secure home she had had, the one place where she had felt most loved and cared for.

CHAPTER 24

Shock waves of the east coast crash of 1873 and failure of wheat crops in the midwest finally reached the west coast. The Depression of 1876 was the worst financial crisis San Francisco had ever experienced. On September 7, 1876, in San Francisco, John London and Flora, who listed herself on the marriage license as Flora Chaney, appeared before the justice of the peace, James C. Pennie, and became man and wife. John and Flora joined their fortunes together at a moment in history when almost thirty thousand men in the city, an astronomical proportion for those times, were out of work.

The marriage, like everything around them, was economically shaky. Undaunted, the newlyweds moved into the South of Market section of San Francisco, where many workingmen and their families lived, and John very gratefully took his two little girls from the Protestant Orphan Home. Flora would have the baby Jack brought by Jennie for occasional afternoon visits. Sometimes Alonzo would bring him in his arms, taking a ride hanging on the strap of a crowded electric car. Sometimes the whole Prentiss family would come and leave the baby whle they took a short outing, to return with their packages or with tales of their afternoon adventure.

It was too soon to wean little Jack. When Flora and John married he was only eight months old, and these were times when children were nursed until the age of two or three. Because of his delicate digestive system and the nervous bowel trouble with which it seemed he was born, he would not be weaned for a long time and would stay with Mama Jennie and Papa Alonzo.

Alonzo and Jennie both became primary factors in the lives of the new London family. They, with their children, William and Priscilla, were an example of a family that had succeeded. Alonzo tried to provide John with jobs. Jennie provided Flora's child with the very substance of his life and tender care. They were stalwart friends to have.

John's daughters had much trouble learning to get along with their new stepmother. Flora did not have the experience or awareness of what being a mother would entail and had no real inclination for parenting. Eliza, accustomed to mothering her own little sister, extended her love and motherly nature to include the baby, Jack, whenever she saw him. In her ability to give a kindly love and have a caring attitude she was like her father.

Eliza was eight years old when her father remarried, a few years older than her sister Ida, and she never forgot the day she was introduced into this new family situation. Flora arranged to have Jackie there for an afternoon, soon after their marriage, when John went to the orphanage for the little girls. They wanted to create a domestic scene and pave the way for a family unity.

Jackie had outgrown the baby basket in which he napped while at Flora's, so John set up a little crib for Jack to be in when the girls arrived, for he was much too active not to be contained. Flora had neglected to get a netting for the crib and was not even aware mothers needed such things for their babies. Insects buzzed around in the Indian summer warmth, coming in and out from the almost hot, sticky sunshine to the oppressive overheated little house. Eliza stared fascinated at the baby with blond, silky hair and blue eyes, his full, moist lips making a little bubble of his spit, his strong little chin wet from baby-drool. At eight months he was teething. His fingers would go into his mouth and a show of sudden pain from his swollen gums would shadow his expression, but he would still try to smile. He looked at Eliza as if he knew all people were good and that the world was a great place. Eliza was charmed by him in every way. Flies crawled on his face. Practical, bighearted, and big-sisterly, she folded herself a little paper fan and stood by him for a long time to shoo away the flies. As she gazed at him during that time her sympathy for him as a small, helpless creature was aroused. She knew what it was like to need someone to care for her. She was told he was her new little brother. She accepted him that day. Already cast by fate in the role of the dedicated big sister, she responded with all her earnest heart.

So Eliza and Ida also became linked in friendship with the Prentiss family. Happy to be reunited with their father, they were still somewhat dubious and cautious where Flora was concerned.

Will and Priscilla went sometimes to play with these two new friends, going with their mother, and sometimes Jennie took Jack when they were in school, venturing by horse carriage or electric streetcar or by cable car, one of those fantastic contraptions in which underground cables pulled the conveyances and passengers up hills so steep that horses would mightily strain and could even dangerously slip. While riding the cable car was as breathtaking for most people as a carnival roller-coaster, it gave the most sumptuous view of the city and the panorama far out over the bay toward Oakland, except when the fog lay over the bay and around the hills. People who came there from every part of the country said they had never seen such fog to make a place so mistly, ghostly, mysterious. No wonder, some thought, a place of the dead spirits seemed possible, more probably reached here, if any place.

But Flora was no longer enacting the ponderous solemn ritual of access to the dead, which Jennie had never seen. It was hard to give up, for Flora wanted to be important to people and she felt important when people came to her seances. She had allowed them to feel the exhilaration of the spirits in their still varying personalities as present in the room, by her power. A few people would be seated at a table, the small fingers of each hand barely touching the thumb tip of the next person in a ring of stillness of anticipation. The mystery, the imminent oppressive fear or nervous exhaustion in which they waited for the contact would affect each person. Then there would come a series of eerie thuds, knockings, or movements of the table. Voices, sometimes deep, hollow, solemn, sometimes light, airy, weird, spoke through Flora's mouth their messages from beyond. She was caught up in the drama of it. There was a certain luxury of expression, yet controlled and directed somehow by the medium, Flora.

The business was sustaining to Flora. John was not interested in the spirits and discouraged it, so she gave it up before their marriage. They were not rich, but John would provide if Flora would put her fertile mind and erratically abundant energies to homemaking for John, Eliza, and Ida. They soon, within a year or so, no doubt, would also bring little Jackie to their home. Meanwhile, it was a benefit to have him with the Prentiss family, for all the London family benefited, too, from their friendship.

Jackie when brought for the occasional afternoon would sleep in the crib. If he woke, he could have a sugar-tit made of butter and sugar mixed in a small lump, bound with string in the center of the handerkerchief-sized cloth. He would be pacified by sucking this between feedings, while Jennie took Will and Priscilla with her to Market Street. She would return with her grocery shopping and special treats in one of the horse-drawn carts, which would wait while she collected Jackie to take him back up the hill. Or Alonzo would come, too, and then the Prentiss and London families would visit.

John and Alonzo shared in companionable conversation. The children would play with spinning tops, play hide and seek, hopscotch, or jacks, or jump rope. Jennie would modestly retire to another room to nurse Jackie, change the cloth he was diapered in, and burp him against her shoulder with soothing pats on his manly little back for his digestive troubles.

Wherever the London family moved, the friendship of the Prentiss family continued. They moved to a farming area of the city, called Bernal Heights, but John was not yet in a position to quit other jobs to farm. They moved again into a section crowded by working people, at 920 Natoma Street, and for over a year were crowded into a flat in an old three-storied frame building where Flora also had a boarder come in. She wanted to use the money for a Chinese servant, for she was preparing to take Jackie, which she had put off due to the ordeal of the last move. They were not really settled, she said. But a roomer to help their finances justified her having someone to do the housework. Though she felt she was already burdened with two children, she thought she should not put off the care of Jackie any longer. She could not admit she did not want motherhood after all, for the premise on which she had bound John London to her was that they would unite their families. She could not give grounds for him to think she was an unnatural mother.

John did not want another mouth to feed at the time but could not let his feelings, be known as it would seem he had reneged on what he thought was Flora's wish. He had to prove himself a man of his word.

Alonzo and Jennie had their own reasons for wanting to delay as long as possible giving Jackie into Flora's hands, even though they knew John was a good man, and they blamed themselves for loving Jack so much when they had known they could not keep him. At last the time for all could no longer be stayed. No one in their innermost feelings wanted to make this change. Jackie, almost three years old and weaned for months, though he had become accustomed through his visits to the Londons' home, was unsuspecting of his future.

One day, his little clothes and favorite toys having been gathered into a bundle in his comforter, it was as if a time had come. Jennie, Alonzo, Will, and Priscilla did not stay long at the London house that day. Mother and Father, as Jack copied Eliza and Ida in calling Flora and John, were ready for Jack to be a permanent part of the London family.

As Jennie stood in the doorway, the child held her with all his passionate life. He loved her. She was always there for him. "Mama," he pleaded as he clung to her.

"Now you be good, Jackie," she said, and she was gone, with all of the Prentisses, looking sad. Of course she cried that night and again, many nights, crying for Jackie from the distance of her own place, as he cried for her in his. He loved her. She loved him.

Jack fretted and cried and was given his supper milk in an unfamiliar cup. He did not understand when night came why Mama and Papa had abandoned him, and John walked the floor that night and for several nights after, soothing the whimpering child to sleep. Flora took it as a rejection and a personal affront when Jack was desolate and homesick, dropping around during the day for his other family, far away and inaccessible to him on Nob Hill.

Flora, who had for long repressed her angry and violent emotions over the loss of Chaney, found an anger at the suffering child, a rekindled secret hostility.

But Eliza, with the sympathy that exists between children, attempted to give Jack back his surrogate mother in the person of her small self. His stepsister washed his little face and hands, brought him warmed milk in a cup and held it for him, to help him drink it. She played with his toys with him, sang him songs she had learned at school, and with Ida would roll to him a ball or build for him a house with the small blocks or amuse him with other toys brought for him from Jennie's, and she tried to give him only good.

But she came home from school one day with a sore throat, which by night had become a high fever. She complained her head hurt. In the next days Eliza was increasingly ill, delirious. Jack, whom she had carried around and held, caught her fever. They were confined to the same sickbed, and the doctor pronounced them seriously ill victims of the diptheria epidemic that was bringing even grown men and women to their deaths.

Grief-stricken, Jennie and Alonzo were sickened at heart to hear that Flora had told the doctor that since she and John had so little money they could hardly even afford to bury the children, they planned to bury them both in one coffin. Jennie could hardly believe Flora was so egocentric that in the most serious illness of the child Jennie and Alonzo had raised she did not send for them. It grieved them to be counted as nothing in their feelings for the child they held so dear. They tried to forgive her as having been totally distraught. John, they knew, had gone wildly off to Oakland clear across the bay, as he had heard of a doctor there considered quite remarkable for being able to bring people through the crisis. John found this doctor, who came and, John believed, almost miraculously saved Eliza and Jack.

John began to see the children's illness as an omen. John had lost one son in San Francisco within his first weeks of arrival there. His introduction to the city was as a place of death for his family. Now he had almost lost a daughter. He became suspicious of the city's humors and vapors and ghostlike fogs. He was strongly determined they must leave it for their health and salvation. He had not been successful in finding a stable living for them in San Francisco. God knows, he had done everything from selling Singer sewing machines door to door to hard physical labor at the IXL Emporium stockroom, opening crates. He had tried hard at carpentry, but outdoor work on the chilly hills of the city was not for him, as his own recurrent illness proved.

Jennie, after Jackie's near-death, was also made anxious about the welfare of the beloved child for whom her arms still yearned. She knew all too well he had almost not lived through infancy. She could not let so many years of her love and hope be lost to life and thought she must encourage whatever was best for Jack. If the London family was going to move to Oakland, she and Alonzo would go back and forth across the bay or do whatever was necessary to keep close to Jack, their own love, their other child.

CHAPTER 25

It was as if some fortune-teller had foretold that Jennie would lose Jack to an English person who would take him away across water. Having Jack taken by a couple from England across the ocean would have been something she could not bear. Having Jack taken across the bay to live in Oakland by the Englishman John London was something she would have to make the best of. She thought she could handle it; it was not, she knew by now, as bad as it could have been. But it was still as if the wicked fairy in a story had said, "The child shall not die but sleep for a hundred years." Each time between trips on the ferryboat over to see Jackie seemed to Jennie another hundred years. Will and Priscilla would look at their mother and father with mournful eyes, as if to say, "How could Jackie be taken from us? Could we be taken away, too? This was a bad thing to happen to our family. It was cruel."

John London was an innocent man to cast in the villain's role. He was just an ordinary person having a hard time trying to do his best. He would never act like, or look like, "the bad guy!" He was a kindly-faced man in his midforties with a full beard. He had been born in Pennsylvania

57

of English stock and, after serving in the Union army, gone to Iowa, then come to California. He had been a deacon of the Methodist church and before he came to California had held a variety of jobs. He had worked on the railroad, farmed, and been a sheriff, a collection agent, a watchman, a deputy, a canvasser, a carpenter, and a builder. Of all his work he liked farming best. It took money to get started on a farm. He had been saving, but there wasn't enough for tools, seed, and renting land and something to live on until the crops came. Now the illness of Eliza and Jack had taken the little savings he had, and the dream of a farm seemed far away. Still, they took their belongings on the ferry and moved across the bay. John was sure it was a move in the right direction. He felt compelled toward Oakland, and, with John's compulsion, Flora had come up with a get-rich scheme. She knew how people came to California for gold. Gold was very big and important in people's minds. Well, she would sell people gold leaf to put on their picture frames. She would go to business establishments, even bars, and sell the owners on the idea of making their paintings' frames glitter with gold. She would even stand right up on the bar and show them how to apply it, if she had to. Every bar competed with others to have bigger, gaudier, more provocative paintings and would want to have gold frames that would gleam and shine and catch the eye. People would be more motivated to buy more drinks and celebrate more in a plush atmosphere where there was the glint of gold, she was sure, and she would sell to other people, too. Everyone loved gold.

While Flora went out to make money in this way, John operated a vegetable stand at Seventh and Campbell, the Point. They first lived on Third Street in Oakland, but John kept his eye out for a storefront they could rent to open a store and very soon found a place on Seventh, near Center and Peralta, where they could live in four rooms behind a little store, and they were in business. If they didn't grow food, they could still sell it, getting what few items they could at the farmers' market each day, and week by week they began to develop a trade, adding a few more items each time.

Flora didn't strike it rich in the gold-selling venture, but she did meet a very slick-looking man in one of the bars, Mr. Stowell. He had money that he could be persuaded to invest in a half-interest in the store.

Flora did not want to stand behind the counter and wait on customers; she did not have the personality to be nice to people all day. She was given to fainting spells and headaches if she had to do things like that, so John needed a partner to help do the work of the store. Eliza had helped, because it was summer, and had taken care of Jack and Ida. Now the girls would go to school, and Flora could see the three-year-old Jackie would just be underfoot. But with the Stowell family in partnership they were able to expand, renting together a big house to share. Some records place this house on Sixteenth and Wood and others on Twelfth and Wood, and the period is described well in books about the life and times of this family, notably *Sailor on Horseback* by Irving Stone. The gruesome details: Mr. Stowell cheated them, stole all the money, merchandise, and even furnishings from the store, and left the London family with nothing but the clothes on their backs and the girls, Eliza and Ida, to feed.

Jackie, at least, would eat well. For quite some time he had again been living with the Prentiss family. Financially successful, they had moved to Alameda, a peninsula a short buggy ride from where the Londons were living.

Flora and John had soon realized neither of them could be tied down to an active tot while they worked, and returning him to Jennie's care was the logical thing to do. They were immensely relieved when the Prentiss family moved to the East Bay, near them. Jennie had urged Alonzo to make the move because she loved Jack and realized he would get very little nurturing from Flora and felt she could best keep him with her if they lived closer to the London family so Flora would be assured of his near presence.

It was much cheaper to live in the East Bay, and the natural beauty of Alameda suited Jennie just fine. Alonzo knew both Oakland and Alameda were on the threshold of development as cities. There were few houses but a vast potential. Jennie and Alonzo decided to help stake John to his farm. He was able to lease ten acres of what was known as the old Davenport property. John had his start at last. He would pay them back when the crops sold. Everything was going to be fine. Everyone at last was going to be happy.

CHAPTER 26

The Printed News

1852   *Chipman, one of Alameda's Forefathers, felt it important to note (in his diary of 1852) the first cricket in Alameda, his eyes viewed.*

1863   *Mrs. E. K. Taylor was overwhelmed to receive seeds sent from her husband in Australia (which are believed to be) Alameda's first eucalyptus trees.*

1864   *The Encinal Railroad laid its first four miles of track. Official runs were made to the villages of Woodstock, Encinal, Alameda—and then back. The only problem occured when obstructing branches succeeded in knocking off the engineer's hat . . . causing the railroad a slight delay several times that day!*

1874   *The longest unbroken coil of rope was manufactured in Alameda, by the Pacific Cordage Company. No other company in the world could beat their recorded length of 1,380 feet.*

1875   *For violating Ordinance #7 (fast, reckless driving) Policeman #1 pursued a young man speeding merrily through town on his bay horse and buggy. When apprehended, the youth was found guilty and charged an $8.00 fine, warning him not to let it happen a second time.*
    *Before patrol wagons started making the rounds Police used wheelbarrows to cart prisoners across town.

1878   *Floating above Alameda's shores, thrilling more than 3,000 Sunday sunbathers—was Hercules, a giant hot air balloon. Owned and flown by Professor Martin.*

1878   *One Bathing Resort that accomodated large Sunday crowds was "The Terrace Baths" of Alameda. They offered: 240 dressing rooms, 4,000 bathing suits to rent, small rooms with hot salt-water baths and upstairs seating where spectators could relax. The 300 ft. beach frontage appealed to lovers of the surf while women, children and men went for a swim in what was soon to rank as the largest swimming tank (measuring 300 by 500 ft.).*

1878   *Several complaints from citizens arose regarding the legality of sunbathers' clothes. The law states that bathing suits must be worn from the shoulders to the knees; anything more revealing would be dealt with by Police!*

1883	*Permission for removal of any Alameda Oak trees, by construction companies, was needed from the Board of Town Trustees. The city-fathers care about their town and objected to uprooting its natural heritage from the ground.*
1885	*Goddimers were top-to-toe, water-proof hooded wraps that the young fashionable ladies wore when the rain in Alameda began to pour. This was also the year that boys' undershirts and drawers sold for 25 cents at the Theodore Green & Company Store.*
1886	*The 1885 assessment of the State of California ranked Alameda County the second richest place.*
1887	*New electric globes were being broken by the flight of wild ducks who had not grown accustomed to shining lights at night.*
1890	*514 Australian lady-bugs were shipped across the sea by Albert Koebele, who recognized the need to use natural predators as a means of pest control. When he saved $2,000,000 worth of orange crops, he was awarded a watch of gold.*
1895	*A race track for trotters and pacers in Alameda was new and thousands of spectators came anxiously to view the 1 mile straightaway, measured 100 ft. wide with 2 cyclists paths situated on either side.*
1896	*At a negotiating meeting for the canal project, Dr. John T. McLean (Alameda's Health Officer) justified his plea for the cutting of the canal by uncorking several contaminated sewage bottles, which released a vile smell. The Federal Director discussed the project with more zeal thanks to Dr. McLeans' determined strong will. *Alameda Tidal Canal is the 2nd largest canal cut in the Western Hemisphere, separating what once was a peninsula from Oakland. Only the Panama Canal Cut is larger. Alameda is the largest Island City in the Western United States.*
1898	*Cream Team Lager and XXX Porter were favorite beers brewed by Mr. Schuler & Son for several years. The Palace Brewery in Alameda established its name and its popular beer was its claim to fame.*
1898	*If a boxer wanted to become a champion, he needed a rigid training program to prepare. Croll's Gardens was the best training center known to boxers everywhere. Sometimes it was necessary to send boxers out to shovel coal or bundle them up in the boiler room of a San Fransciso bound Ferry boat. James Corbett, Rudy Fitzsimmons & Jack Dempsey were all champions that trained at Croll's.*

It was 1879, and Jennie and Alonzo when coming to Alameda had settled on the north side of Pacific Avenue, between Willow and Chestnut streets. The present house number is 2063 Pacific Avenue. Originally the house was a barn. It was rehabilitated for human living, which included moving the building in line with the other houses, close to the sidewalk, in the old driveway, and doing a great deal of carpentry work. Remodeling his own house was Alonzo's first work in Alameda. William was ecstatically happy to work alongside his father. It was his first man-sized job.

Their polyglot of neighbors of almost every ethnic group became Alonzo's and Jennie's friends. They listened to talk about cutting through the estuary between Alameda and Oakland and how Alameda would become an island. It was already an island unto itself in which the races did not live apart but mixed. There were over one hundred Negro families in Alameda, more than twice as many as in nearby Berkeley. The newcomers shared in a community, small but of all races: German, Italian, Irish, English, and more. Conversation was the cultural and social life of the people. They had leisure to talk through long days in which they could tell each other truths about themselves, time to enjoy seeing the children at play with each other. It had less prejudice than any place Jennie and Alonzo had lived, so they marveled at this, as at a really new world, once a dream.

In San Francisco each household kept to their own space, marked out by backyard fences and busy streets. It was a place, Alonzo thought of secrets and pretensions, passions and separations, and material strivings. But in Alameda large pastures for horses and cows were all that were fenced. The older children could roam over practically the whole length and breadth of the land, measured about seven miles in length and four miles in width, surrounded on three sides by water.

No one caused harm to others. Alameda prided itself as a community with no criminal element. There was an empty jail, used only by an occasional vagrant for whom it was kept unlocked or by a recurrent drunk who was usually found asleep on the beach by a policeman and would be taken for his own sake, before the tide came in, either to his home or, depending on the mood of his wife, to the otherwise unused jail, to continue sleeping it off.

Almost all of the land, as far as the marshes, was covered by trees, so thickly branched they met overhead, interlocked with each other so the sun could hardly be seen. They were filled with thousands of finches and gold canaries flickering in the leaves. Little woods creatures abounded: opossums, raccoons, rabbits, squirrels, and deer, and almost every variety of shorebird: egrets, least terns, clapper rails, brown pelicans, gulls, ducks, geese, and more. There was fertile soil, a favorable

62

climate. People on ships and boats passing on the bay could smell the pungency of earth and its spices far out over the waters.

Alameda by 1879 was being considered by its city fathers and some potential developers for becoming a popular resort area to attract fashionable people for holiday and recreation, providing means of support for a growing number of small merchants. But this was still mostly in the talking stages, and Alamedans in general were unsophisticated by city standards and believed themselves content. They believed themselves to be enterprising, hardworking, creative, and goodwilled, and the small, new city of Alameda already had a brewery, a rope factory that made the longest rope in the nation (a record never broken), a brickworks, Clark Pottery and Tile Works, several dairies, the fairly new Croll's tavern on Webster Street, and a town hall on Park and Webb that housed the fire department, police office, and town jail. The first commercially made peanut butter in the nation was manufactured in Alameda.

Houses were going up; pioneer style with shed roof, square posts, and horizontal wood siding, false-front buildings, Italianates, Queen Annes with towers and turrets, rounded bays, decorated barge board, fish-scale shingles, curved windows, and beveled glass, the board and batten with decorative trim and square bays that were called stick houses. These Victorian era styles would sell for one or two thousand dollars in the West End. The East End would boast a cluster of fine mansions in a section called the Gold Coast. Already there had been two enterprising newspapers, the *Encinal*, founded in 1869, and the *Alameda Argus*, founded in 1877.

Jennie liked to take Priscilla and Jack with her to the Family Store to choose her own groceries. Customers could be attended by two sisters people called the old maids, while their father played dominoes with his cronies on a board set across a barrel around which were placed chairs for the kibitzers. Their brother would go out in the delivery wagon, a doubledecker with the upper tiers displaying layers of tomatoes, potatoes, carrots, celery, cabbages, summer squashes, melons, and onions colorfully in view. Priscilla and Jack peered into the store's glass counters as high as their eyes could reach, smelling the prunes and dates and figs, oranges in wooden crates, and other produce. There were jars of huge pickles, pickled pigs' feet, and barrels of crackers, dried beans, and rice. The children admired the store as a wonderland. The sisters admired the children. Priscilla was nine, tall and willowy for her age. Following Jennie, she pulled the almost five-year-old gold-haired Jackie to the store in the big slatted wagon so sturdily built it had lasted for many years. Jennie and the spinsters indulged in long, warm conversation, and Priscilla and Jack went to wait by the wagon, to watch life and movement flow past the store on the board sidewalk.

A boy came down the street in a goatcart. Two men rode by quickly on cycles that had one enormous wheel in front and two tiny wheels in back, seated so high up their derbies seemed to touch the clouds. Women in bustles and flounces and high-buttoned shoes walked delicately under parasols. A boy only a year or so older than Priscilla came selling newspapers. He carried them under his arm up and down the street, calling, and waving one with a flourish. "Could I look at one of those?" she asked. He showed her the front page and headlines he was calling out, and she saw how the paper was organized in neat columns or words. "Do you see, Jackie? Someone put all the words together in a new way." Jack looked impressed.

"You got money to buy?" the newsboy asked her hopefully but doubtfully. She shook her head in regret. He took back the paper. "Well, this is important news today, and somebody's going to buy it. I've got ten more papers to sell. It's my job," he said importantly. "Every day I sell the news."

"Do you make the papers? Do you write those words?"

"Who, me? Hey, that's rich! No. Them that do get a lot more money than me. See, I goes to the newspaper plant and picks up my bundle. That's it." He went off quickly toward a man walking up the block. She heard the boy call out in an excited way, "Whuhxx-tree! Whuhxx-tree!"

"A plant? Like a beanstalk, Jackie? He gets them from a plant, maybe a tree? He picks papers like people pick beans? Will we ever know these things?" she said.

When they went home they would play store, making shelves and putting out an assortment of rocks and leaves and flowers, each arranged in its own space neatly on the shelf. Very businesslike and profound, two neighbor children would take part in the store, to "play checkers" with rock-chalked squares on a piece of board and woodchip checkers to be ritually moved around. *Will I grow up to have a store? Be a teacher, teaching the books? No*, thought Priscilla, *I'm going to be a mama like Mama.*

It did not matter that Jennie was not a facile reader, that she had only one book, the Bible, which was her wedding present and her treasure. Some of their neighbors could not read at all. And Jennie repeated stories and songs in rhythmic cadence. Rhythm, the older Africans among the slaves had taught Jennie, was basis for all learning. Rhythmic sound was communication from tribe to tribe, from person to group, long before they came to slavery in the South and even there, over long distances, from plantation to plantation. By rhythm and by song, the slaves had their ways of secret communications, which they believed were not known to white people.

Priscilla did not bring home books from school in Alameda, as there were not enough to go around as yet. William's education was complete. He was going daily to Oakland as an apprentice carpenter, chosen by the black entrepreneurs for the color of his skin as well as his energies.

Eliza, now on the verge of teenagehood, went with Ida to the West End School. They lived only a couple of miles from the Prentiss family, but they did not get to play very often, and Priscilla and Jack had many other nearby playmates.

Priscilla took the stories told by the grownups around her and made them into creative play that the neighborhood children joined in. They got into the spirit of the stories as if they were the characters, each with a part to say, and the action was directed by Priscilla according to her ideas.

Alonzo admired the child's abilities with words, so like her mother's. Alonzo reckoned that with being able to express herself so fluently she was going to be a teacher, one for whom language would be useful and appreciated. He realized she was gifted with words and their dramatic usages.

Alonzo thought that if they hadn't already been invented, Priscilla could have been the inventor of the fairytales she loved to repeat. She had just such an imaginative mind. She could tell the fairy stories in a way that made them come alive. She was telling little Jackie about Jack and the beanstalk, Jack the Giantkiller, and Jack Be Nimble. Every story or rhyme she knew that had a hero named Jack. "The House That Jack Built" was a big favorite. That little boy was enthralled! He followed her around all afternoon, and she never ran dry of words. And so fluid and melodic was her speech she enchanted the other children who came to play. They would want most of all to be with Priscilla, because she had ideas that appealed to them. They playacted the parts of the people in some of the stories she told, playing "let's pretend." They were giants and kings and other characters, dressing the part in picked-flower crowns and pillowcase capes and dishtowel and apron robes and skirts and in Alonzo's long scarf or oldest shirt, with Jack, the youngest, given a choice role. They would be sailors in a wagon-boat. They would be pioneers in a covered wagon. They would be heroes and heroines.

One day Alonzo picked up little Jack and swung the delighted child up in his muscular arms onto his shoulders, saying "You've reached the top of the beanstalk, little fellow!" Alonzo went stalking after Priscilla with elongated steps, calling out, "Who is this—Jack, or is it the giant coming?" He swung the child down. "Thank Cissy, Jack, for the stories!"

Jack threw his arms delightedly around the demure Priscilla and gave her a big bear hug and received one in return.

Alonzo said, "Tell me, Miss Sweetheart, a story about Alonzo!"

"Oh, Papa! What a surprise! I don't believe I ever heard one!"

"What, no hero-Alonzo stories? Then someone must write one!"

"But, Papa," protested Priscilla, "how can anyone write stories? They already *are*. We learn them in school."

"But there are human minds, like yours," said Alonzo, "behind how all those words are put together different in each story. All the words were put together in one big book by a man named Mr. Webster. That book is called a dictionary, and you know about that. Don't you know other people put words together in different ways to make stories? Just like someone takes a lot of loose boards and builds a house."

"*You* do, Papa. You think how to put a house together. But Mama tells the stories. I'll ask Mama how to think them up."

She would go to the ultimate source. But Jennie didn't know. She had heard the stories told by one of the young ladies at the Big House. "They came from long ago and they stay in peoples' memory. That's all," she said.

Priscilla began to wonder about where all the words came from, who were the first persons to think up words. Since Jack was her constant companion it was to him she speculated aloud about words.

Alonzo liked to remind Priscilla that he cared about her interests and thought she had a talent. "Maybe," said Alonzo to Priscilla, "you will write some stories down."

"No," said Priscilla, "they've already been written."

She liked to put stories into action. Maybe she would be a teacher, teach the books. No, she was firmly convinced. She wanted to be just like Jennie, to "be a mama, making good things to eat and the house all shining and to have sweet, sweet babies like me and Jackie were."

Alonzo teased, "Will wants to build the house and you want to clean the house and cook, so who will write the books?"

Priscilla remembered how Jackie grabbed at all the books from the time he was a baby. "Jack will," she said firmly, setting out in her doll dishes playlike sand stew and salad, a mixture of leaves and pebbles. She hoped to learn Jennie's recipes, which were all in her head and never written down, for cornbread, griddle cakes and molasses, johnnycake, and grits. Jennie would put up vegetables, pickle beets and cucumbers, make jams and jellies and butter, and serve oatmeal with fresh raw milk from a neighbor's cow set so the cream rose to the top. The cream would be poured into coffee, over crumbled spoonbread, on strawberries and sliced bananas with sugar, and on milk toast. She would make buttermilk, buttermilk biscuits. She would gather fresh vegetables from their own backyard garden—sweet potatoes, tomatoes, fresh corn, greens of all kinds. Priscilla knew, admiringly, Jennie was an instinctive cook, always in her apron, happily busy, strong, at peace with her neighbors, a good mother, and her daughter's ideal.

Alonzo continued over time to talk about his idea of writing stories. He told the children and Jennie, too, about the book written by Harriet Beecher Stowe and how this book had changed the lives of many people, how it had affected politics, how it had made some people understand that black people were important enough to fight for, what it had meant in his own life. He said one of the children should do this good work of writing a book. He said it was important to build in this way, build with ideas. It was useful and good for people, like building a house.

CHAPTER 27

Mary Foley and Sally Mulcahy, sisters who lived together in the same house, with nine children between them, visited often with Jennie. The women did chores as they talked, their chairs pulled under the trees' shade. One day Sally and Jennie were shelling peas and breaking ends of the snap beans to destring them, putting them into crockery bowls, ready for cooking. Mary brought baskets of laundry to fold, from baby diapers to workshirts, some to be dampened, which she did by dipping her hand in a bowl of water and flecking the drops over the garment, then rolling it, putting it back in the big basket in the shade. Soon, that evening, she and Sally would iron for hours. Mary had her needle, thimble, and thread of many colors ready, for especially the children's clothes must be checked for rips and missing buttons.

The friends shared from their hearts fragments of their lives and what their dreams of the future encompassed. Sally set the bowls aside to take her youngest on her lap and give him her breast, and the talk flowed on. Jack sat on Jennie's knee as she stroked his hair; he listened, absorbed in the words, not always knowing the meaning. It was the lull of the afternoon when the older children were still in school and the women worked and talked of the past.

When the infant was fed and laid on a pallet to nap and Jack went within their watching to sail his boats, made as Alonzo had once made them for Will, an activity that never lost interest for him, the neighbors talked together as the most intimate of friends. Often they talked of traumas they hoped their children would not know in their own lives but which they had lived through, to become the people they were.

Jennie said, "Like the separate stars, every plantation was a world of its own, far apart, isolated, and as many worlds as there were kinds of men to run them. On this one the slaves were housed in cubicles with no furniture, the poorest kind of wooden cell, hay piled on the dirt floor in one corner to sleep on, the slaves there only to sleep, their waking hours only to work, all fed from a big trough in the yard, the only eating utensil their hands. Certain slaves cooked the food in one shed and dispensed it.

"On another plantation the field slaves would file past big kettles of food with its everyday sameness, receiving a portion into a bowl or a gourd, and carried their own spoon whittled from wood like the bowl. Men, women, children old enough to work all day in the field were each to be sustained until the evening meal by a hunk of cornbread in butter-milk.

"All wore long, loose shirts, the men with baggy pants held by a drawstring under their shirttails, the women with long loose skirts, all the clothes the same, all made of cotton grown, carded, spun, woven on the plantation, all made from the same pattern. Barefoot slaves had callous-thick feet.

"On other plantations, the cabins became homelike. Each had a garden or shared in a community garden. They could have all they wanted from the vast surplus of growing food, plentiful game in the surrounding woods, shoes for everyone, the women dressing in multiple garments, petticoats, shimmies, drawers, dresses, kerchiefs, a change of clothes, allowed to enter a section of a church or to hold a prayer service under the trees, for which the women could wear earrings, hoopskirts made for themselves with grapevines, and clothes held by buttons carved from wood or bone.

"There were rich plantations where the slaves were not sold away, plantations where the slaves were not whipped, where they became their own overseers, where a doctor would come and a preacher, others where there would be cornshucking frolics, weddings, even for slaves. Yet at others slaves would be bought for breeding, thrust together with one another as stud animals and brood animals are used, for breeding, and slaves bore welts and lash marks and scars from wet leather whips, cat-o'-nine-tails, and wet rope, and turpentine, vinegar, or salt water was poured on the wounds. There were scars where they had been hit by boards, by willow whips. Oh, I cannot tell all the horrors.

"I think of people, us black people, all over the country praying for freedom. What else but God inspired that woman to write a book so white people of the Northern states would be urged into war to free us and inspired other things that happened. I think there is some purpose, some good to come, what keeps me religious, keeps me reading the Bible, reading of the time the Jews were brought out of slavery, too, how knowing this of God unites all us people who have suffered. And I think, too, how some people had rules from the Bible, this good book, to live by that kept them from being as cruel as some of the others. I think if the white people of the Parker plantation had not had these rules, they too would have treated their slaves as slaves on most other plantations were treated.

"Think of these thousands of prayers and prayer songs, spirituals, in a land of slavery, for people to be brought forth from their tragic human condition in slavery. Then what singing and shouting, eyes streaming with tears, to hear you have been set free.

"But never free from memory. I had a friend, Caroline, a white child from a plantation where the whipped slaves' screams permeated her childhood. When she grew up her dreams returned those screams still. If I sleep, if on the Parker plantation there was not that same cruelty or evil toward their slaves, in some way this Bible must have made them aware. I think how much worse my life would have been if they had not had this."

Sally Mulcahy, dimpled and curly-haired, with a dark, thick mass of hair and pale, fair skin that sunburned, was twenty-three years old, years younger than Jennie had been when she married Alonzo. She had met and been wed to Andy Mulcahy in steerage on a ship bringing her to be a bond servant in New York, by a priest who was thoroughly on the side of romance and the marriage blessing. Andy had paid off her indenture, helped by his brother, who was traveling with him, which left them nearly penniless. He, then and still, believed Sally a prize worth more than money.

The Mulcahy brothers and Sally were fortunate that her sister Mary, fifteen years older, urged her to come to stay in California, encouraging the Mulcahy brothers to work in Alameda at the rope factory or the brewery. They had arrived with one baby and another on the way. These were now eighteen months and four months old. As the Foleys had seven of their own, the small house swelled at the seams with nine children and five adults, but the two Mulcahy brothers, newly arrived, did not stay, for they quickly heard of a chance to sharecrop in Livermore, a valley, hot and fertile, to the south. They would live in a lean-to there, work to acquire land, build a one-room shack into which to move Sally and the little ones, and then build another room for the brother and continue their growth as farmers and family. Sally dreamed of the proud day of rejoicing when her husband would be coming in a big wagon for her and their children, when the crops came right. All their life experience, even the concept of bondservant, prepared them to sacrifice long years of deprivation for an ultimate goal. They did not complain.

Mary, meanwhile, doted on her sister, for no matter how much better the new land and a frame house and enough food than a dirt-floored sod hut and ever hunger and even with a fine, kind husband and seven children, it was possible to be homesick for the family and land left behind.

Mary had come from Ireland when Sally was only two, but she knew her at once when she saw her, for it was almost like looking in a mirror. Mary had longed so many years for that certain thick brogue and a sister's hug that she felt her joy overflowing because Sally was now in her presence. Mary came alone from Ireland, having just turned fourteen, knowing no one in the strange new land, the strange city, New York. The people and servants among whom she would for years do the hardest and most menial housecleaning, for whom she would be a kitchen scullion, were cold and alien.

"A slavey, that is the way it was," Mary said. "We sold ourselves for a long period of time, had to, to eat and live, out of the famine in Ireland. People would advertise. Men then would be coming through the county, with papers to sign, even for those who could only make an X for their name, bringing us to America to people who paid our passage for so many years of work. There were some came to cruel people who beat them and boxed their ears and gave them little enough to eat, came to households where the man forced himself on the girl whose bond he owned. You came to people you couldn't know what they was like, and it was frightening, for you could not get away, being they owned you and you had no friends in a new, strange land. If you got sick or had to send money back home and borrowed you never got free of the debt, but worked on and on.

"Me the saints protected, Saint Brigid, Saint Patrick, and Good Saint Anne, and the Holy Mother herself arranged my marriage, it's sure. For I met my darling Foley at church when I was but a few months here, and from the age of fourteen he courted me seven years, walking me after Mass back to a block away from where I was bound, for we were not allowed to have callers. So we could only walk and talk and dream toward our freedom and our marriage day.

"By the time we could marry, we had found a way to come on a wagon train across the wide continent, and it took us four years traveling. I weep when I think of that long travail. How people struggled so hard to get the wagons through, abandoned belongings, furnishings, the dead, on the way." She wept. "Our first child is buried along that hard way with a wooden cross we made for a marker."

70

Jennie thought of one time Alonzo came home almost with the morning stars drunk. That was the last time she had ever seen him so. He had wept with his head in her arms and mourned their daughter who had never breathed on this earth. Somehow he had taken the blame that she was stillborn, as if it was for him some punishment, some penance. Jennie had never felt this. Pure grief, yes, for a life not lived, a baby that she and Alonzo never got to hold and tell of their love, but no blame. She had tried to make him feel as she did, that that child was to be appreciated and thanked as a noble soul who had started the process by which Jennie would have the milk to save the child Jackie and that there was some reason and consent to this by a wise and loving soul and its creator, God. She believed their daughter had this part in this other child's destiny, as they too had, and that what they did for Jack they did also in tribute to that stillborn daughter. Someday they would meet and know her, when they too were pure spirit. Until then, she had given to the world a gift.

Whether Alonzo could ever see it her way. Jennie was not sure. But after that night, he had no longer gone to the bars. And she felt he looked at Jack with understanding and compassion and that it was the beginning of his real love for the baby boy.

As if anyone needed permission and encouragement to love! Perhaps the fact that friends and family dear to him had once turned from him because of what was revealed about his race made Alonzo more sensitive and needy for love, grateful to Jennie for her constancy in love. Well, she thought, no matter what he was or did, she did love him.

Mary put down the threaded needle with which she had been tightening a seam to hold together for yet another wearing, inserted it into the thread on the spool, and looked seriously at Jennie while she said her mind. The women had comforted each other with their arms around each other and heard each other's pain, yet somehow completed what had to be done for care of their families, with few such pauses in their pattern of work.

"It breaks my heart to hear such things as happened to slaves in this country, as my heart has broken and bled for Ireland." And all that Mary said was in a brogue so thick and rich, as was Sally's, that Jennie, now that she had learned it, translated in her mind. "Enslaved as we were," said Mary, "by the English Protestants for love of their religion, and hatred of ours, for greed for our land, which was lush and green, for fear of our beliefs, which we held with a passion. Sure, we Irish had known other forms of bondage besides this economic slavery. Long ago there were Norsemen and Vikings who raided the coast, who pushed Irish off their lands, pirating women away or selling men, women, and

71

children on the slave blocks in northern Ireland, selling Irish and other white people captured with swift sailing vessels, slaves rowing in the ship's galley, slaves serving them on land, and some Irishmen involved, too, in this evil business.

"Saint Patrick himself had been brought to Ireland as a fourteen-year-old slave, and he spent seven years there, learning the language and the hearts of the people before he escaped across the water in a small, round one-person coracle boat. He returned, a man grown and a priest, to rid Ireland of snakes, it is said. But what was the snake in the garden of Eden but a symbol of evil? The big *S* stood, in Ireland, for *slavery*. Patrick voluntarily came back, for he vowed to rid Ireland of the evil that was slavery, and he did. Oh, legends get lost in time. Some Irish tell it now that the S sign stood for real snakes and that real snakes were the issue. Some for shame of their slavery past tell the story a different way. This is how I learned it. And more, when these same marauders who set up their camps on the barely livable coast of Greenland stole women, it was for temporary use, never intending to keep them for mates or to keep the children they bore, but to abandon or kill the babes and replace the women they would abandon or destroy, wanting no bonds in their seafaring life.

"But the women, taught this new religion to them, taught love and family. And it changed the culture of these men. And they settled Greenland with these slave women. But centuries later new persecutors were on Ireland's shores and again the Irish talked to each other in symbols, calling Ireland the shawl-covered woman or Kathleen, for to speak of patriotism for Ireland or wear the green meant the hanging tree. And there were many women as well found hanging, their babies with them, hung with the long, loose hair or the long, tight braids of the mother wrapped about their throat. While in the English House of Lords those statesmen made speeches proposing that as the Irish continued to have babies they should through starvation be forced to eat them and solve both the Irish hunger and population problem.

"But even though the Irish have fled their own land by the hundreds of thousands, the men becoming Irish brigades in the armies of so many other nations that they found they were meeting and killing each other in service of opposing nations on so many foreign shores, and there were thousands upon thousands that are emigrants, as are we, we still try to bring forth children, to value them and keep them safe, to bless the family.

"Wherever we are we try to love the land and thank God. Oh, it's a great story, how the ancients colonized Greenland with families by the very knowledge and power given them by the teachings of Patrick and taught those wild and cruel men how to love. How they've stood with moral courage against the domination by the British. How a spiritual strength brought us, too, to freedom in this country. Jennie, you know I love you, and there are feelings and a knowing that we share."

Alonzo had come home from work and had pulled up another chair under the trees and sat through the long and rambling discourse as Mary expressed herself. He had some opinions of his own and wondered whether he should enter into the conversation. Now that there was no pretense over who he was and what his background was, knowing he and Jennie were accepted for their race and secure in their friendships, he had begun of late to open his mind to talk as he never had before. He had spent other such times listening to these women and some of the others who gathered with their children around Jennie, occasionally speaking with them as he learned they were of equal minds in concern for justice, in their abilities for compassion. It was a healing time, to know he could express himself to agree or disagree and still be a cherished friend. Some of the women had equally companionable husbands who would join in of an evening, and after the children were put to bed, with the doors and windows of their houses open so they could easily check on their children, the grown-ups would sit on a lawn or a porch and talk under the stars.

Alonzo found himself becoming quite a talker, saying to Jennie and Sally and Mary some things that Jennie had already heard, because it was a pleasure to repeat his gleanings of history and his own sense of the purpose and meaning of those bits and pieces of history to their lives.

"All this time," he said now, mostly in response to what Mary had just said, "I have had an idea about the English. But how does it fit with this view you tell so well? My view of England comes from an old political cartoon in the newspaper of Queen Victoria standing with arms outstretched on the shore welcoming slaves to freedom. It was also to freedom in the English territory of Canada, north over the border, the underground railroad would take the slaves brought from the South of our own country.

"When I found out I was black, that that was my social condition, I became so interested in how other countries treated people in this condition that I read every newspaper I could, thinking and learning.

"It was right after the Civil War that cotton prices rising began to increase the value of the Egyptian crop, because the South could no longer produce, without slaves, and so by 1869, because of cotton, many Egyptians had become millionaires. Great Britain sent them entrepreneurs showing them how to make waterworks, post offices, sugar plants, steam yachts, theaters, opera houses.

"Controversy over the Suez Canal put Egypt with its involvement in slavery into the newspapers of America daily, and these I read avidly.

"Slavery was part of the Moslem way of life, in fact, essential to it. And I, for a time, consumed with desire for knowledge of Africa, a heritage I assumed when I became labeled Negro, read everything, listened to everybody."

Alonzo went on to say how reports he read about the Atlantic west coast of Africa said there was a primary reservoir for slaves along with ivory, copal, coconuts, tortoiseshell, cowrie shell, and rhino horn. Arabs, Indians, and Persians brought by caravan and ship thousands of slaves bought or stolen from African tribes. Slave traders from both Arabia and India were dealing in Swahilis, who were the hybrid mix of Semites and Negro natives, and there were even higher prices possible for Abyssinian and Circassians from the north. Natives running from slavers roamed the forests like packs of starving beasts.

"Over time, the newspapers recounted, the British empire had struggled to abolish slavery in Africa, even in those places where thousands of Arabs owned large plantations of coconuts and spices worked by thousands upon thousands of slaves.

"English interests sent explorers into Africa and exploration of the Nile and its source was their activity, but suppression of the slave trade was their secret intention and ultimate goal."

These explorers, of whose exploits Alonzo had become enthralled, were already history by the time his interest was aroused. They were Livingston, Speke, Grant, Burton, and the flamboyant Samuel Baker and his wife, a rare woman.

Burton's adventures especially interested Alonzo. Burton, of Irish parentage, had a life of unorthodox bravery. He studied the language and customs of various tribes in Africa, had lived with monkeys to study monkey language, was concerned with the geography of the land, botany, geology, meteorology, and by age thirty-six had written so well of his difficult and heroic travels that his published *Lake Regions of Central Africa* had already made him famous. His book *First Footsteps in Africa*, published soon afterward, would make him even more famous.

All of these adventures and intentions had seemed to culminate with the November 17, 1869, opening of the Suez Canal blessed by Moslem, Greek, Orthodox, Coptic, and Roman Catholic priests. Newspapers reported the military bands and heads of nations attending: Eugenie of France on her imperial yacht leading the way, followed by the Kedive Ismail, absolute monarch of Egypt, known for his abundance of women and slaves, and the emperor of Austria and a flotilla comprised of a Prussian sloop-of-war and seventy vessels of both steam and sail, all made a ceremony to declare Africa now an island. There were four days of celebration that were to include, but did not, as it was not completed in time, the inauguration of the opera house built in Cairo for which Verdi was commissioned to write *Aida* to commemorate this opening of the Suez Canal and entertain the more than six thousand guests expected at these festivities.

So many ideas of history had been packed into the short chapters of his life, Alonzo said. Was there ever a time to come that would equal the portent of their lives, Alonzo wondered, his and Jennie's, their neighbors' and their friends' lives? Would their children's lifetimes equal their own for interest and excitement?

The neighbor children and Will and Priscilla had long since gathered around the adults and were hungry for supper. The women collected up the paraphernalia of their work and the children helped to carry things into the houses so the delicious business of fixing and eating their evening meals could begin. With a pat on the shoulder, a gentle word, each went on to their next duty, leaving the world's business unfinished. But Alonzo was well satisfied to have expressed some of his thoughts. It was a never-ending story. He took off his shoes, stretched out his legs under the trees, and let his mind relax in the patterns of light and shadow.

One day in the far future a writer named Alan Moorehead would write of things of which Alonzo had been curious, had tried to learn by letting others talk and by reading the papers for years, and more than Alonzo could ever have dreamed of, into a book called *The White Nile*. But that was after Alonzo's lifetime and from sources Alonzo could never know. What Alonzo spoke of here and ever so much more are in that book. Alonzo felt that for his time he had an open, questing, exploring mind. He had heard many stories, traveled across a nation, been of two races and cared for both, and fought in a war that changed his country and the fate of black people of whom he was now one, and in his family the races were united, and equally loved.

A small child-shaped shadow, made long by the late sun, passed over him as Jackie came to him and snuggled by his side. "What did you build today, Papa?" he said as he stroked the muscle-and-sinew-strong arm.

"Hullo, Son." He brushed back the blond cowlick that often curled on the child's forehead. "Hmm, today we put in windows. We put the glass panes in their sashes and hung them in their frames. We tied the iron weights on the rope cords. Remember, I showed you how we do that when I fixed the window in your bedroom? When we got through, those windows went up and down smooth as you'll ever see. And, Jackie, when I was pulling one of those windows up and down, testing it, I put out my head and guess what? I was looking eyeball to eyeball with one of the cows that had wandered over to see what was going on. Was I surprised! And was that cow surprised, too!"

They laughed together.

"Papa," said Jackie, he had remembered something exciting, "Flann and Danny, the biggest Foley boys, twins, caught a fish in the estuary. It was bigger then me. It took them both to carry it home."

"That's great, Jackie. You told me that yesterday. It was a salmon. There are a lot of them. They grow as big as a man. We share fish with the Foleys. They gave us fish for supper last night. That was sure a good supper. I'm ready for supper again!"

"Papa, will you tell me a story before supper?"

"Now, your mama Jennie is the best storyteller, and Priscilla."

"I like your stories, too, Papa. I like to hear you talk."

"I'll tell you what, Jackie; you tell me a story. I like to hear you talk, too."

"We-ull, would you like to hear one about the house that Jack built or about Jack and the giant?"

"Any story about a fine boy named Jack interests me very much. I'd sure be mighty proud to hear you tell a story. Now how are you going to begin it?"

"I'll say once upon a time there was a boy and everyone called him Jack because that's who he was, Jack, just like me. And sometimes there was good and sometimes bad and scary . . . because he had these things called adventures. . . ."

CHAPTER 28

Flora was not happy after all. When John had spoken often of a farm she had visualized fields fertile with full-grown grain, a winding tree-lined lane through which visitors would come in their carriages for social pleasantries, envying the fortunate Flora her country life-style, with her home almost like a resort, with fresh foods, and leisure to enjoy cool lemonade and glasses of wine in the soft, warm air. She knew there would be some hard work in the beginning, but not that it would be so tedious, the days so long and boring. She had not dreamed of John as this man in work clothes gone all day in the fields, bending with hoe as if a farm were nothing but work, work, work, to come smelling of sweat, hungry, to the table and then quickly to sleep, to labor the next day. A long wait for the crops.

76

As if this wasn't enough, John's plan was to take the ferryboat to San Francisco with the best-looking of the produce, where with a pushcart he would go up and down the streets as a hawker, calling out, "John London's sweet corn! J. L. sweet corn!"

She would be ashamed to appear again in the city dressed as she was used to, in her handsome braided and beribboned coat-dress with the bustle, wearing that expensive ostrich feathered hat in which she looked most elegant, the former gift of a doting, even fawning, client. She had never expected that after these years John would have risen no higher than a common street peddler. She had given up the wearing of her wig of black curls. She seldom saw people socially. Alonzo and Jennie, though living closer than ever, came less often than before. Flora did not push for more closeness. When she saw how the children and men gravitated toward Jennie's kindness and understanding she was made jealous by a realization that Jennie's qualities were lasting, intrinsic, unaffected, and natural and people valued them. She felt, by contrast, people did not value and appreciate her own qualities. But was it her fault she was prone to nervousness, heart palpitations, female trouble, and attacks of prostration? People did not understand her sensitiveness; that was the problem.

Eliza had unshirkingly assumed the household burdens. She cleaned, scrubbed, washed the clothes for all the family, prepared the vegetables from the garden, and did all of the cooking. Flora told her often it was fortunate that she did not have a fragile nervous system and have to so frequently lie down as Flora herself did. Flora claimed a weak heart and that she was subject to "fits." Her emotions were the vortex around which the whole family revolved. She knew others considered John kindly, long-suffering, tolerant, and hard striving for their living and that he could not make demands on Flora. He learned how to indulge her, as the children, pliable, learned. Flora was the center of their life together, a volcanic, tumultuous center erupting emotions, like fire and hot ash, on whomever she chose. It was as if the family lived along the earthquake fault. Several times on a bad day Flora could leave them shaking and trembling, for John stepped warily where she was concerned and controlled his own feelings. Eliza tried to be staunch, for everybody's sake. Ida softened and crumbled.

For several years the spirits had stayed subdued. Flora for a few months before and many months after her marriage to John had her erratic tendencies and self-will briefly under control. During the time John was making a sincere effort to realize his dream uniting them with their children on a farm, back to the land, out of San Francisco's worst depression, hoping his health held and that Flora would continue to be thrifty, they seemed to have a promising future. John saw the lush, rich

77

growth of corn and other vegetables to be harvested as a manifestation of his prowess, a unity of his energy with the earth's cyclic energy, a verdant promise. He had no way to know that Flora's behavior grew out of a dormant, dark, incalculable obsession to be the center again of something more important than the daily round of chores or drudging for a living that John seemed to find meaningful.

At just this time of Flora's restless inner urgings for an undefined importance, the newspapers carried photographs and stories of a tent encampment of spiritualists along the shores of Lake Merritt in Oakland. There were pictures daily of women and children and men by the water's edge, enjoying their camp meetings, and reporters portrayed their experiences as exciting news for the east side of the San Francisco Bay.

John had farmed and harvested and was going back and forth to San Francisco, selling the crops. Flora planted her own seeds according to her own nature, in the form of notices she put up in local stores by which she again hoped to draw people to her. Partly from boredom, partly from what she saw as their continued poverty, for John's efforts were not bringing in the big sums or the living style she had once fantasized, Flora visited the encampment of spiritualists and put up notices about herself. She did not want to arouse some of her old customers. She did not want them to see the style of living she had now adapted to. But she encouraged some from the tent camp to attend a seance she was planning to hold in "the parlor" of her Alameda farmhouse. And she had thought up an idea not one of them previously had imagined, something that would assure their interest and excite their curiosity. And she was the only one who could offer them something so rare. Flora thought it was brilliant how she had just conceived of such an idea. She thought it was a great stroke of good fortune that she had thought of such a thing. It made sense to Flora in her scheme of things. She got the idea that the cherubic looking blond, angelically blue-eyed little Jack would be the medium. Surely if he were the child of Professor Chaney and she herself, both of whom had this inclination to be a channel for mystic messages, he must have some inherent qualities that would make it work. Every spiritualist needs must have some unique drawing power or attraction, whether a flair for how they dressed themselves or the atmosphere they could create, more unusual than others, to attract patrons.

Flora did not tell John. He had made it clear he did not care for seances, but he was gone most of the time anyway, from before dawn to after dark in San Francisco. She planned to do this during the time that Ida and Eliza were in school. She did not tell Jennie and Alonzo, although they could have seen the notices she had posted, but they did not. Actually, it was something Alonzo had told them all, recently, about his visit to the newly reported, but ancient, Indian burial mound in Alameda had given Flora this brainstorm. She was still planning the details but was very excited about the possibilities. It was just outrageous enough for the newspapers to eventually write about her and her "child medium," just enough so as to make Flora a talked about and popular person again, and if her fame occurred, she glimmered it would establish Jack as Chaney's son, when the time came. Newspapers would report on this *unique* child reputed to be son of the noted Professor Chaney formerly of San Francisco, and he would read it and come. *Then* she could decide whether or not to snub him and coolly show she did not need such as him anymore—or, well, who knows? She would see when the time came. At any rate, she would be proven to have a son he would covet. With such gifts, Chaney could not dare disclaim Jack. Perhaps Chaney was by now much changed. She often wondered what he was about. She was now not sure whether she wanted his love or revenge, but thoughts of him still rankled. As for that child, Jackie, he too had been a disappointment, but this would make up for the problems he caused her.

Jack had already learned from his visits to Flora to move humbly and in fear, trying to be anonymous in her presence. Like Ida, he would stay out of her way. In fact, he would wish he was far away, as far as Mama Jennie's house, his real, true home. One time he had been at Flora's only a short time when he slipped away and was found by Eliza. She had an idea he would be on the way back to the home he wanted, down the one straight road, too long a road for such a young, though gallant, little fellow to go alone.

Since they had been in Alameda, Flora had not made any concentrated effort to have the little boy with her. As before, Alonzo or Will brought him sometimes on Saturdays, John's only day to take them for an outing. If they had the money and John was not too tired, he would treat them to a picture show. Flora, though occasionally Jack stayed a day or two every couple of months, wanted Jack there more and more seldom, claiming her weak health as the reason. Flora did not get satisfaction from having him around. Eliza on the occasional weekdays Jackie did spend with the London family just took Jack with her to the West End School. Eliza had endeared herself to the teacher for her seriousness and maturity, as she was as useful there as elsewhere. She assisted the teacher by helping less willing and able classmates with their lessons at recess or during class.

The teacher's desk sat on a platform in the front of the room. Jackie, too young to be enrolled as a student, when permitted to visit on occasion by special permission would sit on the platform edge with a slate and chalk, enthralled with learning. The stories and books, the singing, and the reciting of numbers and geography place names all seemed the finest knowledge any child could have. He longed with all his heart to go to school. It was to him a place of happiness and security, as he could be there with Eliza. Alone with Flora he did not feel safe, due to her uneven temperament, her bouts of drinking, and the times when Eliza and John would concern themselves attending to Flora in her moods while Ida, and Jack, too, stayed as inconspicuous as possible.

Then came the terrible day Flora had planned for the innocent Jack. With heavy Indian blankets she shut out the window light and darkened the room. Candles sent feathers of smoke and the smell of hot wax, and in an abalone shell incense burned to which Flora had added a pinch of chaparral and sage to give a desert pungency to the stuffy air of the blanket-draped room. Indian-file, and in awed silence, several unknown women entered, dim figures in the candlelight. These would be the participants in the seance, and they seated themselves in a circle around the table. The child Jack, barely five years old, nude except for an Indian loincloth, with Indian symbols painted on his face and chest, had the horrible experience of being forced by Flora to lie down on this table in this dark room ready for these strangers to enter, place their hands on the table around him, and wait in silence.

Flora pounded a hypnotic rhythm on an Indian tom-tom. Suddenly there was a wild war-whoop kind of yell that sent shivers along the scalps of all present. Jack was terrified and could not utter a sound. He had been forbidden by Flora to cry out no matter what happened. Then a strange, hollow chanting that all surmised must be an Indian chant was heard, and as the smoke rose and the room filled with the dense smell of chaparral, Flora announced that the Indian, Plume, had entered from the great beyond and would answer questions. Timidly one woman spoke. Plume answered in an Indian language and an otherworldly tone of voice, which Flora translated for the women in a strained monotone as if she too were otherworldly. And so each woman, some hesitant, some more firmly, asked questions and was spoken to in turn. The tom-tom began again, and Flora after a long while seemed to come from her trance, thanked the women for the contributions of money they had given her when they had arrived, and invited them to come again as she planned to hold seances for four days, a ritual number for the four corners of the earth, and those who attended all four days would have a special surprise on the fourth day. She could not reveal what would happen, but they would never forget it. A feather Flora identified as an Indian headdress feather supposedly had also fallen on the table in front of one of the women during the seance, and if she brought it tomorrow she would receive a message; she had been selected by that token. The Great Spirit had looked favorably upon her. Perhaps the others would receive one the next time they came. So the women left and Flora went back into "the parlor," took the child off the table, washed his face, and had him back into his clothes, the Indian blankets down and windows up to air the room. It had been a fruitful event for her, financially as well as emotionally gratifying. It had been interesting to start the seance at "high noon." She felt her imagination had surpassed itself this time. She ignored the cowed and trembling child who crouched at the closed door with his arm over his face, weeping.

When she had straightened the room and suddenly noticed him she scolded him sharply, "Stop that nonsense, now, stop that at once!" He was certainly an irritating child, she thought querulously. He had no ability to appreciate what she had just done.

CHAPTER 29

Jennie and Alonzo were angry and very troubled over Jack's condition. He had had screaming nightmares since his return from the few days spent at Flora's. Jennie and Alonzo had given him a stable and happy home life. He played with other children. His feelings were respected. They did not understand what could have brought him to almost a nervous breakdown. What he said did not seem normal; he appeared almost on the verge of madness or hallucinations. Jackie had never lied or made up frightening stories. Well, Jack and the beanstalk and a giant that ate bones and blood were very scary, but he knew that was just a fairytale. He knew the difference between a made-up story and something that really happened, and they never let any story scare him; they always explained it. He could talk to them.

Jack could not have made up what he was telling them, over and over, as he woke sobbing from sleep. They knew about Flora's seances from the past, although they had not attended one, but this sounded unlike anything she had ever done. The horrible dark room, Jack's being made to stay on a table with the hands of strangers, scary people he could not see, placed around him, and frightening raps and voices, a scream, war whoops, the disembodied voices, the unnatural-sounding voices. As they pieced it together this is what it seemed to them had happened.

Alonzo said, "In the past Flora received contributions from people of like minds who came to her house meetings in San Francisco to hear voices, to get messages from supposed spirits. Has she decided to manipulate Jack? To use him to earn money?"

Jennie had experienced Flora's exploiting the living for her own ends, her whims and vagaries and unexplainable purposes, so she had never put any confidence in or, attached any credibility to Flora as a medium. For if she did not serve well the living, how could she any better serve the dead? Jennie knew how insensitive Flora was to those around her who depended on her daily for her emotional as well as physical well-being. Eliza was made to be a drudge, Ida neglected and loveless, John's dream negated, Jack's needs simply ignored, or so all this seemed to Jennie. She knew how Flora did not care and even found it a convenience that Jack spent months with Jennie; then suddenly, as when he was an infant, she had compelled him for an occasional afternoon. She would have a spell where she would desire his presence and command he stay for a day or a few days, then, just as impetuously, become bored or annoyed by having him underfoot. To have him returned to Jennie "so she could get her rest" would be one way she would put it, as she neglected him for months on end.

Jennie and Alonzo both guessed correctly that while Flora overtly rejected him she wanted to keep Jack on hold as a memento of her loss, perhaps for use as a future tool of revenge toward Chaney, and she would unconsciously persecute Jack by neglect or her cold attitude toward him because he would always remind her of a failure.

Even if Flora had found a use for Jack, a way for him to earn his keep with her, if she did not sense the psychic damage the seances were causing the child, then Jennie must step in, said Alonzo. He and Jennie must talk to Flora and John about Jack's welfare. It was touchy. They had never given a reprimand to their friends.

How unlike her friendship with people like Sally and Mary, Jennie thought, was her friendship with Flora. Sally sat by her now as she sang to Jack, holding the sobbing and shuddering child on her lap, as he had had another day of frequent crying and talking about his fears of Flora's house and the things in "the parlor." Sally's milk-white skin that usually had an easy sunburn, giving a rosy glow to her face, seemed pale with concern. They had told each other things each had never heard before, she and Mary and Jennie, though some of each woman's experience was far removed from what past experiences the others might have had. They could talk out old traumas and feelings, even tell of things the others might not agree with, coming from separate cultures, but everyone would try to understand.

Sally wanted to help Jennie bear the anger. "You and Mary and I have been friends, no matter how our ideas have differed, embracing differences and trusting each has reasons to think as she does, respecting feelings. You're angry for Jack's sake and think Flora won't listen to the child's fears or to you speaking for him," she said.

"What can I say to Flora?" Jennie sighed. She remembered how Flora would only talk and never listen. They did not share conversation as Jennie could with Sally and Mary. "I feel I can only talk at her and not with her, even about something as serious as this."

Rosy Sally's dimple and her pink cheeks were subdued in solemn pallor. A child's spirit was a sacred thing, and she was totally serious in her response to Jennie's concern.

"Sally, you call on the spirits. I've heard you. Tell me the good in it, please, I need to know, because this is what Flora does . . ." Jennie began.

"There's wide differences, Jennie. First of all, I don't know Flora, but if she's not all goodness I wouldn't want her as a go-between to the spirits for me, for I'd be thinking she wanted something besides goodness from it. The spirits I speak to are ones that have done saintly acts for love of God when they were in their mortal body, were living people, and anyone can speak to them, not just some special person. They each became a saint by doing service to humanity, to be an example of God's will, how they believed God wanted them to be in their lifetime. That's different from just calling on any spirit at random, for money or to get attention, saying you can do it. I never see or hear the saints, the spirits I speak to, but I think they can hear me and can see God's face and, like any friend, would help me with the cause of my prayers by adding their voices to God on my behalf. And being a friend is all their business now, having no household chores and other distractions that cause me sometimes to forget my prayers. I bake soda bread and scrub the kitchen floor, and if I forget praying, well, my friends the saints keep praying for me. It's for my spiritual progress, don't you see? It's different from what a seance is. Them that has a curiosity and that can't wait for heaven for their answers keep paying people like Flora to get beyond the secret of death for them. I don't know if the holy Lord matters to them in this, if faith and love for Him in His glorious mystery enters in. And I don't know what you can say to Flora when you speak for Jackie.

"But, Jennie," the rosy glow came back and she blushed with fervor and the dimple showed itself in her radiant smile as Sally said, "I'll pray to the saints and the Holy Mother herself to give you the words! I'll make a pilgrimage to the church and light a candle so as when I'm not there on my knees for you the light will burn and the smoke will rise to

God as a symbol and reminder that my prayers are there for you. Anyway, you know from your Bible that even in the lions' den or the fiery furnace, God goes with the ones that love him, and he loves us all."

"Thanks, Sally. I know it. It's just good to hear it again, to have somebody keep telling it. We have to teach it to Jack, too, how he is loved, so his fear can be as nothing. But he's not ready to hear it yet."

"Let him come play with Mary's and mine on Saturday, and you and Alonzo go visit Flora and John. The Blessed Mother, whose own son suffered, will be with you to make peace for this suffering little child."

CHAPTER 30

Alonzo could hardly believe his ears, as what John was saying was not like John at all, but like one of Flora's fantasies coming from John's mouth.

Their conversation had started out normally enough, as Alonzo walked around the acreage with John, looking over the farm, while the women talked. John had done most of his work alone and without machinery, and they talked at first of farm inventions that, Alonzo had heard, would have changed the economic conditions of the South, keeping the old plantations going without slave labor. There were always dreams of some machine or another. The combine, which had come with the reaper, the binder, and the threshing machine, had been used successfully in California since 1854, drawn by horses. Corn harvesters and cotton harvesters were new. The potato digger, predicted to come on the market in about 1886, was the latest idea.

But John, though enthusiastic about farming, was going to leave the Alameda farm. He would be over to give some payment to Alonzo soon for the stake he and Jennie had given them. About all that could be realized out of the crops this year had been taken, and John was not going to put money into a new planting and the long wait again for the proceeds. No, he and Flora had made a decision just yesterday. They were going to move to Emeryville and he would help to manage a racing stable. Just like that it came, a change in their lives, so suddenly he himself was still amazed that he had made such an agreement. The men would go into the house later, and Flora could tell them all about it. It was her idea, really, that and the strange way it had come about.

Alonzo wondered uncomfortably how Jennie was getting on there in the house with Flora. He had an unreal feeling, as if he were in dreamland in the field with John. The men sat down on a log, and Alonzo suggested that John tell him more.

When they arrived at the London home, Jennie with a basket of pies she had baked and some homemade bread and preserves, had gone straight to the kitchen when Eliza came to the door and Alonzo, seeing John out in the back, had joined him there.

Eliza had been ironing, and Flora reclined with a cool cloth on her forehead. Jennie suggested some tea for Flora, who rose, pleased, to greet her, and said, never mind, she would make the tea and they could both take some while they talked.

Jennie, seeing the great ironing Eliza was struggling with, said, "Child, now you just let me do this and Flora and I will have a visit, and maybe you've got some schoolwork or something else you'd like to do."

Eliza gave her a quick look of gratitude. She had been ironing with the kitchen door opened, a hopeful token that a breeze might relieve the heat of the task. Sweat curled the fine ash-brown hair about her face and beaded her forehead and upper lip.

At a nod from her stepmother, Eliza felt she could leave, and Jennie spoke pleasantly to Flora. "Now, don't stir yourself; let me put on your kettle and make you some soothing tea. You're feeling poorly from the heat? I'll just spell Eliza on this bundle while we talk some. No need to fret that young lady—she sure is growing, isn't she?—with things between grown women."

Jennie set the mood that it would be serious conversation. Flora sat at the kitchen table and sipped at the tea. Jennie put the iron back on the burner to heat while she collected her thoughts, then spoke with the thump of the iron as she moved it over the dampened cloth spread on the starched shirt. Steam rose as she talked, and she finished the garment while the iron was hot and began the same process with another.

By the steadiness of her voice and the tone of it, by the emphasis of her words, she tried to let Flora see the gravity of the situation. She would speak for the boy, still in his innocent, unspoiled years of childhood, barely out of babyhood, not even of school age, totally dependent on the adults around him for help and understanding, for his developing nervous system, for his health, his sanity, his direction and guidance, for a child's right to live free from terror and recurrent nightmares. The seances were beyond his understanding.

Flora had never been so talked to by Jennie before. Jennie's attention focused strongly on her impressed Flora into compliance, by attitude, by content of her words, and by steadiness of her gaze whenever she raised her eyes and looked into Flora's eyes. Flora felt almost hypnotized by the intensity of Jennie's feelings. She had not felt that impressed in a long time.

To Jennie's surprise, Flora suddenly said, "Why, Jennie, I'm not going to be having seances!"

Jennie could hardly believe her ears. She was overwhelmed with happiness. "Oh, thank you, thank you, Flora. I'm so glad to hear it!"

Flora went on. "Yes, at the last seance a remarkable thing happened. One of the ladies who came, a Mrs. Roanoke, whose husband owns racing horses and brings them here to Alameda, stayed after and we had a long talk. Seems she felt guided to offer us a house in Emeryville and a position to John, helping to manage their stables. We've talked to her husband about it, too, and it's all decided. John is going to give up this farm, and we will move within two months, when the last of the produce is sold and we can be packed, maybe sooner." Her nearsighted eyes glistened with pleasure and gazed off into future fantasy even as she recalled to Jennie how the Roanokes had sealed the bargain by entertaining them at the fancy Kohlmoos Hotel just built on Linden Street, encompassing the block from Lincoln to Haight avenues. The Kohlmoos brothers' vision was for a watering spa to attract a rich elite to Alameda, but even bigger things were happening in Emeryville with a horseracing track.

It was Jennie's turn to be stunned. This change of events was like a bolt out of the blue for her.

"That's the way the spirits work," said Flora. "I just haven't been happy here as I want to be and John has more ability than can be realized on this little old plot of land, so I convinced him we should better our luck by this offer. The Roanokes are awfully rich, but she just can't find anyone they can depend on who has the right combination of skills, so it seems like they were guided to our door."

Alonzo and John entered in time to interrupt what Jennie might have said. The four friends sat around the table to share some of the sweet-potato pie Jennie had made and brought. Flora and John unfolded more of their sudden plans, at least as far as they had thought them out. They would have a better house to live in than on the Alameda farm. John would surely rise in position as the Roanokes acquired more horses and winnings. They would have an exciting life getting acquainted in the racing circle. Who knows? They might invest in a horse in the future. There was money to be made in racing horses. John would pick up experience in horses, their training and breeding, as the work was being done by the trainer and the stable hands and the jockeys. John was going to help build and oversee new stables for Mr. Roanoke. Flora could hardly wait for the move; oh, yes, and would it be all right if Jackie just stayed with the Prentisses until they got good and settled in their new house? Jennie was right about that child having a delicate nervous system. Flora was even flattered a little to think in this regard he was like her. It would not do to upset him with change yet. They would arrange for him to come later.

To have Jack stay was the one thing Jennie had been thankful to hear, and the other was that there would be no more seances for Jack.

As she and Alonzo walked home, deciding they needed the time together to talk, Jennie said from now on she would be careful what she prayed about, for it seems her prayers were answered. But the answer was strange and as hard to understand as the problem.

Flora and John had much to say to each other, too, for their decision was so new it could not be said to be well thought out. But that was not the important thing, for this had been a mind flash, a psychic experience. It defied explanation that Mrs. Roanoke had found Flora and had believed Flora and John to be the couple she and her husband had been looking for and that John would actually agree to the impetuous arrangement. Actually, John's reasons would have surprised Flora if she had known. John was sensitively aware that Eliza and Ida were carrying a heavy burden and that Flora was not going to become the hardworking farm wife he needed. If she could not change, he would, to get better living conditions for his children. If Flora was happier with their goals, she would be a better helpmate and better-spirited toward the children. If he had a better-paying position, they could afford household help for the family as they had briefly had in San Francisco and Flora, Eliza, and Ida would be in a less stressful relationship with each other. He was aware Flora was disappointed in their economic situation on the farm. He could change that in time, but meanwhile the girls were getting older and too little time was left of their childhood, which he wanted to make happy for them, they had had so little joy in their short lives. When Flora presented her solution, he had spontaneously agreed. He felt it was satisfying to farm, but he loved his children more.

Flora at last felt her own power had worked in her favor. That was the purpose of the psychic experience, this benefit by which a person could be sure of the spirit's direction and receive some reward from it. She acknowledged that mystery that brought Mrs. Roanoke to the seance; and that gave that lady the assurance she needed to choose Flora and John. She had immediately invited Flora to one of the races that very next day. Racing was a fad and the sporting crowd celebrated at the new Kohlmoos Hotel, at Crolls, and at other Alameda landmarks. Flora had made as definite an impression on Mr. Roanoke as on his wife. She did have a way of ingratiating herself. She had a chic diminuative figure in her modish San Francisco clothes. The ostentatious hat was still fashionable, and she wore it with a flair. Fortunately, she had not roughened her hands with work. The Roanokes' friends also were impressed with Flora.

Mr. Roanoke accepted Flora's praise and recommendation of John, furthered by his wife's conviction that there was spirit guidance for this choice. A gambler on the horses knows how to act on a hunch. John was hired even before he and Mr. Roanoke met, and when they did, it was all worked out within the same week. His new employer liked at once John's obvious honesty and sincerity and willingness to work, as well as his having some background in building and farm management, which seemed to apply to Mr. Roanoke's needs. Flora's assertiveness had paid off.

She was pleased, too, at the way she had handled Jennie this afternoon and gotten her to agree to continue providing free child care for Jack. Flora wanted to become socially important in the sporting crowd, that new East Bay social set revolving around horseracing, and a tagalong child would not be an asset.

Jack was plumb silly about those seances, reacting like that, thought Flora. *I was doing nothing to hurt him. After all I* am *his mother! And even if Jennie was right about them affecting him, Jennie doesn't know everything. Jennie hasn't the slightest idea how to be important.* Flora brooded. *Jennie and Alonzo think goodness has importance. But they will probably never be important people. They proved it when they lived on Nob Hill and didn't even try to mix with society.*

Flora herself was more ambitious than John. It was up to her to think of the get-rich schemes and to look out for opportunities. She knew she often completely exhausted herself from her brain working and working on big ideas. *I feel,* she thought, *that I am going to be a very important person. Too bad Jennie has no concept of the importance of being rich and popular or famous.* Then she caught herself with a start as something basic to her belief struck her! *Oh, my! Here I am thinking all this as if she had a choice. Why, I'd forgotten. . . . She couldn't become important. . . . She's black!*

CHAPTER 31

Before Flora and John moved from Alameda, Alonzo and Jennie visited them to say good-bye. John paid Alonzo a portion of the money he had advanced him to start farming. He assured Alonzo that he and Flora would soon be wealthier than they could become by farming and he would pay the rest later.

Jennie and Flora had a serious talk about Jack's forthcoming education, since Jennie would enroll him in school in the fall. Jack had never been named officially. On his birth certificate he was still "baby boy, born to Flora Chaney." Now Flora must decide under what name he would be enrolled in school, for this would establish the identity he would bear publicly for years. Flora was feeling quite pleased about John at this time. She thought that now he took direction from her he would be an achiever. For now, she should forget Chaney. She decided on the name John Griffith London, the Griffith from a nephew of Flora's, Griffith Everhard; although she did not keep in close touch with any relative, she remembered the boy with fondness.

It was a season of good-byes. Flora and John, with Eliza and Ida, moved to Emeryville, near the eastern bay shore, by a hugh shell mound made into a park. Their home adjoined the racetrack. Sally Mulcahy with her two little ones moved jubilantly, but with many kisses and caresses and affirmations of love and prayers always for all the Foley family, the Prentiss family and other neighbors and friends of Alameda, to their cabin in Livermore, the flat, hot valley of farmland to the south.

And, though they had not foreseen they too would be making a move, Jennie, Alonzo, Will, and Priscilla readied themselves to leave Alameda. It was not for themselves but for William that the family made the move.

But Alonzo had loved Alameda and been happy and felt a sense of peace there. William, at the young age of almost fifteen, had come to an adult determination to further his own business career. It was a time when youth was no barrier to work. Children twelve and fourteen years old were laboring ten to sixteen hours a day in jute mills, canneries, steam laundries, and other sweatshops and in the fields, for the sum of ten cents an hour or less. William was one of the lucky young people in that he was sure his work would support him well. Thanks to his training he could hold his own with any man. Though he could still be considered an apprentice in the building trades, he had, from working with his father, developed many aspects of his craftsmanship, sharpened his skills, and acquired his own tools. He was ready to prove himself and had found some black contractors in Oakland who, taking an interest, employed him. Will believed the chances for a black man were far better in Oakland than the other places he knew of or had heard of.

Alonzo spoke for Alameda as having a start toward becoming a city without prejudice if only he and the other black families there continued in the development of it, but Will liked the promise of Oakland, a bigger city, where he was becoming established with friends and was popular for himself and respected as a craftsman, and he did not want the daily commute.

89

And Will was proud that he would have the life of a young black that his father with his white face could never have known.

Jennie and Alonzo were not ready for their firstborn child to leave home. They did not see him as old enough to be on his own, and there was no reason for him to be when they could help him. Will's father had been much older when he had developed his own business, in his early twenties, and a family man, too. Jennie wanted to make sure Will got enough to eat, those breakfasts of eggs and grits or oatmeal, with home-made bread in thick buttered slices; the slabs of pork boiled with green beans or mustard greens; a choice of fish fresh from the estuary, rolled in corn meal batter and fried. No young man alone would eat right. Since William G. had a loving mother to cook for him and iron his shirts, Jennie and Alonzo had decided for William's sake, to move to Oakland and keep the family together. The business world could be rough on a person, especially a young kid. Alonzo wanted to be close to give guidance and advice, even though William would be working with others, strong black men building their careers.

In Alameda, Alonzo was his own person, independent, free, truly individual. The hunting and fishing and knowing the habitat of wild creatures and being present in a place of such primeval beauty appealed to him. He opened up to people as never before, relaxed, and also was drawing ever closer to the land and could appreciate what John London expressed about the growing of things. He sensed the earth turning under his feet, pulsing with life, sending its juices through green plants in season.

Always one for a sense of place, Alonzo had absorbed the city, San Francisco. Now in Alameda he learned best to appreciate the earth in its resilient cycles and glory in its pure, unchanged beauty. Here was virgin land, trees with their thousands of birds, and he, a builder, did not even want to bring about its change.

He stood one day in an area known to have a burial mound at the east end of the peninsula. There was something spiritual about it, a place of spirits. The original people had left; no one knew when or how long ago. No one had seen them living. Someone had unearthed one of the hallowed dead from this great shell mound, an Indian grave mound, and Alonzo had seen this body, as it had been laid there, face turned to follow the path of the sun. He had gazed on this person who lived before him in time. As he looked he heard the far drumming of the bay water as a constant rhythm against the shore, one wave coming after another. He wondered if the people coming after he was long gone would respect this place as well. He felt a spirit of peace, as if there were tangible spirits of peaceable people in whose presence he had his being. He never forgot that moment when he first felt an interaction with the earth as a living entity and that deep intimacy with creation and the essence of his own being.

For Alonzo this had been a religious experience, to feel the great energies of the earth through time as vibration, as rhythm, to feel the strong presence of spirit. He was strengthened by being there, in the presence of the dead whose bodies had been given into the earth's keeping, their faces turned to follow the path of light. He felt his own unity with time and space, with others having had life, and with spirit everlasting. He felt what it was he honored by being there and the acceptance of himself as having meaning for the world, too. His meaning was also through Jennie and the lives she had fed from her breast, William, Priscilla, and Jack, now given the name London. *I feel in myself a unity with all this, a history and a destiny*, he thought. And he was glad he had received that feeling, to take with him as he moved on.

Invocation

Good wild juices and the fat of clams
covered our lips,
> *We felt the earth*
>> *move change the earth alive with us*
>> *the earth's skin coating our sweat in cooling mud*
>> *our tattooed faces shone*
>> *as oysters abalone seed filled shore marsh.*
We knew and named and numbered oak hoard deer herd
elk whose big guts stored their feed like hollow logs
quail squirrel rabbit seal sea-otter and more
whale washed ashore salmon sturgeon longer than a man
spawning the estuary
> *we timed harvests under trees so thick we could not see stars*
> *through goldfinches starbursts of flowers*
> *a fragrance hanging far over the bay.*

> *We saw the strange men coming and laughed au au au au*
> *slapping our thighs. We taught them lore*
>> *shell and obsidian/flint/basalt/medicine stone tubes/*
>> *find grain chert/jasper/antler/deer ulna/*
>> *cannon bone split/iris fiber/bulrush/tooth/quill/reed*
>> *by buckskin bound/useful tools and beautiful.*
>> *They called a wilderness what only was bewilderness to*
>>> *those who had not counted acorns known these roots.*

91

We laid our dead facing the sun path
for the spirit journey
  for the next thing that would happen
  lowered them gently bodies into the earth body
  shelter from the coming cold
  to ornament the earth
  placed iridescent mallard breast gift basket
  pumice shone charm stones
  layers deep in measured order not to be disturbed
  by animal by bird land 3000 years deep
  petrified bone let bodies rest
  facing the racing sun trail waiting the passing sun
  the sun going west.

Our dead for road bed were dug
midden made best road black blood bone fragment shell
skulls 1 inch thick marked where the brain pressed Your
children tossed them as toys pocketing our arrow heads
You taught asphalt cement paint face into white mask
collect plastic artifacts
          what better than seeds animals
what better have you brought the land you who do take
and not give are your children gentle
          is your peace sweet?

Alonzo felt a spiritual bond with Alameda, still, Alonzo could see that Will believed in Oakland as the place for a young black man's future, the new frontier Alonzo had come West for and dreamed about. This dream was opening up for his son. The parents were proud of William's skills. His talents and interests were so like Alonzo's. He was motivated to work in a most professional way, interested in all phases of carpentry.

The year was 1881 when Alonzo and his family moved to Oakland and rented a cottage on the corner of Dennison and Kennedy streets, in the southwest end of what was then called Brooklyn Township. Close by was the section, also on the Oakland side of the estuary, where many people of color had found places to live. The waterfront was still mostly mud flats. A former mayor had tried to claim all of the waterfront as his personal property, slowing up development of the area. Squatters built shacks there. Many of these ramshackle houses and houseboats were now lived in by black families. William had a strong desire to be as close to the black community as possible in every way, and he was satisfied. Alonzo and Jennie had never lived in such a small, shabby house, but there was not another to be found. There had just been not enough houses built for the growing population.

The Prentiss home was located about fifteen blocks from John Swett School. Jackie and Priscilla were both enrolled. Priscilla walked Jack to school and home. They were inseparable except for their separate classes. She would look for him on the playground. Her friends, too, took pleasure in having the little boy with them. Priscilla Anne was of great help to Jennie where Jack was concerned.

Of course, the family made every effort to remember to call the boy Johnny. School was a very important step in the life of Jackie Chaney, now John Griffith London. It was agreed that for Jack to have a chance he would have to be identified with a family line. Flora bragged that her own Welsh forebears had been in America since before the Revolution. She was pleased to make it known that the London name could be traced to an Englishman who had fought with George Washington.

Alonzo took Flora's bragging with his old habit of silence, which he could assume now when useful. He had heard by now that in England people had sold themselves into slavery and the poorest were in dreadful bondage, that even Captain John Smith, made so much of in American history, had once been sold as a war prize and had written in his journal about the settling of this country: "Poor whites were lifted bodily from the streets of London and brought over and sold from the ship." Alonzo did not think Flora needed to put on airs in front of Jennie.

John London had gone through a hard time to find a place for his two daughters, so it was easy for him to understand the need to help the nameless young child when it came to enroll him in school. He was a sympathetic person and agreed that Flora's child should adopt his name. Though there were no legal papers, for years at school the boy was publicly called Johnny.

No one consulted the child, but he never forgot his name Jack, the name that Jennie gave him. He kept it as his secret choice and believed if he ever made his mark on the world it was by this name, Jack, that he wanted to be remembered. If he could not use it at school, still he knew it to be his own and would keep it in his mind until he came into his powers.

Their rented home at this time could not be made satisfactory to Alonzo and Jennie. So many people lived as they did, in hastily built, simple, boxlike structures, where the earth had been scraped raw and ugly for that purpose. People walked through mud on undeveloped streets. Jennie and Alonzo kept on the lookout for a vacant home to move to, but homes continued to be scarce as the population of Oakland was fast burgeoning.

In 1883 they found one on East 15th Street, not much better but closer to John Swett School. Alonzo kept the other cottage in his name for William, who was romancing a girl and moving toward independence from his youthful past into his future.

Out of the clear blue and after over a year of separation, Flora one day showed up on the doorstep of Jennie's home and demanded that Jack leave immediately with her. She gave no explanation at the time for her long absence from Jack's life or her sudden reasons for compelling him to leave with her. She did not fill in the missing time or tell why she and John and his daughters were leaving Emeryville and moving to a farm in San Mateo near Colma, a bleak coastal area where farming was poor.

Jennie had no choice but to gather Jack's belongings as quickly as possible. So, with hugs and kisses for him, unexpressed feelings of anguish, and desperate attempts to choke back tears, she sent the child with Flora. Flora claimed mother's rights to do with him as she willed. At this time a mother could place a child, leave him, or reclaim him according to her own needs.

Jack's protestations that he wanted to stay at Jennie's, his looks of despair and fear at going with Flora, were negated by Flora. Jennie strengthened herself to help the child. She could not allow him to be torn apart, claimed by two women who would rend the child in two different directions. Jennie knew her Bible. "Honor thy mother," it says. Jennie knew the story of how the king threatened to cut a child in two by sword and give half a child to each woman who claimed him. The true mother would sacrifice her interest in the child to let him be whole. She could not divide Jack by setting her feelings against Flora's. She had to leave the door of friendship open for Flora, too, so that Jack could come back when Flora needed him to, as she might again.

"Go with your mother, child," said Jennie. Unsaid in her heart was *Jack, don't forget me. I know I have been all to you that a real mother can be.*

Years later Jack scrawled some notes from which he planned to complete his own version of his life, a writing ambition never realized. He wrote of this period, the time he was separated from Jennie, as the most wretched time of his life. He wrote that he felt starved, his hunger neglected by everyone else. No one knew what the child was going through or if this hunger, so ravenous in his mind that he described it as like wanting to snatch bread and meat thrown away by other children up from the ground and devour it, dirt and all, was in some way concerned with his very real hunger for love. The mother who nourished him was gone, maybe forever, far, far away. And the London family moved again, from San Mateo to Livermore.

94

Eliza and Flora in later years puzzled over those childhood diary entries and said there had been food enough to eat and did not know why Jack wrote as he did or understand his hunger. But Jack could never explain this hunger and at that time Flora fed Jack a kind of poison. In her passion to wean Jack away from Jennie emotionally, she could not attack Jennie as a person, for the care Jennie had given Jack was too real and had to be acknowledged. In one area only could Jennie be devalued, as being different from Flora, John, and Alonzo because of her black skin. And this difference could be used to Flora's advantage.

Flora began to make insidious remarks that soon became openly blatant, starting with talk against the dark-haired Catholic Italians who were neighboring farmers. Somehow Jack must be made to see he should not associate with or trust certain people. Flora had long given up wearing her black wig, and she and all the London family had light brown or blond hair. She would present the light-skinned, blond races as superior, as, indeed, she thought they were. She could not mention Jennie by name but could cast racial slurs on all dark-haired, dark-eyed races, twisting the mind until Jack could see dark skinned people had qualities that made them inferior. People with "foreign" ways and ideologies, especially Catholics, whose ideas and allegiance still went back to Italy, where their Pope was, and the Chinese, who were trying to take jobs in this country and whose beliefs were a mystery to Flora and feared by her, were all people Flora felt it would be right for her son to join her in not trusting. None of these had done anything for Flora and maybe were a threat to what she believed, as Jennie could be.

Jennie had tried to put a scare into Flora about her seances, intimating they did not allow Jack to have a whole, sane, safe, healthy life, that the child could die of fear-induced nervousness, nightmares, a tortured spirit. She made a strong case against using Jack against his will. She told Flora these things so emphatically that Flora was intimidated. It was the first time Jennie had stood against her, but it showed Jennie was different from Flora and therefore not completely her friend. Now Jennie was far away and Flora could do as she pleased about the seances, but she held back. There was no one who would attend, no patrons, and after the Roanoke incident John would not consider spirit guidance reliable. The remote neighbors on surrounding farms were Italians, Catholics, and their religion would not let them share this interest of Flora's. Another reason to declare them inferior was that Professor Chaney had hated Catholics.

Perversely, everything Flora tried to discourage Jack from he seemed to be drawn to. He would go off to those farms across the fields, and the Italians would give him books and camaraderie, good humor, and even wine! They drank it at all ages! He was glad at their parties and watched them dance and celebrate under the olive trees and among their vineyards. And yet, because of what Flora put into his mind, he feared them and held back. Dressed in his shabby farm clothes, he watched a celebration of love, the first he had ever seen, a wedding reception. This was all he had known of romance, and it became an ideal for him. He was a starving child again seeing, hungrily, the embraces, laughing, crying for joy, and hugging and kissing of friends and families. He saw there was a world he was apart from, that he desperately wanted to partake of and didn't know how.

A beautiful book came into his hand from one of those families, and it became the substitute, as close as he could get, to that world. It was a story of peasants, farmers, and artists, writers, the creative process. In the book an illegitimate boy rose out of poverty, out of a life that, young as he was, Jack understood, to become famous, exalted as a writer-composer of music. It brought back to Jack the pleasure he had known, embraced by Jennie on her lap as an infant, knowing books. And this book was about someone like him, if only he could rise from his own illegitimacy and poverty into fame, by writing. The book was *Signa* by Ouida. Jack also read *Alhambra* by Irving and *African Travels* by Paul du Chaillu and thought how Alonzo would have liked that one and wished they were together again, telling stories as before. He lived with Jennie and Alonzo in his mind, went back to them over place and time. He read more, and these books and the joyful, passionate, wine-drinking Italians he watched apart were life to him. Whatever gloomy prejudice Flora was impressing was not in his conscious mind. But her teaching seeped, nonetheless, without his even being aware, he was so young and vulnerable and alone, into his subconscious mind. Forever after he would have a dual being; one open to people, eager to love all and to explore the world, loyal to any human, drinking with them, and searching romantic love and one judgmental, despising himself for drinking, negating races, failing in his fantasies of family and romantic love, and never knowing why. His was a mind early divided.

One day, a glory day for Jennie, a wagon with the smiling, rosy Sally Mulcahy and her husband and children pulled up at the Prentiss family home in Oakland. Out tumbled Jennie's former neighbors for a reunion, a brief one, because they were taking produce to Mary and the Foley family in Alameda and could not stay. They had come very much out of their way on their long wagon ride to bring Jack. It was an act of charity, for they knew what it meant to Jennie and Alonzo and the little boy, too. They lifted down out of the wagon the few things that belonged to the child. There was not much, just a change of clothes.

| S | 49 | Ohio. |

Alonzo T. Prentiss

1 Lt., Capt. Lovejoy's Co., 49 Reg't Ohio Inf.†

Age 42 years.

Appears on

Company Muster-in Roll

of the organization named above. Roll dated

Tiffin Ohio, Aug. 26, 1861.

Muster-in to date Aug. 26, 1861.

Joined for duty and enrolled:

When Aug. 23ᵈ, 186 .*

Where Ottawa *

Period 3 years.*

Bounty paid $ 100 ; due $ 100

Remarks:

....

....

....

....

....

....

† This organization subsequently became Co. I, 49 Reg't Ohio Inf.
* See Muster-in roll shows enrollment of all men of this company as of same date. See enrollment on subsequent card or cards.

Book mark A B 376 0 G C

C. H. White

(750) Copyist.

| P | 49 | Ohio. |

×

Alonzo T. Prentiss

1 Lt., Co. *I*, 49 Reg't Ohio Infantry.

Appears on Returns as follows:

Dec 1861 to Feb 1862 Present,

Mar 1862 Resigned Feb 2. 62

....

....

....

....

....

....

....

....

....

....

....

....

× also Prentice

Book mark:

G. G. Slitter

(546) Copyist.

From U.S. government files; papers honorably discharging Alonzo Prentiss from Company 1, 49th Ohio Infantry, Union Army of the Civil War. Other documents regarding Alonzo Prentiss's army career and the army pension he later received are also on file in Washington, D.C.

DECLARATION FOR INVALID PENSION.

TO BE EXECUTED BEFORE A COURT OF RECORD OR SOME OFFICER THEREOF HAVING CUSTODY OF ITS SEAL.

AA AA

State of _California_

County of _Alameda_ } ss.

On this _8_ day of _July_ A. D. one thousand eight hundred and ninety-_ _
personally appeared before me, _a Deputy Clerk_ of the _Superior_ Court, a Court of
Record within and for the County and State aforesaid, _Alonzo J. Prentiss_ aged _71_ years,
a resident of the _City_ of _Oakland_ County of _Alameda_ State of
California who, being duly sworn according to law, declares that he is the identical
Alonzo J. Prentiss who was enrolled on the _29_ day of _Aug._
186_1_ in _1st Lieut. Co. I, 49th Ohio Vol. Infy_

[Here state rank, company, and regiment in military service, or vessel, if in the Navy.]

in the war of the Rebellion, and served at least ninety days, and was honorably discharged at
_ _ on the _18th_ day of _March_ 186_2_ That he is _Totally_
unable to earn a support by reason of _Rheumatism and_
age

[Here name the diseases or injuries from which disabled.]

That said disabilities are not due to his vicious habits, and are to the best of his knowledge and belief
permanent. That he has _ _ applied for pension under application No _ _. That he is a pensioner
under certificate No. _ _.

[If a pensioner, the certificate number only need be given; if not, give the number of the former application, if one was made.]

That he makes this declaration for the purpose of being placed on the pension-roll of the United States
under the provisions of the act of June 27, 1890.

He hereby appoints _J. H. Sheppard, 1000 E. 16th St. Oakland_ State of _Cal._
his true and lawful attorney to prosecute his claim. That his post-office address is _Oakland_
County of _Alameda_ State of _California._

Alonzo J. Prentiss
[Claimant's Signature.]

Attest:

Fred Tusher

Samuel Wilder

Also personally appeared _Samuel Wilder_ residing at _Oakland_ and _Fred Tusher_
residing at _Oakland_ persons whom I certify to be respectable and entitled to credit, and who,
being by me duly sworn, say they were present and saw _Alonzo J. Prentiss_ the claimant, sign his
name (or make his mark) to the foregoing declaration; that they have every reason to believe, from the
appearance of said claimant and their acquaintance with him for _ _ years and _ _
years, respectively, that he is the identical person he represents himself to be; and that they have no inter-
terest in the prosecution of this claim.

Samuel Wilder
Fred Tusher
[Signature of witnesses.]

Sworn to and subscribed before me this _8_ day of _July_, A. D. 18_90_
and I hereby certify that the contents of the above declaration, etc., were fully made known and explained
to the applicant and witnesses before swearing, including the words _ _ erased and the
words _ _ added; and that I have no interest, direct or indirect, in the prosecution of
this claim.

[L. S.]

Robert Cadman
[Signature.]

Deputy

[Official character.]

Record and Pension Office,

WAR DEPARTMENT.

Respectfully returned to the

Commissioner of Pensions.

Alonzo A. Prentice

Co. I , 49 Reg't Ohio Inf

was enrolled ____ Aug 23 ____ , 186 1,

The medical records show him treated as follows

No record of service.

From ____ , 186 , to ____ , 186 ,

he held the rank of ____ 1 Lt

and during that period the rolls show him present

except as follows

By authority of the Secretary of War:

E. T. Ainsworth

Col. U. S. Army, Ch'f

Washington, D. C.
(COMMISSIONER OF PENSIONS.)

(119)

DIVISION.

Department of the Interior,

BUREAU OF PENSIONS,

Washington, D. C. Nov. 13 , 190 2.

Respectfully returned to the officer in charge
of the Record and Pension Office, War Department, requesting a full military and medical
history

_____ of the soldier.

Please examine all records likely to afford
any information as to diseases, wounds, or injuries incurred by him while in the service.

Claim No. 803387

Name Alonzo A. Prentice

Co. I 49 Reg't Ohio Vol. Inf

_____ Commissioner.

6-41

Card 1 (top left):

S. | 49 | Ohio.

George E. Perkins (?)

.... Co. I, 49 Reg't Ohio Infantry.

Appears on

Company Muster Roll

for Aug. 23 to Dec. 31, 186_.

Joined for duty and enrolled:

When Aug. 23 ...., 186_.*

Where Ottawa, O. *

Period 3 years.*

Present or absent Not Joined.

Stoppage $ .... 100 for ....

Due Gov't $ .... 100 for ....

Remarks: ....

Name not on Co. Muster Roll

"Recapitulation leaves him
present for duty.

* See enrollment on card for this record's roll.

Book mark: ....

(358c)

Card 2 (top right):

P | 49 | Ohio.

Alonzo J Prentiss

1 Lt , Co. I , 49 Reg't Ohio Infantry.

Age 42 years.

Appears on **Co. Muster-out Roll,** dated

Victoria, Texas, Nov 30, 186_.

Muster-out to date ...., 186_.

Last paid to ...., 186_.

Clothing account:

Last settled ...., 186_; drawn since $.......... 100

Due soldier $.......... 100; due U. S. $.......... 100

Am't for cloth'g in kind or money adv'd $.......... 100

Due U. S. for arms, equipments, &c., $.......... 100

Bounty paid $.......... 100; due $.......... 100

Remarks: Joined a 1st Lt at
original org'n as set forth
Resigned accepted Nov
11 '62.

.. mark: ....

Rox

Copyist.

Card 3 (bottom center):

S. | 49 | Ohio.

George E. Perkins

.... Co. I, 49 Reg't Ohio Infantry.

Appears on

Company Muster Roll

for Dec. 31, 186_.

Joined for duty and enrolled:

When Aug. 23 ...., 186_.*

Where Ottawa, O. *

Period 3 years.*

Present or absent Not Joined.

Stoppage $ .... 100 for ....

Due Gov't $ .... 100 for ....

Remarks: ....

"Recapitulation leaves him
present for duty.

* See enrollment on card for this record's roll.

Book mark: ....

(358c)

3–402.

Certificate No. 829405

Name. *Alonzo S. Prentiss*

Department of the Interior,

BUREAU OF PENSIONS,

Washington, D. C., January 15, 1898.

SIR:

In forwarding to the pension agent the executed voucher for your next quarterly payment please favor me by returning this circular to him with replies to the questions enumerated below.

Very respectfully,

M. Chandler Frank

Commissioner.

First. Are you married? If so, please state your wife's full name and her maiden name.

Answer. *Yes Daphna W. Prentiss   Daphna C. Parker*

Second. When, where, and by whom were you married?

Answer. *March 1867 At Nashville Tenn I have forgotten the officers name*

Third. What record of marriage exists?

Answer. *I have nothing now but the record in family Bible*

Fourth. Were you previously married? If so, please state the name of your former wife and the date and place of her death or divorce.

Answer. *Yes Ruth M. McConnel she left me in Nashville in Aug 1865*

Fifth. Have you any children living? If so, please state their names and the dates of their birth.

Answer. *I have none living by my last Wife there are three by my first Wife Thomas Wilson, Born Dec 25 1843, Lyman Edwin born Oct 30 1849 Ruth Edna Prentiss born Nov 7 1852 she is now Ruth Edna Williamson, all of these three living in Ohio*

Alonzo S. Prentiss
(Signature.)

Date of reply, *Feb 7*, 189*8*.   O–8   5301b750m1-98

OFFICERS' CASUALTY SHEET.

Regimental No. _____

State of Ohio.

Name _____ *Bradliff* _____

Rank _____ *H* _____ Regiment *49* _____

Arm _____ *Inf'y* _____

Casualty _____ *Resd* _____

Day _____ *10* _____; Month _____ *March*; Year _____ *62* _____

Cause of casualty _____

No. and source of the order accepting resignation, &c., _____
_____ *10 Sept. 62* _____

Remarks _____

_____

E. H.
Clerk.

(171)

Headquarters of the Army,

ADJUTANT GENERAL'S OFFICE,

Washington, February 13, 1862.

Special Orders, }
No. 36. }

Extract.

x   x   x   x   x

2. The following officers having been reported on adversely by Boards of Examination, and the President of the United States having approved the reports of the boards, they are discharged from the service, to take effect at the dates opposite their respective names:-

x   x   x   x   x

1st Lieutenant Alonzo T. Prentiss, 49th Ohio Volunteers, February 15, 1862.

x   x   x   x   x

By command of Major General McClellan:

L. Thomas,

War Department,
ADJUTANT GENERAL'S OFFICE.

November 14, 1892.

Adjutant General.

A true copy:

For office use only.

Rec. Pen. Office.

Assistant Adjutant General.

C. | 49 | Ohio

Alonzo T. Prentiss

1 St., Co. I, 49 Reg¹ Ohio Inf.

NOTATION.

Book mark: R. & P. 376900

Record and Pension Office,

WAR DEPARTMENT,

Washington, Nov. 27, 1893.

It has this day (_Nov. 27, 189 3,_)

been determined by this Department from records
on file, and information
furnished by the 2 Auditor
that the resignation of
this officer was accepted
to take effect from Mch.
10, 1862, by A.O. No. 10, par.
5 of that date, Dept. of the
Ohio.

O. G. M.

(440)

State of California,

ss.

COUNTY OF ALAMEDA.

I, JAMES E. CRANE, County Clerk of the County of Alameda, State of California, and Clerk of the Superior Court of said County (which is a Court of Record), do hereby certify that James E. White *whose name is subscribed to the annexed* affidavit *is now and was at the date thereof a* Notary Public *of said County, duly qualified and authorized by law to* take aff fidavit *, and full faith and credit are due to all his official acts as such* Notary Public *And I further certify that the signature of* James E. White *affixed to the annexed* affidavit *is genuine.*

IN WITNESS WHEREOF, I have hereunto set my hand and affixed the seal of said Superior Court, at my office in the City of Oakland, County of Alameda, this 6th *day of* January *A. D. 189* 4

James E. Crane
County Clerk and Clerk of the Superior Court of Alameda County, State of California.

By J. W. Stetson
Deputy Clerk, etc.

State of _California_ County of _Alameda_ ss.

In the matter of Claim No. _808587_ _Alonzo J. Prentiss_

Co. H 9th Regt. Ohio Infy. Vol.

On this _third_ day of _January_ A. D. 1894, personally appeared before me, a _Notary Public_ in and for the aforesaid County, duly authorized to administer oaths, _Jacob Samuels_ aged _48_ years, a resident of _City of Oakland_ in the County of _Alameda_ and State of _California_, whose Postoffice address is _976 East 24th Street_ and _Cyrus S. Prescott_ aged _63_ years, a resident of _City of Oakland_ in the County of _Alameda_ and State of _California_, whose Postoffice address is _1137 East 20th Street_ well known to me to be reputable and entitled to credit, and who being duly sworn, declares in relation to aforesaid case as follows:

(Note. Affiants should state how they gain a knowledge of the facts to which they testify.)

This is to Certify that I have known Alonzo J. Prentiss Co. about Nine (9) years and know him to be a man of Moral hability and that he has complained of Rheumatism for some time that said complaint did not come from immoral habits and his charicter is good. Signed Jacob Samuel
976 E. 24th St. E. Oakland

The above Statement I Know to be true

Cyrus. S. Prescott

The above statement was written by me Jacob Samuels at No. 1128 23d ave E. Oakland California on the 3d day of January 1894 and was indorsed by Cyrus S Prescott at same time and place from our personal knowledge of the Claiment and in making the same we did not use and was not aided or prompted by any printed or written statement or writing was read or dictated by any other person

_We_ further declare that _we have_ no interest in said case and _are_ not concerned in its prosecution.

Jacob Samuel

Cyrus S.
(Signature of Affiants.)

3—1081.

PENSIONER DROPPED.

United States Pension Agency,

SAN FRANCISCO, CAL.

FEB 11 1905 ,190

Certificate No. 879405

Class INVALID

Pensioner Alonzo J. Prentiss

Soldier

Service J 49" Ohio

The Commissioner of Pensions.

SIR: I have the honor to report that the above-named pensioner who was last paid at $ 12 00 , to Dec. 4 , 1903 has been dropped because of death; date unknown.

FEB 10 1905

Very respectfully,

John L. Fiedler.

United States Pension Agent.

NOTE.—Every name dropped to be thus reported at once, and when cause of dropping is death, state date of death when known.

o-9

Jack London, at age ten, with his dog, Rollo.

Jack London at age eleven,
January 1887.

Prentiss home, 2060 Pacific Avenue, Alameda, California. Photo taken in 1979 by Mr. Eugene Lasartemay.

In Oakland, with her grown son William going through the gate, Jennie watches over her family from the doorway. Priscilla and Jack sit on the doorstep. Collection of the Northern California Center for Afro-American History and Life.

Jack London as a student at
Oakland High School, 1895.
Photo distributed by The World
of Jack London, Glen Ellen,
California.

Mother of the Disard boys, who were
Jack London's friends.

Lucy Cauldwell, Jack London's first sweetheart. Her grandfather had left his Jewish heritage, changed his name from Cohen to Cauldwell, married a young black girl, Marie Craddock, and brought his family to Oakland where they were actively involved, as was Jack, in the black community. Friends thought Jack and Lucy would marry, but she married their mutual dear friend, Edwin Dewson. Photo courtesy of Theo Bruce, Lucy's great-grandniece.

Jennie Prentiss, circa 1874. In 1914, at the age of eighty, Jennie served as midwife to her young friend Esther Jones Lee at the birth of her daughter Esther. This photo may have been given in commemoration. Photo courtesy of the late Mrs. Esther Jones Lee. Collection of the Northern California Center for Afro-American History and Life.

Mr. John Jones, wealthy tailor and abolitionist circa 1874. He helped to establish the Prentiss family in Chicago and advised them to go to California. Photo courtesy of the late Mrs. Esther Jones Lee. Collection of the Northern California Center for Afro-American History and Life.

Captain William Shorey and family. Captain Shorey was the first black captain of a whaling ship in the Northern Pacific. Photo from the Collection of the Northern California Center for Afro-American History and Life.

Mothers' Charity Club, Oakland. Organized 1907. Motto: "Lift as We Climb." Object: charitable work. Membership: thirty. Meetings: the first and third Mondays of each month at the homes of members. It is believed Jennie Prentiss is *front left* and Mrs. Shorey *front left center*.

Jack London's first daughter, Joan, with Jennie Prentiss. Courtesy of the late Joan London Miller, Pleasant Hill, California. Collection of the Northern California Center for Afro-American History and Life.

Joan London at fifteen months, with her mammy Jennie, Jack's foster mother. Courtesy of the late Joan London Miller, Pleasant Hill, California. Collection of the Northern Californian Center for Afro-American History and Life.

Jennie Prentiss with Jack's daughters, Bess and Joan London. Courtesy of the late Joan London Miller, Pleasant Hill, California. Collection of the Northern California Center for Afro-American History and Life.

Picture of Jennie Prentiss at picnic with Jack London, relatives, and friends, 1911, Glen Ellen, Sonoma County, California, on Jack's Beauty Ranch. Photo courtesy of the late Irving Shepard, Glen Ellen, California. Collection of the Northern Californian Center for Afro-American History and Life.

Jack London with Wallace Towns in the Klondike, Alaska. Photo courtesy of Royal E. Towns, Oakland, California.

A tree monument. At the base of the tree is the gravesite of Jennie Prentiss, Mountain View Cemetery, Elks' plot, Oakland.

Eugene P. Lasartemay,
author, historian, archivist.

Mary Rudge, author, educator, lecturer.

MRS. VIRGINIA (JENNIE) PRENTISS
IN HISTORICAL CONTEXT

B
920.932
B38n
Beasley, Delilah. *Negro Trail Blazers of California* (1919). The author spent 18 1 2 years either researching or writing this, yet much work in Black history remains to be done.

B
B389
A1
Bonner, T. D. (ed.). *Life and Adventure of James P. Beckwourth* (1931). Beckwourth Pass was named for this Black mountain man.

R
917.3
D838q
Drotning, Phillip T. *A Guide to Negro History in America* (c 1968). Pages 16-24 concerns California. Two Blacks were at the presidio of San Francisco in 1790. Twenty-eight of the original forty-four settlers in Los Angeles were Negroes. Others participated in the gold rush. William A. Leidesdorff was appointed U.S. vice-consul in 1845 and is buried in Mission Dolores.

973.8
F854r
Franklin, John Hope. *Reconstruction: After the Civil War* (c 1961). "Franklin points out many fallacies which still impede the solution of problems left by the Civil War."

326
L82one
Logan, Rayford. *Negro in American Life and Thought: the Nadir, 1877-1901.* John Hope Franklin says this is extremely valuable concerning the difficulties and disillusionment of Blacks after disfranchisement.

323.1
M258h
MacWilliams, Carey. *Brothers Under the Skin* (1943). Old but still one of the best surveys regarding several of America s minorities.

R
920.932
T425p
Thurman, Sue Bailey. *Pioneers of Negro Origin in California* (1949). This first appeared as a series of articles in the *San Francisco Sun Reporter.*

326
W871s
Woodward, C. Vann. *Strange Career of Jim Crow.* Rev. Ed. (1966). The harshest segregation policies did not originate in 1870's but in the 1890's. They were initiated in the western states of the South and only gradually spread eastward.

Friends of the
Oakland Public Library

PRESENT A PROGRAM
CELEBRATING THE FOUNDING OF THE

*Jack London Collection
and Research Center*

AND HONORING THE

*East Bay
Negro Historical Society*

Thursday, November 19, 1970—8:P.M.
West Auditorium . . . Oakland Public Library
124 Fourteenth Street, Oakland, California

Program

Introduction
Mrs. John Keats DuMont
President, Friends of the Oakland Public Library.

"JENNIE PRENTISS—JACK LONDON'S BENEFACTOR"
by
Eugene P. Lasartemay
a founder and the Curator,
East Bay Negro Historical Society

"JACK LONDON—Oakland's Misunderstood Son"
by
Russ Kingman
authority on London
Director, Jack London Square Association

MOTION PICTURES OF JACK LONDON IN 1916
First showing of recently-discovered film taken six days
before London's death. Courtesy of Russ Kingman

"PRINCE OF THE OYSTER PIRATES" *
Dramatization of London's youth
showing his relationship with Jennie Prentiss.
From "Death Valley Days" — TV series.

Reception and Refreshments

* This thirty minute film will be shown after
the reception for those who care to stay on.

Guests of Honor

Mrs. Sadie Calbert

Mrs. Estella Earl, representing the Coffey family

Mrs. Russ Kingman

Mrs. Eugene P. Lasartemay

James Calbert, Principal, Prescott School

Paul Faberman, Chairman, Library Advisory Commission

Ted Smalley, Director, Oakland Civic Theater

Royal E. Towns, West Oakland Old-Timers Reunion

FROM OUR LIBRARY STAFF:

Mrs. Frances Buxton, Chairman
Jack London Collection and Research Center Committee
and Senior Librarian, California Room

Miss Sumika Yamashita, Young Adult Division

William Brett, Director of Library Services

Edward Nylund, Art and Pictures Department.

ON EXHIBIT:

Pictures and memorabilia of Negro pioneers and other
history makers from the collections of Royal E. Towns
and the East Bay Negro Historical Society.

Londoniana from the collections of Russ Kingman and the
California Room, Oakland Public Library

Program celebrating the founding of the Jack London Collection and Research Center at
the Oakland Public Library. The ceremony was attended by Jack's youngest daughter,
Bess London, who heard the speech by Eugene Lasartemay previously heard and appreciated by her sister Joan London who subsequently helped Mr. Lasartemay in many
ways and encouraged this book.

Jack stood shyly there with a new, sad look about him Jennie had never seen before. She could tell he was glad, pitifully eager, to be home again with her, but he also had received, somehow, some way, a deep emotional wound. That showed.

"This time," said Sally in a moment of confidence when it was possible in all the bustle, "he'll be with you a long, long time, I'm almost certain . . ." and she briefly told Jennie what she had learned of the troubles of the London family. How they would resolve them no one knew. Sally had not really known the London family in Livermore, but knowing she was coming to Alameda to see her sister, Sally had visited Flora and offered to carry any message or news to Jennie in Oakland. She had been most surprised and pleased to have been entrusted with bringing Jack. Subject always to her mood and whim of the day, Flora impetuously decided to send him, based on her own worries about the Londons' economic situation, which she did not communicate, and because he had been an annoyance to her, reading, moping about, and disappearing for long hours, maybe to those Italians. There was no real message other than that the Londons would probably be moving back to Oakland.

While obviously grateful to be back with Jennie, Jack seemed estranged from others, lonely, as if a shell had grown around him, no longer the easy-talking child Jennie had raised to be trusting and cheerful. Continuing to think over the bits and pieces Sally told her and what she surmised and later learned from several sources, including Flora herself, Jennie understood what the London family had been going through during that time. She was aware how deeply Jack, apart from his family, had been affected.

Jack had come, on his own, to realize his natural mother and stepfather had no love for him. He was bitter about this. He had experienced a steady and unchanging love and family warmth at Jennie's, seen the passionate exchanges among the Italians, romantic and expressive, made more poignant to him when he was an outsider looking on.

In spite of what Jennie said to assure him that his mother cared in her own way, that people had different ways of expressing their loving, Jack kept his own feelings. He knew he was right, and that feeling stayed with him all his life.

The London family had lived as if impoverished on the rocky Marin coastland where John tried to grow potatoes and other crops and they had struggled to save every cent. Then they were able to invest in land in fertile Livermore, the warm inland valley, as Sally's husband and others had done. Flora had gone calling on owners of big hotels in San Francisco across the bay to help John develop a better-paying market for his produce and had found one who wanted to buy all the eggs that

126

could be delivered. It turned out there were other bed-and-breakfast places that would do the same, and it seemed this was where the market would be. Flora convinced John that they should sell eggs instead of vegetables. At first John protested that he had no knowledge of chickens or desire to be a chicken farmer; he wanted to raise vegetables. But he was always intrigued by the idea of new inventions and still persuaded by Flora and her enthusiasm, so, though John at first did not want to take the risk, they bought electric brooders, newly on the market, and did well for a time by also taking in a boarder, a man with three children, the oldest only three years younger than Eliza. Eliza, Ida, and Jack were counted on to keep the farm going by helping to do the work.

The sixteen-year-old Eliza suddenly married this man, a Civil War veteran old enough to be her own father, and took on the additional responsibilities of mothering his children. The idea of having a boarder to alleviate the family burdens had seemingly backfired, as Eliza took on his burdens. The lonely, isolated Ida threatened to run away. She would not work herself as an unappreciated wageless slave the way Eliza was willing to do. She felt betrayed by Eliza giving her attention to others, for Ida needed her sister's attention. Jack had seemingly grown sullen at home, where he was worked continuously, and absented himself more and more. The electric brooders failed, the hens died, the business was lost, and John and Flora were in danger of losing their land.

Jack worried over the fact that his mother and stepfather might show up again in Oakland and force him to move back with them. He did not want to live with them again, in Livermore, Oakland, or anyplace. They had worked him hard for his age, and he had tried valiantly, knowing they did not want him just for himself, that he had to prove his worth to them with continuous effort. He was disturbed at Eliza's marriage, for it had not been a romantic wedding, he thought. The Italian reception under the trees had been all he had seen of how to marry and celebrate. He had been impressed with its expression of joy on the part of all there. He feared Eliza would not be well loved.

Eliza had mothered him, which he needed. He felt deserted that she would take on other children. As she was only three years older than the oldest child for whom she would be a mother, he also thought she would be more like an unpaid servant, the same as she had been for Flora. That was Jack's feeling about how Eliza had been treated.

Jack knew Ida also felt abandoned and he believed Ida would run away, but as she was barely thirteen he was not sure how she would be able to do that. Jack had often thought of running away to Jennie, but remembered she had told him he had a duty to go with his mother.

How glad he was to be with Jennie again and be accepted back. She had taken him in her motherly arms, and if pain was in her own eyes at how miserable he had become he did not see it as she looked out over his dusty and tousled hair. She only said, "Well, Jack! I expect you'll want a good bath after that dusty buggy ride, and let's get some food in you; you've got ribs and elbows and all kinds of bones showing all over. Papa Alonzo and Priscilla are going to be mighty glad to see you! I expect Will's going to be stopping by around suppertime. He's got a place of his own and—well, we'll tell you all those things later. We'll get you in school and—oh, Jack! I'm just so glad to hug you!"

CHAPTER 33

In 1884, the Prentiss family moved to 528 18th Street in Oakland. Will, at eighteen, was a man grown and on his own. Priscilla and Jack were enrolled in Cole School, which was located between Union and Poplar streets in the western section of Oakland.

Most people who knew of Jack living with the Prentiss family, wherever they lived, assumed he was one of the Prentiss children. People were just allowed to believe whatever seemed right to them. Alonzo looked so white people naturally thought Jack was his son. Jennie and Alonzo long ago had come to feel Jack was their own. But they respected Flora's wishes and always enrolled him in school under the name of London.

Priscilla, at eleven, continued to be responsible for escorting Jack, who was eight, to and from school. But soon he wanted to go alone. His sensitivity to race, an education begun by Flora, was beginning its slow torture. Had Flora not damaged the foundation of his being, the strength of his love for Jennie could have better enabled him to bear the ordeal ahead.

There had been less than thirty years of integration for the schools of California. Before 1857, attendence at a school for whites was denied to Negroes, Mexicans, Indians, and Orientals. The parents of the students attending school with Jack had not experienced an integrated education, and many passed their prejudices onto their children, particularly whites.

Jack's education in bigotry, begun at Flora's when she tried to instill in him prejudice as to whom he should associate with and that people of fair skin and light or blond hair were superior, continued under the taunts of schoolmates. The children of prejudiced parents were quick to make stinging remarks about family ties or even friendships and associations with persons of color. Jack tried to avoid the epithet he was given by white classmates, "nigger-lover." During his first years at Cole School he suffered from cruel remarks, from the insulting names that were shouted at him. He could not meet the wanton challenge. It was a trial that brought him endless despair. Even in the classroom, there were days when he would slip down in his seat. He hoped the teacher would overlook him and not bring his presence to the attention of other students. They were unaware that the people who fostered him loved him dearly and how great his need to love and be loved was.

It came about that Jack resorted to defensive violence early in life. When he was pushed to it he would fight. However, he employed strategy. He would take another route to Jennie's house, or he would walk past her house until all the children were out of sight.

When he was teased at school because of his closeness with Priscilla, he would not make friends or bring other children to his home because they might tease and hurt Priscilla and Jennie, too. He would protect his home.

When Jennie learned his suffering on this score there was no soothing counsel or understanding of what to do about racial intolerance that she could offer, for Alonzo had protected himself and his home and his job security in the same way in the past and they knew no better way to resolve the problem. She would help Jack endure and admire his spirit, which was never broken, though sorely battered and bruised.

What did help Jack was his chance discovery of the Oakland Public Library and unlimited books. This opened up to him a new world in which he could transcend the limitations of being a child in an unfair society. In the library, though outwardly it was only a ramshackle board building next to Oakland City Hall on 14th Street, he could go far away from his everyday pain and the cruelty of children at school. He could associate with the ideas of fine minds, the ages and countries and philosophies and adventures spread out for him in colorful bindings, and he had only to choose to open the books to be transported.

The librarian, Ina Coolbrith, mentor to Jack London and Isadora Duncan and her poet brother Raymond, and other children as well as adult writers, kept her own life secret with all its trauma until biographers discovered its drama after her death. She herself then became a story immortalized in the library in a book like those she had cared for.

Ina Coolbrith became the first poet laureate of California, co-editor of California's then best literary magazine, *The Overland Monthly*, with Bret Harte and Mark Twain. She held a salon for writers of all persuasions, gave Joaquin Miller his name, and sheltered his half-Indian daughter, Callie Shasta. Ina Coolbrith herself knew what it was to be a victim of prejudice, one of those who were driven out because of religious prejudice and who had fled across mountains, never again to reveal they had been Mormons. She had lost an infant and suffered cruel physical and mental abuse from a husband from whom she was divorced. She had changed her name and hidden her past. Suffering was a secret in her life, and she could recognize it when she saw it and did what she could to prevent it in the lives of others.

Something in the child Jack's look of untold horrors and unfulfilled dreams went straight to her psyche as if one soul spoke to another. The love of books knows no limitations of age or sex or race. Ina Coolbrith expanded upon Jack's affinity for books instilled by Jennie and opened further by the few books he had received from the Italian farmers. Ina Coolbrith was a fit guide to the world of the intellect, and from the moment Jack saw her as if enshrined in a holy place of books, she took him into her aura. Jack was filled with awe and adored her for the rest of his life, once writing her of his long respect in a tribute letter. She saw him as a hungry, growing young mind, ready to devour the whole library in great hunks, taking out quantities of books in huge, indigestible gulps. She tried to direct his appetites, finding for him the most substantial and the most delicious of all the literary offerings. She fed his tastes, which were eclectic. He was almost insatiable, reading constantly. He took books to the eating table and to bed and lost himself in them on the playground, gone beyond suffering, anger, and the world's prejudices into paradise. And so he read for years.

Jack graduated from Cole School as a straight A student at a little over fifteen years of age. He had become a disciplined and practiced writer in school because, due to a personality and opinion clash with his music teacher, he was required by the principal to spend each music period out of the class in solitary work, assigned to write essays instead. By the time of his graduation, which he did not attend, thinking he had not the proper clothes for it, his reading and writing prowess were equal to that of any college student.

Though he wanted desperately to continue in school, the economic problems of Flora and John London had intervened in his life to the point that Jack was compelled out into the world on their behalf, to try to make it as so many people of the era had to do. He was fortunate for his time. He had a ninth-grade education. But muscles and brawn were what the jobs he could find were all about. Muscles and brawn, physical speed, and endurance were what he had to sell. An education would do him no good as a work slave; it would be stamina and strength that would count. Now he was leaving youth's pleasures—learning, reading, and the precious social friends he had at last made, with whom he had shared the last joys of childhood play. Those friends, left behind at school, would play awhile more, while he sweated in the jute mill for ten cents an hour for ten-hour days and in the canneries. He felt lucky to be hired, as he knew he was, rather than go hungry or let Flora and John, who turned to him for help, go hungry.

CHAPTER 34

Remembrances

My name is Mrs. Jane Wright, Jane Disard before I married, and I can relate many adventures of Jack with my brothers, Charles and William, and the Dewson boys, Ed and Joe. My family and I are the source of this remembrance. In the 1880s Lucy Disard, Victoria Dewson, and Jennie Prentiss were working together diligently helping others in the church who were less fortunate than they. Do you remember the Mothers' Charity Club of the First African Methodist Episcopal Church? Even before the club was formed in 1905 through the efforts of these women (it lasted one year and united with the California Women's Federated Clubs and was responsible for the instituting of the Fannie Wall Children's Home and Day Nursery in 1914), these women did their good works in the church.

There were no Baptist churches for Negroes in Alameda or Oakland, so in 1881 Jennie joined us. I recall that upon my first sight of her family I thought she had a white-looking husband and a white-looking child, Jack. Sunday after Sunday Jennie was seen walking straight, neatly dressed, with her children, including Jack, to church.

Jack made friends while attending Sunday school at the First A.M.E. church on 7th and West streets. The building was formerly Oakland's first public school. First A.M.E. was the first organized church of the black worshipers in Oakland and was established in 1864. But about Jack, his best friends there were the children of the Disard family and of the Dewson family, the two women who were Jennie's best friends in church work.

James L. And Lucy Disard resided on Filbert Street. Their children, Ida, Martha, Jane, Flora, Mary, Lucy, Charles, and William, became friendly with Jack and the children of Alexander and Victoria Dewson. The Dewson family lived on Myrtle Street with their children, Evelyn, Ruth, Gussie, Lora, Edwin, Joe, and Alexander. These children were light-complexioned also, so Jack fitted in very well with them as play-mates. In pairs and groups they were often seen together around town, especially Ed and Joe Dewson and Charles and William Disard, boys that Jack mixed with and became fast friends with.

These boys were ganged together in fighting and playing. Swimming down in the estuary was one of their sports. They took responsibility for keeping the Disard home warm in their own way. Always ingenious, Jack and Ed pirated coal from a coal yard somewhere in the vicinity of Seventh and Market streets in Oakland. No one knew, for many years, their source, for my parents would not have accepted that.

Ida, Martha, Flora, and I, along with Lora and Ruth Dewson, were best friends of Priscilla Anne.

Even after Jack was attending high school, he was often seen with one of our group, Lucy (Cohen) Cauldwell, a beautiful girl, with whom he was close friends. They were so close and such a beautiful couple together that some of us believed there would be a marriage.

How early young Jack's life and attitudes were shaped, having lived in a Negro community where he was loved, with Negroes who fathered and mothered him.

Jack was never a problem to Jennie, although the condition of his clothes often indicated that he had many fights with other boys. The Dewson and the Disard boys were on his side, if they were around.

Jack had a healthy appetite and always had a strong, determined look on his face. Jennie believed that he enjoyed it most when he excelled in rough games, especially wrestling. The mothers talked often of the exploits of their children. Jack went over to Alameda regularly when he got older, would hang around the tavern run by the Croll family, a German family there. He got along with people of all ethnic groups. He learned to box for sport and did this all his life. I heard that his second wife, Charmain, put on gloves and sparred with him even on shipboard when they sailed to the South Seas, even when she was at last pregnant. Others have said this. It is in other books.

After he was famous as a writer, written often about in newspapers, he stayed close to Jennie Prentiss, so we saw him around. I think he always had a longing for Jennie's kitchen, where as a child he would be eating his favorite food, spoonbread and cornbread, with lots of butter.

If Lucy hadn't married Edwin Dewson, I wonder if she would have married Jack. When we were growing up together, we thought of him as one of us.

I am Theo Bruce, the great-granddaughter of Isaac (Cohen) Cauldwell, and I add this history of my family, for whom, according to the African Ministry of Cultural Information, Cauldwell town, one of the first four towns in Montserrado County in Monrovia, Liberia, was named;

Great-grandfather Cohen, who as a young man ran away from his Jewish parents with a young black girl, Marie Craddock, changed his name to Cauldwell and came to California in January 1855 by way of mule back across the isthmus, then on a ship, the *Northern Light*. After reaching San Francisco, he went directly to Sacramento, stayed for six years, came back to San Francisco, and finally came to Oakland. He was a farmer, sailor, miner. He and his wife, Marie, had two sons and two daughters. One of the Cauldwell daughters, Lucy, married James Disard. One of the Cauldwell boys had a daughter named for her aunt, Lucy Disard. This daughter, Lucy Ann (Cohen) Cauldwell, once a girl friend of young Jack London, grew up to marry Edwin Dewson.

This is the family heritage of Jack London's first sweetheart, but no biographer of Jack London has mentioned her name. The Disard, Dewson, Cauldwell, and Prentiss families were close friends. They were known to be good-spirited, a strong community of loving people, and as for Jack London, they knew and loved him well.

CHAPTER 35

Oakland in the 1880s! The time and place to be young. There was a band pavilion in Washington Square, on East 12th Street and 8th Avenue, with park benches among the trees where people would socialize. Men would sit in the park and play dominoes. Some people had leisure. Business was growing, too. Telephone poles had gone up. Stores and offices flourished in the heart of the oak grove where ancient trees coexisted; the city's largest building was at 5th and Clay. The Salvation Army band, tubas gleaming and cymbals ringing, marched daily around the square appealing to all to do good works.

Open motorcars, mostly horse-drawn carriages, and frequent parades of Company F, Fifth Regiment of the Second Brigade of Oakland Light Cavalry, forerunners of the National Guard in Oakland, made the streets colorful. Men and boys in straw boaters and felt derbies, boys black and white, side by side, turned out to watch the smartly groomed horses and parading men wearing high cockades with shining emblems on the front, visors and chin straps, rows of buttons on their coats, and gauntlet gloves.

South of MacArthur Boulevard, Sausal Creek widened into swimming holes for kids. There were boat houses for rowboats and sailboats, and racing crews practiced regularly at Lake Merritt. Traveling theaters came in wagons covered with canvas or in tents to provide amusement. On 8th Street a wooden bridge connected Oakland with East Oakland and the fashionable Tubbs Hotel, erected by Hiram Tubbs, one of Oakland's energetic early citizens. Horse cars ran to the hotel past grazing cows and on to Badgers Park in East Oakland. The hotel looming impressively across empty fields, with its water tower, windmill, large museum, pavilion, theater, restaurant, and sailing pond.

From San Francisco came men with long beards, "beavers," or bravado mustaches, long-stockinged women in voluminous multiple petticoats, heavy skirts, and bonnets tied with huge bows to enjoy the resorts. They especially would frequent Lake Merritt, only a fifteen-minute walk from the ferry landing, where they could ride the pleasure boats and cheer the regattas. The adventurous camped in tents by the lake.

People on both sides of the bay liked the ferries, which were like floating cities, with restaurants, bars, and even blankets and bedding for night rides! Musicians strolled the decks with accordions or violins. There were Irish harps, and Italian orchestras. Girls tossed their long hair, played tambourines, danced, and passed hats for coins. Beauty contests were held on board with groups verbal about the charms of the girl of their choice. Those of the comfortable middle-class with business in San Francisco were glad to come home to Oakland on the ferry to their own peaceful band concerts in the park or wide porch swings on their home verandas.

Oakland policemen waxed their generous moustaches, put on their bucket helmets and uniforms with big brass buttons, and went through the city, where mostly order prevailed. Oakland did not have problems as extreme as that wild boom town San Francisco, notorious for raucous entertainment, saloons, brothels, and unlevel basalt-block streets littered with tattered handbills and broadsides, patrolled by pick-handle-and-hickory-stick-carrying vigilantes. There anger and frustration of race tensions and unemployment were still rampant.

Almost thirty thousand San Francisco men, more than the whole population of Oakland, were unemployed, and about half the labor force was Chinese. In 1877 Kearney led five hundred men to city hall demanding, "Work, bread, or revolution," threatening to capture San Francisco and plunder it. Now San Franciscans were agitating to totally exclude the Chinese, who had already been malevolently exploited. The original tribes of California's people, reduced to serfdom for life, had been decimated, the Mexicans crushed and negated, and the blacks excluded from many trades.

By contrast, Oakland was being settled mostly by family groups of all races. Its population numbered 1,543 people in 1860, and it was then the thirty-eighth largest town in the state. By 1870 the population had increased to 10,500; by 1880 it had tripled and Oakland was the second largest city in California. It had grown with small tradesmen of all races; barbers, weavers, tailors, bakers, shoemakers, staymakers, silversmiths, engravers, tobacconists, glaziers, auctioneers, blacksmiths, and more, coming to escape the boisterous anger and volatile prejudice across the bay.

Contributing to Oakland's growth was also a steady influx of Jewish small businessmen who, with other tradespeople, expanded their shops northward along Broadway. Six of the seven men's clothing stores were owned by Jewish businessmen, and these "modest clothing houses along Broadway, between Second and Fourth, comprised a significant part of Oakland's original business district. In 1862 [Samuel] Hirshberg built a two story brick building on Broadway near Third, one of the very first brick structures in a town whose wooden shacks were often gutted by fire. Two years later, this section of Broadway (today's Jack London Square) became the East Bay's initial paved street."[1]

Oakland's Jewish community was very eclectic as to national origin. Included were such leaders as "Isador Alexander, from Prussia, who had trained his Chinese employees in the art of bootmaking; Aaron Cerf, an Alsatian . . . Jacob Letter, from Russian Poland, and one of the very earliest Jewish settlers in the area; and Joseph Julius Bettmann, a Bavarian storekeeper . . . businessmen who opened dry goods stores . . . perhaps the first of whom was Samuel Hirshberg, whose small concern reputedly carried everything from a needle to an anchor.[2] It will be seen how progeny of this community enhanced Jack London's intellectual life.

Among the Jewish families was the family of Gertrude Stein, who lived in an East Oakland home surrounded by ten acres of rose hedges and eucalyptus trees. There, at the age of fourteen, Gertrude Stein had her first memorable aesthetic experience. A sunset in Oakland so impressed her she remembered it the rest of her life. Gertrude Stein was born February 3, 1874, Jack London January 12, 1876; at one point in their lives they saw the same sunsets and were influenced by the same city, Oakland, and each in their own way left their mark there.

A literary love drama of the 1880s also enacted itself on the same Oakland stage. Robert Louis Stevenson and Fanny Osbourne cast themselves in starring roles for the life scenario that took them, in 1888, away to Hawaii. During June of that year Harry Bird, son of Urban Bird of Woodstock, on the west end of Alameda, close to where John London had farmed, delivered milk daily to Robert Louis Stevenson's yacht, the

Casco, which was being outfitted for the trip. Young Harry rowed out every morning with a pail of fresh milk from his father's dairy. The Samuel Orr family, the Scotch operators of an Alameda oil plant using *kuiki* nuts from the Sandwich Islands and other South Sea islands where Stevenson planned to go, were related to Fanny and also lived in the vicinity of the land John London farmed, part of which was the Clark Pottery and Tile Works, where Jack would someday buy the tile to roof his Wolf House.

Robert Louis Stevenson and his wife and her son and daughter stayed also at a vine-hidden cottage at 305 Spruce Street, adjoining the Clark Pottery and Tile Works and the tract farmed by John London, where members of Stevenson's wife's family, the Ed Koehler family, still lived one hundred years later, in 1988.

Robert Louis Stevenson was already a famed writer when his yacht sailed out the estuary through the bay and into the great Pacific. At the time, Jack London was twelve years old. Crowds of people turned out to see Stevenson off. People talked about his venture for months. Stories about the noted author appeared frequently in the newspapers. None of this went unnoticed by the impressionable young Jack London. Already he was frequenting the waterfront, fascinated by ships and the freedom they promised taking every odd job on any boat offered, wanting to learn how he too could sail away on adventures. He knew, too, that he would be a writer. He already made up his mind.

Oakland celebrated the passages of its Bohemians such as Robert Louis Stevenson, whose romance with Fanny, who was married when they met and fell in love, had its scandal. Oakland also recognized efforts to make a family city, a good business community, a center of religious fervor where people could thrive as God-fearing citizens.

Over the years churches were built through sacrifice and dedication on the part of their congregations, and on holy days and Sundays women in muffs and capes and leghorn hats, with bouquets or blossoms pinned on breasts or at gloved wrists, men in frock coats and spats, strutting with their canes, children following, walked in vast hosts to worship.

One of the oldest Oakland churches was the Presbyterian church built on Harrison between 6th and 7th streets in 1854, then the First Congregational, built on the west side of Broadway in 1869 between 10th and 11th. The wooden synagogue built on 14th and Webster and dedicated by a small group of Jewish people August 15, 1878, was designed for the future, for it was large enough to hold five hundred people.

The African Methodist Church began in what had been Oakland's first school building, which had been built at the northeast corner of 4th and Clay about 1853, was moved to 6th and Washington in 1862, sold to A.M.E. in 1864, and then moved to 7th and West streets. It was on 15th between Market and West when Jennie Prentiss attended, and in the 1980s A.M.E. is at 34th and Telegraph.

During the 1800s there were movements in Oakland toward educational enlightenment, too. One of the city's social and political leaders, Dr. Samuel Merritt, a mayor during the decade following the Civil War and for whom Oakland's lake was named, lived in a mansion on College Row where the University of California began in Oakland and where it stayed from 1860 to 1869, with offices at 12th and Franklin. He was one of the many civic leaders who wanted to keep the university in Oakland, where its influence was felt early on.

A continuing subject for many news feature stories of the time was the moving of the university, the naming of the university, and the philosophy of George Berkeley, an Englishman for whom the neighboring town to which the university was moved was named.

Abraham Lincoln had made the university possible, as well as a town to hold it, by signing into being in 1862 both the Emancipation Proclamation and the Land Grant Bill (the Morrell Act) to promote education: "Without education, emancipation did not emancipate. The freed man exchanges one thralldom for another . . ."[3] The city of Berkeley grew out of the university, which moved to the lands granted for education and was named by the college trustees, inspired by Berkeley's one " 'serious' poem 'On the Prospect of Planting Arts and Learning in America.' Although not new (it had been previously used by Voltaire, Dryden, and others), Berkeley's idea being that the center of world history moves West like the sun was irresistible. 'Civilization,' born in the East, moved west, to Greece, to Europe, to England, and then, finally, to America. Berkeley, California, at the western end of the country, home of the new university, represented the new Golden Age to be born in the Americas, the last refuge of the muse."[4]

To achieve an education at this university became one of the highest goals of some of the youths in Oakland. By the time Jack London was of an age to understand the meaning of higher education it became his goal. Will Prentiss had not considered the university. Education for his chosen work took place on the job; his goal was to marry and support a family. Priscilla, too, still had her goal, "to marry and be like Mama." John London had gone from job to job; he would end up, after years of being unable to work due to accident and ill health, in a final job as door-to-door peddler in Alameda. Alonzo had never considered a business other than carpentry, his life's work. The people they knew considered having a trade more practical and more urgent than pursuing education.

Having a business was the respectable, respected thing to do for self and community. Many Negro families in Oakland established themselves in business very early in the city's history.

One such family was the Scott family. The patriarch of the family, Charles Humphry Scott, had a store next to the post office at 5th and Broadway. They were listed in the first U.S. census and were great Catholics. They laughingly said, "None of us Catholics ever had trouble getting social security because the church always kept good records." Alfred Scott's sister married Bill Towns, who had a barbershop at 12th and Broadway. Their son, Wallace Towns, went to Cole School and also chummed around with Ed Dewson and his younger brother, Alexander, and Jack London. They were in the same social group at school.

Ten years after their Cole School chumming, the boys, Jack London and Wallace Towns, got "gold fever," talked over going to the Klondike as Argonauts or Sourdoughs, as they were called, and in 1904 did sail on the same ship, sharing adventures in a search for the gold, which none of the Oakland men and boys who sailed on that same ship with Jack ever found.

The cabin in which Jack lived in the Klondike and into whose walls he had carved his name was later sought out, brought to Oakland and reconstructed in Jack London Square, in the prime Oakland business district, commemorating his memory long in the future, far from the 1800s, when Jack London wandered the wharfs where Jack London Square and the Port of Oakland offices now stand.

Notes

1. Fred Rosenbaum, *Free to Choose* (Berkeley: Judith L. Magnus Memorial Museum, 1976).
2. Ibid.
3. John Boe, "'Who Is George Berkeley?," *East Bay Express Newspaper*, October 9, 1987.
4. Ibid.

CHAPTER 36

Capt. William Shorey, because he was Alonzo's friend, always kept an eye out for Jack at the docks. He would let Alonzo and Jennie know about the time Jack was spending with the sailors and dockworkers, and because he had developed a real fondness for the boy and knew that

Jack looked up to him, he could give advice to Jack that the boy respected. Because there was a rough element involved around the ships, this advice was often needed. The waterfront still abounded with opium smugglers, harpooners, sometimes violent ashore, human wharf rats who preyed on others, and desperate and unscrupulous men not above shanghaiing a needed crewman whose able body they would sell for a long voyage. There was bad and good, and it was hard for a young boy to keep balance.

Captain Shorey, master of the whaling ship *Emma F. Herriman*, spent many hours at the Prentiss house. Both he and Alonzo were great cribbage players, which resulted in welcome recreation ashore for the captain after periods at sea, sometimes a year long. The homey Prentiss house was always open to the captain and his family. Jennie and his wife established a friendship, sharing in the doing of charitable works extended to sailors' families.

Captain Shorey when first commissioned had to prove himself a skilled sailor, navigator, and trader and a forceful leader to achieve the status that he held. He started early in life as a seaman on a whaling boat, and in three years he had become a licensed officer. On his third cruise he sailed as master of the vessel.

Capt. William T. Shorey was born on the island of Barbados, British West Indies, the son of a sugar planter and a beautiful Creole lady.

During the many years Shorey was cruising the Pacific Ocean as captain of a whaling ship he had thrilling experiences that were often prominently mentioned in the daily press in several cities. In one case he left the port of San Francisco February 1901 and returned in November 1901. Many vessels had been wrecked during the season, and no one expected the return of Captain Shorey. When his ship was sighted, the *Examiner* sent a reporter out in the boat with the pilot who was bringing the bark into port. The newspaper stated: "Whaling bark passed through the typhoons. Only vessel on the coast having a colored captain, safely reached harbor after trying experiences."

Captain Shorey's visits brought exciting news of the adventures of the many ships as men told them to Captain Shorey. Jack, wide-eyed, sat and listened to these tales repeated and to Captain Shorey's adventures. He was tremendously influenced. When the story of the Sea Wolf was written by Jack, it included some of the experiences of Captain Shorey.

Because Captain Shorey also became attached to young Jack, he would always bring gifts for him. Many of the gifts were made by the captain while at sea. Jack envisioned that he too would sail away for an adventurous life and return with gifts for his friends.

When Jack was but thirteen years old, Captain Shorey took command of a sleek brig named the *Alexander*. It was not as large as the *Herriman*, but it was a graceful vessel. Jack would take his friend Ed Dewson to the Oakland estuary and they were permitted aboard the *Alexander*, where they learned skills from the seamen, who would show the boys how they sewed sails and steered the vessel and told them how whales were tracked and killed. They had souvenirs from exotic ports and articles they had made such as walking canes and chess sets. Some had learned the art of scrimshaw and made metriculous designs on whalebone, which they turned into watch fobs or bracelets or carved into fantastic shapes. Some made miniatures of their favorite sloops, carefully erected in wine bottles. Captain Shorey himself had a cribbage board made from walrus tusk, inlaid with tropical wood and mother-of-pearl.

By his friends, the seaman of different vessels and the dockworkers, Jack would be given salmon. The men handled the catches for the Alaskan Packers and liked to be generous with the young boys who hung around admiringly. Jack loved salmon, and Jennie learned a dozen fine different ways to fix salmon, to the delight of her family, especially Jack, who felt he was helping to provide for the family.

Jack saved enough from the jobs he got on the different boats to buy an old and rather battered skiff for six dollars and eventually outfitted it to be seaworthy with oars, sail, and a paint job that made him proud. He had done most of the work himself over months to make it fit. For the next months he spent every possible minute teaching himself to know the sea, running risks, as wild a sailor as possible, but he learned the tides and the winds and the navigation laws, self-taught as captain of his own small vessel.

Jack was strong and healthy and became a compctent sailor. He, like many young boys before him, felt the call of the sea. Captain Shorey and Alonzo were always able to talk young Jack out of enlisting on a whaler or Alaskan fishing vessel. Not all captains were as concerned as Captain Shorey. Many ships were leaky "coffin ships," "hell ships" to which men were often taken by trickery or force for the long voyages. Men were sometimes beaten, kicked, whipped, and even killed on the long trips. Nerves grew taut and scurvy was rampant. Their quarters were frequently cramped and filthy, the food wormy, and the ship rat-ridden. They had no associations such as unions for their protection or to hear their grievances against cruelty and incompetence.

Captain Shorey and Alonzo knew that more than anything else Jack really wanted to go to high school and on to college. They reminded him there weren't any schools in the Pacific Ocean except schools of fish and that if he stayed in Oakland surely a way could open up for him.

Flora and John were in Oakland, however, and pressuring Jack to help them, to continue to contribute to them. Their financial need was very serious, and by law parents were entitled to all the wages of a minor child. They had always come to Jennie to insist that Jack be made to work for them. So Jack had carried two paper routes, before and after school, and turned over the money to Flora, along with money from his work on the boats. She would ask for it. There had been a tremendous conflict, emotionally devastating to Jack, when he held out for himself the few hard-earned dollars with which he bought his boat. Now he was being forced by the Londons' circumstances into a wage-slave factory job. He set his jaw and entered, as they said in those time, the school of hard knocks.

CHAPTER 37

Was ever a father finished educating his son? Alonzo thought as he prepared to give Will a lecture. He had been meaning for some time to have a heart-to-heart talk with the boy, who had come under the influence of some strong and verbal racists. Alonzo, who had lived all his childhood as a white person and had white parents and family whom he still thought of with compassion, could not see the good of Will's new attitude.

Will and Alonzo had never had a confrontation on any issue. Will had not been a rebel against his parent's upbringing. They had given him a tremendous amount of love, and he gave them love in return. But Will's new ideas were causing Alonzo a great deal of concern.

"Will," he began after what had been a pleasurable game of cribbage, the two of them alone, when an opening had come for Alonzo to speak his mind, "Son, we were living peaceful in Alameda, blacks and whites together, no jobs barriers on account of race and all friendly with each other, but I can tell you, and your mama can tell you, we know what it's like when the white people don't love black people."

Will looked at his papa in surprise; this was hardly what he had expected Alonzo to say. He had surmised that there was some disapproval of his friends Cully and Rash and their ideas, because he had noticed an inadvertent pained look on his papa's white face sometime when those two got to ranting on about the black man's power and how whitey was going to get his, they'd see to that.

"Yes," said Alonzo, "your mama was a slave and white people held slaves. And not just white people, in this country the people of the Creek nation and the Cherokee nation, those and others of the tribes, were holders of thousands of black slaves. And," he added emphatically, "there were even black people that were free men that held black slaves in this country. In Africa, too, black people sold their own people into slavery, would hold their own black slaves in their own country, took slaves of their own race but of different tribes, and the tribal leaders had the power of life and death over their own people, who were like slaves to them."

"Yes, I went to war swept along by the sudden ardent feeling of myself as a hero for my time. I thought of myself as a white man, and I went to war with other white men, and what white people were fighting for, many of us, was to right a wrong that was being done to black people, to bring justice in this country for the black race. We'd risk our lives for that freedom.

"Now there were no black people that were going to look at any white person and thank them. No one wore a badge of their identity, after the war was done, to say what side they fought on. No one who fought in the name of justice for the black race expected to be appreciated by the black people for what they did; they did it because it was right, not because they would be thanked.

"But when I'm among blacks who don't know what I am, a black man myself, I have felt race hatred directed toward me for this, my white face, a hatred so profound it devastates the spirit.

"Just as some of those whites, once I was labeled black, rejected and despised my race.

"So what is the difference between the two races, if each has the same faults as the other? If the black people that are most angry for what white people did show that they too would do the same thing to white people, for revenge or just because they're capable, aren't they, haven't they become, just the same as the thing they hate? Where will it end if one can't prove they are better and stronger than the other at making peace? Whether it's for a race or a nation, that's the only strength that counts for the good of this world, and, I guess your mama would say, 'to get you to the next.' You go to church with your mama, so I'll leave that up to you.

"But, Son, I didn't think I was raising you to be against white people or Chinese or women or any other human being.

"When you were little and you and Jack would get into something— maybe that time he broke the first boat you made and you were ready to come up against the side of his head with a board 'cause you were that mad—your mama read you that story of the first brothers, how Cain killed Abel because he was angry and jealous and felt like what he had wasn't appreciated. Well, we're supposed to have *evolved* since that time.

"Didn't your mama say, 'Now we forgive'? Now you know I don't go to church. You know I don't say, like your mama does, 'Jesus says,' but I got my own reasons. And my reason is that I'm black, but I'm white too, and you're white, too, and what are you going to do? Are you going to hate your own self that you got a drop of white blood in you? And look at Priscilla; now you got to admit that black and white make beautiful babies. She is one beautiful and fine girl, that sister of yours.

"Now I know your mama, she's mighty proud that she's black. She thinks she is pure black, too, so I would never say anything to hurt her pride, but I look at her sometimes and I think, why, she's even got eyes that have golden flecks in them, not deep dark black, and her skin . . . Now she thinks she is real black and so do others, but I think she is more a chocolate. I mean a chocolate cream. And she never saw her own papa. She doesn't know who her papa was. I mean we black people in this country have got to be *tolerant*, because there's not one of us has got a pedigree proving there's no white blood in us somewhere down the line. And maybe all people do go back to the same two ancestors; some say so.

"For certain, we go forward and in a new generation we take our own new values. I want to go forward in you and tried to give you that plan for people to live together in peace, beginning with me and you, with your own ability to give compassion and love.

"Someone lays the first board. You are a builder. You know how it's done.

"And if you don't feel that in yourself, then there is still one more thing. You were raised with Jack. I raised him same as you and Priscilla, and it is my hope you love him as a brother. How could you not build a world for your white brother, too, and the children I hope you each will have?

"So what can you say to me, Son, now that I've said this long piece?"

Will was silent. Cully and Rash, his new friends, had put Alonzo down for his old-time ways and, yes, because he was too white-looking. They had pointed out to Will that a new breed of black man was what was needed, tough enough to reject their friends and family who disagreed. If the blacks were going to get ahead and surpass the whites he had to be ruthless, cut throat in business, and cruel to those whose thinking would hold them back in their rush for power. Alonzo was soft—that was it—and even if he didn't have a white skin they would never hire him on their crews because he was old, slowing up from arthritic pains and rheumatism in his fingers and joints. His knuckles were swollen, and he often moved as if his back and feet ached. Cully and Rash had no use for anyone who wasn't the fastest and best. The sharpest and the strongest was what they were about, because there was a natural law, they said, the survival of the fittest, because they were going to get even, they said, and get revenge on the world because the black man had suffered in it. They hadn't explained to Will all the ways they planned to do this, what forms it would take. So far it just meant that they were doing a lot of talking. It was amazing how Alonzo was not bitter for being hated and not loved by both black and white and how the races much alike were, he said.

It took courage for Alonzo to bare his heart to him, thought Will. He chanced his own son might reject him. Will had never heard his father talk like this. He used to be so silent, but over the past years he had been opening up, sharing his thoughts more and more. *The best way I can show him I care is by listening to him*, thought Will. *Let him grow old and garrulous! I might even learn something.*

With real affection, Will put his arm around the old man's shoulders.

Alonzo realized Will didn't have to say anything; the gesture was eloquent enough.

CHAPTER 38

"I couldn't say this to anyone," said Alonzo, "so I say it to myself. It is how I dream, my dream, and it is real, too.

"There was a house compactly on its foundations, like a dream house, but already built by parents, by community, the white curtains already up, the blinds pulled to a certain level, into which I moved and tried to live. That was my life with Ruth. Then one day the door was shut and I was on the outside.

"I know building, the challenge of being a carpenter. What I know is feel of the wood, the grain of it, the surface like satin, the pull and push of the saw, how that vibrates through my whole body.

"So I built a new house.

"That's my love for Jennie, touching her every day, going through my whole being. And the foundation I built myself is solid.

"Building with her, for these children, my love, it's a man's work; it's a life's work."

CHAPTER 39

Flora and John London came back to Oakland having to make a complete new start. This time Flora made an agreement with the operator of the California Cotton Mills, who was bringing young women over from Scotland as mill hands and needed room and board for them, that she would operate such a boardinghouse. John, of course, would be needed in every way to help with the physical maintenance a place of this nature required. They got an old house on East Seventeenth near the mill. John set about at once the labor of fixing it up, painting, repairing, correcting the plumbing, and doing all the other work a battered house entails. Flora had to see to the linens, to stocking the pantry, do unaccustomed major scrubbing and cleaning in which she was not at her best. She would even have to cook for them all until they could hire extra help, for they drastically needed a place to live themselves and an income.

With one problem and another arising from this venture, its initial success and expansion to two houses, then eventual failure, Jack's stay at Jennie's home had become a permanent arrangement, for Flora had no time to be bothered with a child, restless and inquiring, his mind ever curious, always into someting and in her presence sullen, withdrawn, friendless insofar as she could see, and difficult. She had not time or mind to continue his education in bigotry, that subconscious jealous competition, subtle, insidious, and quite unreasonable, burning out of a sick and sinister anger. She was too stressed out with her new and overwhelming duties to consider him at all. Flora hardly noticed how long it was that she did not see Jack. She seldom thought of him.

But when the boardinghouse venture failed and the impoverished Londons moved to the most squalid house they had lived in yet, Flora again cast a speculative eye on the strong and energetic child a few blocks away whom Jennie and Alonzo were feeding and housing and educating as her rightful source of income. She called on the Prentiss family, and it was agreed that Jack would take morning and afternoon paper routes and turn over the money to Flora, as well as any money from the odd jobs he got from his sailor friends at the wharf. She did not force him to live in their shabby place at San Pablo and 22nd, for, she reasoned to herself, he would be another mouth to feed and John could not seem to find work. It was Jack's duty to help support his parents. She was quick to point out that he had completed third grade already and many a young boy with less schooling than that had to go to work full-time in a factory or mill. If he worked hard before and after school and gave her the money, she would not interfere.

145

Jennie, so concerned for Jack's education she would have agreed to almost anything, promised to be supportive of this arrangement. She faithfully got him up earlier to give him a good breakfast, so he could deliver papers before school as well as after, and Flora, who knew when his pay was given, would find him and collect it if he did not immediately bring it. She would come to where he lived with Jennie at 825 18th Street. Sometimes she even waited outside the office of the newspaper where he was paid to get the money at once.

John at last found work, a night job as a watchman at the wharf, and Flora cast about speculatively for ways to make money multiply, for a time losing heavily in the Chinese lottery. She did not hold seances, as her house was not a nice enough place to attract a clientele, but she began to think again of her Indian guides and that exotic, mysterious world where spirits of all past times, disembodied, mingled freely. She had no close women friends in her life and had lost from her home both Eliza and Ida. John could not grasp what Flora thought or her motives. Jennie as often as she could saw Flora and tried to keep her balanced.

So 1885 passed and the other years until Jack graduated from the ninth grade. Ida had carried out her threat to run away from the problems at home and had disappeared. John London suffered serious injuries when he was struck by a train and was again unable to work. There were no social programs for welfare, disability, or accident liability to which he could apply. The family was all the support any person had. At fifteen then, Jack, forsaking his dream of high school, went to be the full-time support of the parents he already had felt did not love him. He gave up fun with the black friends with whom he buddied around, the little boat he had stolen time for and cherished, the long, greedy reading binges and library full of thrilling choices free for his own enjoyment, the warmth and the savory foods in Jennie's clean kitchen, a snug bed, the endearments of his sister Priscilla, still tender enough to smooth down his unruly cowlick and fantasize with him dreams for the future, and the conversations of Alonzo and Captain Shorey that welcomed him to join in. Jack went to live with the Londons in one of the scrap-built squatters' shacks by the estuary, to help Flora take care of the disabled John. There was no indoor water or plumbing, no electricity. The water was hauled in a bucket from a public faucet down the muddy path. They were unable to heat and warm the rough shelter. There was no transportation in the shantytown where the very poor lived, and Jack could not have afforded it if there had been. He walked a hard distance to work and back again and never saw the daylight, leaving before six in the morning and returning after midnight, caught up in the long workdays. The sixteen and eighteen hours that he and others worked was not unusual in those days of few unions. In the cannery where he labored he saw himself as a slave until death, which he felt must come before he could find a way to change his life. Love, pleasure, and laughter could not be part of such an existence. He remembered the Sundays he had gone to church with Jennie, where since a young child he had sung and praised God, how they had all clapped hands and called out Amens, praying for the goodness of the Lord to come upon them.

Slowly, slowly, as the grueling, joyless, tedious days and nights, the cruel hours of work, ground down his spirit in the hopeless, unending labor for the loveless home, he cursed his own strength and youth and powerful muscles that would force him to go on this way seemingly forever and he began to believe that there was no mercy, no loving God.

CHAPTER 40

I was barely turned fifteen, and working long hours in a cannery. Month in and month out, the shortest day I ever worked was ten hours.

But many a night I did not knock off until midnight. On occasion I worked eighteen and twenty hours on a stretch. Once I worked at my machine for thirty-six consecutive hours. And there were weeks on end when I never knocked off work earlier than eleven o'clock, got home and in bed at half after midnight, and was called at half-past five to dress, eat, walk to work, and be at my machine at seven o'clock whistle blow.

And when a workman got old, or had an accident, he was thrown into the scrap-heap like any worn-out machine. I saw too many of this sort . . .

I remembered the wind that blew every day on the bay, the sunrises and sunsets I never saw; the bite of the salt air in my nostrils, the bite of the salt water on my flesh when I plunged overside; I remembered all the beauty and the wonder and the sense-delights of the world denied

147

me. There was only one way to escape my deadening toil. I must get out and away on the water.

—Extracts from Jack London's diary*

They would never complain about it or let Will and Priscilla know, and be worried, but Jennie and Alonzo were aware of days when the rheumatism was so bad in his joints that Alonzo was almost laid up. He kept going, though, but Jennie decided, considering his grizzled hair and years of work and the fact that she was considerably younger and the young ones raised, that she would go out to work. She knew she was good as both a housekeeper and a nurse, and it was in these two types of work that she found all the work she wanted or needed. At first Alonzo protested, but it was pointed out to him that Priscilla liked to cook and keep house and Jennie liked to cook and keep house and with Will and Jack both out of the house the two women didn't have enough to do just for Alonzo. They didn't like to be idle, neither did he, so he saw the point in that. Jennie already volunteered a lot of time to church work, caring for the sick members and performing other charitable acts. This would be the same; she would be doing good and getting paid for it. That made sense to Alonzo, too. Also, she let him see how worried she was about Jack. That young one could wear himself out, get real sick, or even get himself an injury like John London did, so they might best put some by to be ready to help him out if the time came. Alonzo now saw, all these things considered, what a good plan it was and how, since Jennie was so willing to work outside the home, he should be agreeable to it.

It did happen that Jack, considering the estuary and the moonlight making a path over it luring him with a message that his knowledge of the waterfront and its activities might be the way out of the dehumanizing grind of mill and cannery work in which he would otherwise wear out his life, came to Jennie with a proposition that he could join the fishers; she knew they made good money, and one of the sailors had let him know of a good buy on a boat. For three hundred dollars he could own the *Razzle Dazzle*. It was a lot to ask, as much as three years' house rent. Why, those houses Alonzo helped build sometimes sold for only five times more. But it would be a business and Jack could earn money to pay her back. Could she advance him the money? It so happened that she could and did gladly.

*From Jack London's diary as printed in *John Barleycorn* (New York: Century Company, 1913).

CHAPTER 41

The wondrous sunlight danced on the living waters' ever-cresting innumerable patterns of white-lace foam and high, sloshing waves. Masts of hundreds of ships of all sizes tilted and straightened and changed direction in the changing waters. The waves sent their spray high on the wharf that day, and there were gulls that seemed to cheer for him as Jack walked out with his head up and joy in his eyes for that one ship that stood out from all the rest because it was his. The *Razzle Dazzle*, what a name! Sleek as all sloops were, she had a fine, graceful prow that would cut the wave crests and carry him to the free world from the $1.25 days of sweat-slavery wages to the riches, to him vast sums, of up to $20 or more in just one night.

By day he would fish, but at night Jack would act out a plan he had not shared with Jennie for pirating the oyster beds the Chinese so perseveringly cultivated. Every café, saloon, and grocer wanted to buy fresh oysters daily. Others discovered where these beds of treasure lay, and Jack was going to be in on the taking.

For this purpose French Frank had sold Jack the ship and the secret information. Jack knew he would not be alone in this effort, for French Frank planned to buy another vessel with an even faster getaway speed, and it would be "every man for himself" and no loyalty among robbers if the Fish Patrol came. Jack was ready for risk. He believed he would be the best and fastest sailor among the thieves if it came to a test.

Just a few hours ago he had tied his scant belongings in an old cloth to move onto the ship. Flora had been speechless with anger that he had acted without her knowing, but when she understood his message about the money he planned to bring her, and with John pacifying her that it was better than having Jack ship out on a whaler, in which case they would wait months or years for his return with pay, if he were not lost at sea like so many a young man, she controlled her fury, agreeing to "wait and see" if he would bring money. She did not know about the three hundred dollars or that he had bought a sloop, only that he was working fishing. He would tell her more later. As John said, Jack had acted independently, he had not run as Ida had or committed himself to others as Eliza did, but if Flora tried to force him on this she might lose completely. They must wait and see. John was pretty sure Jack's latent fear in Flora's presence, plus the inspiration Jennie always had given him about caring for parents, would make him continue to help them. Privately he was relieved, glad the boy had shown enough gumption to follow his own dream, something John had not been able to do with Flora.

The fifteen-year-old Jack had sealed his bargain with a drink when he handed over the money and received the ship's papers and his first whiskey. French Frank, an old hand with alcohol, had slugged down a shot, and Jack tried to look as nonchalant and weathered an old salt as possible doing the same. His swallows went down like fire and scalding lava, and now, he thought as he stepped onto the rocking deck, he must be quite drunk.

Drunk and hallucinating. There was a sea siren, a mermaid, or something on the bunk that reached out a bare white arm and pulled him under and he was drowning in her long hair and wet kisses were all over his face and his head was going down again and seaweed arms entangled his body and he was a dead man for sure. He couldn't breathe and the ocean was on fire and there was some huge wave surging over and over through his whole body, inside. And his penis was trapped in an octopus crevice and something was surging in his veins and his body was the ocean with hundred-foot waves, hammering the soft sand over and over and . . .

Jack regained consciousness a day and a night later. He had lost an afternoon, evening, and night on that strange, exhilarating, frightening, wondrous voyage, his first. Had he been shipwrecked, Odysseus-like? There seemed to have been Circe and many question marks, the sensation of all night long opening oysters swallowing them whole, his tongue on the pearl.

Diving the endless depths of moving water, he was awake, in sheets, on the floor of the cabin, naked, and she was cooking something and looking over her shoulder at him and laughing, a slight girl but with full breasts and voluptuous belly under a faded dress, barefoot, hair down to her hips, touseled as sea spray. He became conscious and recognized her.

"Maiden voyage?" She looked at him and gave him a big, open smile.

"Wild sea!" he commented. She was French Frank's girl. Jack expected a big knife any minute now.

"I come with the ship!" She was emphatic about that! Well, why not? It was her home, had been for a long time.

"You sure do come!" He could be emphatic about that!

He ate the eggs and toast as she went down, too, blue skirts out like a tide pool around her, on the sheets beside him, running her open palm over his bare nipples and stroking his muscles, and her eyes danced. In broad daylight and sober he didn't have the courage with women to do the same to her, but his eyes were on her moving breasts, round and pointed-tipped, flexing under thin cloth. With every bite of eggs he felt he was tasting smooth flesh, and his mouth watered and his eyes never strayed from the curves of her thighs and buttocks, breasts and shoulders. He thought, *I will love the female body forever. I will lust for sex always. I will never get enough after this.*

He pulled on his pants and she grabbed up some soft fabric and suddenly ran on deck, and he ran after. There was a small audience of men gathered on the wharf, comfortable on the pilings and on their heels, sitting and looking. They had earlier watched the unusual gyrations of the boat for a long time. A boat that rocked against and in opposition to waves was an indication of some interesting inner turbulence, and now they laughed and cheered to see what flag was going up as the girl pulled the lines. It was, entangled, his undershirt and her shift! The sailors loved her and cheered her, and they cheered Jack for capturing Mamie, the seventeen-year-old queen of the oyster pirates. That made him their royal favorite. As far as he was concerned he was now the prince, and all before he had stolen his first oyster. But they had voted her their queen, and he stole her love.

So the ship became the first home Jack ever made for himself, and Mamie, who claimed she had adored and admired him from the first moment she saw him, rolled with him in the narrow bunk and on the floor of the cabin and on deck under the night stars.

Such was his dream. In truth he was still poor and ragged. He owned no undershirt, no socks even, and Mamie, who did appear to have great attraction to Jack in spite of French Frank's jealousy was the black-whiskered young salt "Spider" Healey's niece and visited Jack's ship only under the chaperonage of a Mrs. Hadley, her sister Tess, and Spider himself. She had been voted the oyster pirates' queen. She did look longingly at Jack as if she loved him!

It was Jack's experience that the old men won out over the young. Hadn't the venerable Mr. Shephard taken the young Eliza? To be barely fifteen years old and the envy of older men for holding the admiration of the young seventeen-year-old Mamie gave Jack a sense of his own powers. There was the famous duel with ships that he fought with French Frank, who, not to lose face over Mamie, for the waterfront sailors knew from the dangerously teasing Spider that she was attracted to young Jack and not Frank's own fifty-year-old grizzled self, once tried to run him down. Jack, steering his own boat with his foot on the wheel and a rifle in his hands, held him off. Another time, Frank came close enough to Jack's sloop to fling his knife into the wood of the cabin, purposefully missing Jack by an inch, just to throw a scare into him. Unshaken, Jack, that time with a daredevil named Scratch at the wheel, went after Frank, coming so close their prows almost crashed each other as Jack, always with a dream of Mamie at his side, held out the knife, handle toward French Frank, fearlessly returning it as if it had been carelessly dropped. The older man easily could have murdered Jack and for a moment looked as if he might do so, while Jack gave him look for look, unflinching. Then, with a laugh, Frank took the dare, of friendship, in the spirit Jack offered, and the waters rang with the sailors' bravos as the sloops passed each other unscathed.

There were days Jack fished and he brought Ed Dewson and other friends on board the ship, but there were secret nights about which few knew, when he went to the oyster beds of which he had learned and pirated their treasures. There were rich oyster beds in the upper basin of San Francisco Bay. *Ostres lurida*, about the size of a silver dollar, propagate naturally along the south shore of Alameda. Seed oysters were planted on the mud flats of San Francisco Bay. These oysters had been brought from Shoalwater Bay and multiplied rapidly, with the imported Eastern bivalve, *Astrea virginica*, in and along the tidewater. The Chinese engaged in this new field of occupation, for oyster cultivation was an important industry in Asia and the knowledge had come with them to California.

Jack did give support money to Flora and John. He was concerned about their poverty-stricken condition. He paid Jennie back the money he owed her, and by that time she had heard from Captain Shorey, who had his own reliable sources at the waterfront, how Jack was earning it and she gave Jack a lesson he would never forget! Beginning with history and ending with the humanities, religion, and law, she filled in some gaps in his education as a compassionate human being. Her opinion was that after the Chinese Exclusion Act of 1882 and the violent acts against them before and after the legal cruelties, the Chinese, who had worked the California gold mines and helped to build the railroad as section track hands, who had labored as the least privileged in the most menial, most difficult jobs, had to be enterprising and had to develop their wits and find new ways to make money to survive. Jack should understand the suffering they had been through and should not prey on them as an enemy. Jack was astounded at this thinking. Once he heard it he agreed. It had never been presented to him so.

"But I thought the waters were free for all of us," he protested. "No one claims the fish, the turtles, the clams, the birds when we are out hunting. Natural things, like rocks, like the ocean itself and seaweed, are there for the taking. How can an oyster be owned?"

Jennie explained that the Chinese, making oyster beds, which they planted as farmers planted crops, were farming the ocean and that since

152

they had no land and were prevented by law from owning land, they had found a way to help themselves to support their families and they should be protected in this by kind people. She had heard Alonzo and Captain Shorey speak of this. Jack took it to heart.

The next thing Jennie heard was that soon after, Jack had joined the Fish Patrol, guards of the coastline who enforced laws. They were supported by fines collected from those who did injury to the waters or their fellow sailors. Those sailors who hijacked ships or men who used nets so fine-meshed whole species of fish would be destroyed and the food-chain broken, the fishing industry damaged, would be fined.

Angered, Jack's old pirate rivals set fire to the *Razzle Dazzle*, because the Fish Patrol policed them, too. So Jack lost his home and his continuous dream of Mamie's love, which for him went with the ship, his fantasy ended. But as a deputy Jack continued his exciting and dangerous sailor life for two years on a patrol ship. Then at seventeen he made a longer commitment to the sea. He signed aboard the *Sophie Sutherland*, a sailing schooner bound for Siberia, Korea, and Japan, a three-month voyage.

Jack arrived back in Oakland in the depression of 1892–93 and moved into the cramped home of John and Flora at 1321 Twenty-second Avenue, helping them with his sea pay. The money ran out, and he worked again as one of the lucky ones to be hired for his youth and strength in a jute mill, making burlap, breathing lint, and sweating for ten cents an hour, ten hours a day, six days a week, a work-slave as he had been at the cannery, until his mind and body rebelled.

He relived his adventure in the seal-harpooning voyage by writing a short story, "Typhoon off the Coast of Japan," which he entered in a newspaper composition, winning first prize from the San Francisco *Call* over writers from Universities of California and Stanford. This encouraged him to write more, but he could not sell his writing. He worked on, as a beast, as a machine, repetitious, unthinking, arduous physical movements, continuous hour after hour, day after day in the mill. He saw small children and women exploited by horrible working conditions, as they were in factories and mills and canneries throughout the city.

Jack's first sight in the mill, through the lint-filled, sweltering, odorous air had been of hundreds of women, children, and men in half-light. And one woman fell in her place, a brief ruffle of movement and moaning cry like a shore bird swooning. Before the women on either side could bend to her need, the foreman's frown and gesture forbade them and compelled them to continue a flow of work. He motioned a gawky underfed boy into the space left by the woman. The child stepped over the woman and into her place with a look of fear and triumph. Promoted to this work he would receive two cents an hour more.

The foreman grabbed two other urchins, thin and vulnerable, pale girls about eleven years old who pulled huge rolling bins of jute bags through the factory. He pushed them to help the woman, who was making a heroic effort to subdue her anguish, her cry of pain and horror. The woman had red, tear-filled eyes. Jack had heard her gasp, "My baby, I've lost it . . ." and the murmured word of another, ". . . miscarriage," and the children wrapped closer her voluminous skirts that Jack saw were blood-drenched and moved her, the foreman lifting her shoulders, against a near wall. "No doctor," she pleaded. "My husband—we can't afford it." She told where her sister could be found, the address, and one child was sent to bring help from her sister. There was no time for compassion in the factory. The woman lay still, wet with blood and tears. Her eyes had been sunken in dark sockets, red-rimmed from eyestrain from the dim interior months before the weeping began.

Jack looked secretly at the grublike beings about him that saw no light of sun all the days of their work and thought, *Is this the promise of life? Is this the human progress that has been made in the world, one form of slavery after another?*

CHAPTER 42

In 1884, Jack joined the great frustrated and angry army of men led by Jacob Coxey that grew up across the nation for a march on Washington to demand fair employment for the suffering and hungry people. Led from Oakland by an Irishman named Kelly, hopping railroad boxcars, Jack and others of the unemployed found themselves among the hoboes, each known as a king of the road. The Industrial Army, Coxey's Army, fell apart from starvation and discouragement long before impressing Washington to help them with some government work program, such as building roads for the nation, to solve the unemployment problem. But learning to be a tramp and riding the freights gave Jack a way to see the land, like he had once ventured on the high seas.

Jack was arrested as a vagrant sleeping in a park in New York, where he had gone to see Niagara Falls, in his hobo days. Jailed and taken before a judge, Jack said he was a poet, that as a poet he had a right to experience the sky and the grass and travel to gather experiences for his writing. The judge told him, a poet, as he claimed to be, was not recognized by the court as a paid vocation. Hard manual labor on bread and water in the Erie County Penitentiary was the sentence for vagrancy, for not having a job, a permanent local address, or money. Chained leg to leg with other convicts he would be taken out during the day on a work gang for hard physical labor, for not having a job.

When Jack was free he rode the rails west as fast as he could across Canada and worked his way from Vancouver on a ship back to find things changed for those who loved him in Oakland.

Significantly, he too was changed. He had kept a journal of things he had seen and thought as he traveled and knew now, as a writer, that to develop his mind and skills the most important thing he must do was continue his education. From the time he had looked wistfully after the Oakland High School boys with their light-colored high hats or occasional brown derby, debating and enthusing their ideas as they walked past him on their way to school, to the dreams of the University at Berkeley he garnered from newspaper stories and from the hopes Jennie had for him, Jack had believed it was his destiny to go on with books.

He was nineteen years old, and the students beginning high school were fourteen and fifteen and of more privileged social and economic classes. He would have to work his way and did, as the school's janitor. He grit his teeth and endured. He would continue to endure any embarrassment of clothes, speech, or age, any physical or social indignity. He would overcome these because of what he must do, what he believed he could be. At midterm, in January 1895, Jack entered Oakland High School.

At a future time, when she too went to that school, he told his daughter that he had personally washed every window in that building, the floors, the toilets, the blackboards, all, over and over.

Of course, at school Jack was rejected by some of his classmates because of his age, poverty, and lack of social ease and status. In the coveted awards of ego—"the cutest boy," "the most popular athlete"— among the shallow and frivolous who thought of school as a place of conformity to a peer group, he was out of place.

Surprisingly, as before, Jack found some who liked him. These were students whose minds and sympathies were broad. These were some who were simply intrigued by a person who had had his gamut of adventure and were drawn to his company by the stories he wrote for his assignments and read in class, true tales of travels they had never thought of experiencing, conditions and places they had not known existed.

Jack's English teacher was pained by his writing: his grammer, style, and content. But he was a hero to some students. High school can be time for emerging idealists, thinkers, would-be world leaders. So there were some who compensated for the ones who perpetuated social barriers such as Jack encountered in school before, with those limitations and prejudices. His friendships balanced out those who could not accept him. He continued with his friendships made in grade school, though most of his former classmates were out in the world and he was in school with some of their younger brothers and sisters. Also, he made new friends.

Jack found a favorite friend in Judah Magnes and went with him and his younger brother, Isaac, on long walks, introducing them, to the concern of their parents, to the waterfront. Judah, whose credits would include valedictorian, editor of the school magazine, and champion debator, was a fine thinker, and Jack entered into dialogue with him, intrigued, as he later would be by the young Russian-Jewish intellectual Anna Strunsky, with whom he carried on a long and literary love affair of the mind.

It was together with brilliant and capable young people like this, in formative years, that Jack considered the world's problems and formulated his own philosophy and course of social action. Judah was the son of David and Sophie Abrahamson Magnes, who both ran a prosperous department store in Oakland. Their two beautifully groomed boys were incongruous walking along the docks and wharfs in the slums and unsavory parts of Oakland, where their friendship with Jack London took them.

On account of the shabbily dressed and culturally deprived, unkempt-looking ex-sailor and former tramp and vagabond, now comrade of their sons, worried reports were given back to David Magnes and Sophie by well-meaning customers and friends, in much the same way that, in an earlier time, Captain Shorey had given remarks and advice to Alonzo Prentiss about the dangers of the waterfront and bad companions, out of concern for Jack.

Flora continued to agitate her prejudices. There was a London family branch that was Jewish, and she began to actively disclaim relationship. Jack continued in his own way. He was his own person, with the help of Jennie, for though he now lived with Flora, he tried to keep his mind apart.

Through his new friends Jack met bearded, black-coated men with long garments and forelocks, dealers in scrap iron and old clothes, having lately come from Lithuania, Romania, Russia, and Eastern Europe. Jack and his friends would enjoy exploring Jake Pantoskey's Free Market at Fifth and Washington, where multiple stalls and stands faced outward toward the sidewalks to present food and flowers, shoes and shirts, collections of fantastic old and new items. He learned of the loneliness and discrimination that had brought many of the Jewish people to this country and of the ancient tradition among the Jews of concern for the disadvantaged, of the humanitarian aspects of their religion, and of their federations and benevolent organizations that helped Jewish transients and refugees, for theirs had been a history of exile since before their time of slavery in Egypt.

He heard the names of great benefactors of the city, Frederick Kahn and others, how Jewish community members, even those seemingly least able to help would, because of their biblical perspectives, pledge money to individuals and causes.

Jack became guiltily aware that he had not followed the precepts of Jennie, who had long given food and service to the sick and poor through her church's various endeavors, and that, try as he would, he could no longer have a personal religion. He was drawn to it, yet he held back from all belief. He wished longingly there was something for people like him, who couldn't believe a religious creed, some system he could be a part of.

Judah left Oakland at age seventeen to enter Hebrew Union College in Cincinnati. Jack's high goal was still to enter the University at Berkeley. His happiness at high school was to be continuously published in the student literary magazine, the *Aegis*. He joined a new group in the city, the Henry Clay Debating Society, and for the first time met young intellectuals his own age and older from a wide spectrum, for it was composed of people from all walks of life, from students at the university to lawyers, schoolteachers, ambitious politicians, including socialists, and, most challenging for Jack, brainy, beautiful, and cultured young women of money and position such as he had never had opportunity to meet before, and he was overimpressed by them after so recently having been on the road as a destitute hobo.

As a budding agitator and revolutionary, Jack could have become their enemy. As an impressionable young man who stood in awe of such women, ready to idealize them, he could only be a worshiper or admirer or lover. And so he spent more than a year among them, his heart bursting with romantic love. In this group also was the young lady he would marry, who would become the mother of his two daughters, Bess Maddern.

So he dreamed of romance and loved and dreamed of writing and wrote, and then the great dreams of riches and gold that overpowered so many men came over him, too, and on March 12, 1897, he joined the rush to the Klondike.

CHAPTER 43

Jennie was proud of Jack when he told her he was continuing his education, but when she heard from him that his ambition was to write stories she was dubious this was a way he could make a living. She thought he would teach from the books or learn from them, but she had never known or heard of a single person who made a living by way of writing books. Even after Jack began to succeed, she tried to convince him that he needed some other trade, too, to fall back on. It was the long waiting periods for stories to be accepted, during which time she saw how he suffered, that worried Jennie.

She had been amazed when he returned from the Klondike and went immediately into Anderson's Co-ed Academy, the former Kohlmoos Hotel in Alameda, which had become a cramming school to prepare students for the university. In eight months he completed studies structured to take two years, and he had, then been accepted into the university at Berkeley.

Jack had become very political, and this Jennie understood. Many of his writings expounded socialist ideas, and she knew what and who had influenced him to think along those lines, as she knew her own political source. He used his life experiences, fantasized, slightly disguised.

But she was hurt by his writing, too, because it was about this time that one of Jennie's friends told her that Jack had written a story that referred to her and in this story Jennie was called "Mammy." Troubled by what she did not understand and concerned about what changes in him this meant, she had a long and serious talk with Jack. She saw that on Jack's part he felt very strongly about words. He said words were what he lived to work with. He studied them. He hung them on lines he stretched all around his room and lived among them, reading and savoring them and putting up new ones to learn. He said it made him sick and mad what some people had done with words, destroying them for use by people such as himself, but that he was a rebel writer and wouldn't stand for it. He was reclaiming all the language; the words were his and he was going to make them right. He said *Negro* was a good word, had always been and still was in most cultures. It meant black. Now who could dare to say that it meant anything derogatory? Another was the word pickens, a West African Cameroon word for children. Africans taken in slavery had their words taken away from them. Africans who had lived in that vast area between the Niger and the Zaire rivers had this word for children and when they brought it into the language they used in the South among themselves out of love for their children should not have had that word ridiculed or taken away. Nene, niney, ninnay, now that part of the word *pickaninny*, which schoolmates had taunted him with, he couldn't get the meaning of. It could mean anything from "dear" to "smallest" to "of our tribe," he couldn't even speculate, would just accept the word. But Jack wanted Jennie to know he felt she was his mammy and he would always be her pickaninny. *Society will beat me up for that*, he thought. *I've found that out. I can see what will happen already, my publishers, my white family and friends, they're going to whitewash me right out of the black community when they get a chance. Make me some kind of racist for my words. No one in the future is going to accept my jokes, my familiarity, my identity with the black community. Why would I have been stumping, shouting, speaking out in the parks, reasoning for socialism if I wasn't for black and white equality? This is what socialism is all about, men and women, races, ages of people being deserving of equal wages and goods. As a child I worked hard as the grown people. I had the brute force and muscle to do it with. Women worked their life out right alongside me. Black people worked as hard as they had the strength to do it with, harder than most. The Chinese worked alongside them on the railroad and the docks and ships. White men too. All equally trapped in the sweat labor jobs. Are words really the way to social change?*

Niger, that word tells of a river and home place, of a people. Southern white slave masters had made it a cruelty to say it and *Negro*, which means "black," impossible to use to describe people with pride. They should not have been allowed to get away with stealing language. The word *colored*, spat out, used on drinking fountains, as a label on places to keep people apart, was not used in a complimentary way. *Mammy* and *Pappy* were terms of endearment both black and white children in the South gave to their own parents, a word for a southern mother, then and now, a word also for a black southern mother. Jack wanted people to know that word was affirmation of Jennie's mothering of him and he would be a pickaninny, hers. He was not afraid to call her his mammy in the language of Negroes. Did she understand? It meant he would be at one with her, her son, and she would be his mammy and the mammy of his children, his identity with her, family. Some would say his words were the choice of a "nigger-lover," as he had been called in his childhood. He embraced his destiny with words. He would use them to heal the world's old wounds. He wanted to own the language.

Did Jennie think his attitude could not change anything? Maybe others would continue to use words in derogatory ways. The writer holds a mirror up to society so people can see how they talk. This too had purpose. Can they love themselves? Can they change their words?

And what words in relationship to blacks could do better? The important thing to Jennie was what it meant to Jack, what he meant by it, and she was satisfied. And when he married Bess and they had two daughters, Joan and Bess, the girls called Jennie Mammy and loved her, and the name was their symbol, their term of endearment.

Jennie appears symbolically in much of Jack's writings, as does his ambiguity about his parentage. In *Martin Eden* he would write of the shock received by the hero at the darkness of his own face, browned from the sun. "He had not dreamed he was so black. He rolled up his shirtsleeves and compared the white underside of the arm with his face. Yes, he was a white man, after all. But the arms were sunburned, too. He twisted his arm, rolled the biceps over with his other hand, and gazed underneath where he was least touched by the sun. It was very white." His hero has "full, sensuous lips." "He wondered if there was soul in those steel-gray eyes . . ." He sees composites, black and white.

Jack wrote out in *Martin Eden* how he wished to be a benefactor of the very dark woman. (In the book she was a Portuguese woman, dark of color) and of her children. He wished them to benefit by his writing. It would change their lives; he would get them a farm and a cow. She had been good to him; he would write himself a way to show he was grateful.

His doubts of his own race, the socialist idea of giving profits to the downtrodden, the dark woman he chooses to reward, and the absence of the hero's natural mother, who in the book is dead so he wouldn't have to deal with her, are close to the truths of Jack London's life.

A novel is subtle, threading a way through the psyche like the glint of gold in earth or stream. Is this real? Is it mica, fool's gold? Jack presupposed readers who would dig the lines with the endurance of the prospector, carefully pan the sluicing stream for minute specks, and persistently and vigorously chip between rocks with the miner's pick.

His hero, the persona, the plot, experience of living, his material, the nature of life itself—he brought all his talent to bear in *Martin Eden*, on the purpose and meaning of life of a creative person, with not only the need to write but to expose the flaws of the trade of writing as business and how writers are exploited by this business. It was also an indictment of those who fail to love enough the ones who write. It was about faith, trusting the creative force to fulfill itself, and, when confronted with the world's betrayal of the writer, courageous death.

Jack knew he would be misunderstood and fail at last when the book he considered his most important, which he had anticipated would have world-moving sociological benefits for all, *The People of the Abyss*, failed to do for the whole of civilization what Harriet Beecher Stowe's novel had done for her country—shocked it into action for justice. No one in the United States gave such serious concern to Jack London's book or learned that what was told of England could happen in any country, did happen, and involved the world's concern for change, for when one man suffered, he suffered for all. In Jack's vision for humanity no racial stigmas exist, his society serves all equally.

When Jack knew he had expected too much from the writer's powers or too much of readers he was ready to die for his values. He could continue writing as merely a way to earn a living, grimly aware that such an attitude culminates in the writer's self-destruction. He had written that already! But the mine has more than one vein, the gold cares not for chronological time. Discovery is relevant always. There was always his hope that his daughter, Joan, showing an inclination for writing and some talent, as well as concern for social justice and causes similar to her father's, would continue his work and make his dreams reality. But a bitter divorce and estrangement from both daughters, who in the dispute took the side of their mother, whom he refused to admit he wronged, led to a subsequent block each time he reached out to his oldest daughter, Joan, the one who would write on.

One letter he wrote to Joan, impetuous with longing, told her he wanted to talk with her about many things, close to the core of what moved him. He wanted to talk with her, he wrote ". . . about race." But then no one knows if he ever did.

"I believe I have black blood in me," Joan would say, on occasion, to Eugene Lasartemay as he was documenting work on Jennie Prentiss and Jack London. Joan liked to drink and sometimes when she had been drinking she would bring up this subject. She seemed to have some of the same opinions expressed by Alonzo to Jack—that when you don't *know* your bloodline it makes you better able to love all people.

One of Jack's most significant books, *The Star Rover*, has as its purpose the different mentalities that can develop under certain circumstances. His subject is not the criminal mind but the crimes created against society by the unexplored world, the unexamined experience, and how a mind can evolve to reach out beyond its solitary imprisonment. In *The Call of The Wild* the instinctive spirit of the world is personified in the brute hero, the animal. This wild spirit proves a better spirit than that creature who would set civilization over natural instinct, man. His readers may be generations into the future who are the discoverers of his true gold, the value and significance of his writing as one glittering gold lump, his coin of the world.

Jack's writings have been well-examined by critics who have had fine, intelligent minds but no knowledge of the contributions of people of the black community in the shaping of Jack's work and ideas and the sharing of his experiences. Some of his friends from Oakland's black community sailed with him on the same ship to the Klondike, and he shared even these experiences with his black friends in ways still to be documented. His life on the Oakland wharfs and ships, his school days and his family experiences, have all been shaped in untold ways by the Oakland black community. A mine of this gold of experience is still untapped, unwritten.

It has been said none of the Oakland people who were in the Klondike with Jack came back with gold. Eliza's husband had mortgaged their house to help fund the trip for Jack and himself, only to have to turn back due to the hazards and hardships for one of his age. Jack alone came back with riches. These were his journal-notebooks in which he made continuous recording of characters, moods, descriptions of places, arguments, ideas, plots, and his own poems, raw material for stories and books he would write, which sustained him for all the years of his life. The claim he had so excitedly staked in the Klondike for himself, thinking he had discovered gold, turned out to be based on mica, fool's gold, not the real thing. His writing was the real thing.

When Jack returned to Oakland from the Klondike, he found John London had died. Flora had adopted Ida's child, Johnny Miller, a five-year-old boy, and was changed in a positive way. She was at last able to give unselfish love. She was visited often by the spirit of John London, whom she could speak with, see, and hear.

CHAPTER 44

Jack had learned from Jennie of the messages of Rev. George Washington Woodbey, which were being spread through Oakland by members of the church. These messages were referred to from the pulpit and the subject of much dialogue in the homes of the black community.

George Woodbey's ideas came to him at a time when Jack was most open and ready to hear them, ready for education, having come back as he did from the experiences with Coxey's Army of Unemployed, from his associations with men of the road and his hard time in prison. He had learned firsthand of the uncountable numbers of people out of work and otherwise disadvantaged. Before these travels he had known of these conditions yet been inclined to attribute them to the flaws within people.

Of his own family, mother and stepfather, Jack's examples, John had ill health and other disabling incidents, so he was often not fit to work. And Flora had a difficult personality. In the instance of the boardinghouses, for example, the Londons had, as usual, incurred debts and exhausted their resources through their own mismanagement. Flora, always a speculator and entrepreneur, had been led by her whims into gambling and risks. She drank and played the Chinese lottery; then she could not account for the mortgage payment money or the debts owed to the butchers and produce men from whom she shopped. The Londons lost the boardinghouse business. Was that society's fault? There were so many flawed people who did things wrong and were hungry and home-less. But apart from these instances of personal failure there was that prejudice against national origin or color or religion, used to keep people unemployed, downtrodden. There could not be something wrong with *all* of these people.

Jack considered Jennie and Alonzo, who did so much with what little they had, who were thrifty and cheerful and even when things were going wrong economically for them were able to give comfort. Jack had not realized until he saw the homes of people of wealth that by these others' standards he was shabby. He had not known that while looking at himself as Jennie and Alonzo did with their eyes of love. Now he saw that for all their industry and thrift, they had never had property, money in the bank for their old age, trips to Europe, a share of the earth's resources; the gold, the oil, the timber, and the farmlands were claimed by others. Eliza's husband had risked all, mortgaging his home so he and Jack could have an equal chance to find gold. They endured as others did, risked as others had risked, even their lives, on the perilous waters, yet, having done equal labor, some came back millionaires, while most came back with debts and impoverishment. Was it their fault, and did they deserve to continue to be hungry, ill-clad, homeless?

Jack had seen the men on the road and knew (as he would later write, in *People of the Abyss*, of the sleeping men he looked on in the flophouse) they "were lovable, as men are lovable. They were capable of love." He also knew that they had no better chance from society, as it was, to house themselves better, to have a decent job.

Reverend Woodbey, Jennie explained, taught that the Bible—both Old and New Testaments—was a socialist document with close affinity to such classics as *The Communist Manifesto* and *Das Kapital* and other writings of Marx. As a Jew, Woodbey emphasizes, Marx was able to do "the greatly needed work of reasoning out from the standpoint of the philosopher, what his ancestors, the writers of the Old and New Testa-ments, had already done from a moral and religious standpoint.

"Woodbey welcomed [the label socialism] . . . and believed its princi-ples were in keeping with the best in the American tradition."

163

Woodbey was in advance of nearly all Christian socialists. He was preparing a publication called *The Bible and Socialism: A Conversation Between Two Preachers,* which he later published in San Diego, "being convinced that Socialism is but the carrying out of the economic teachings of the Bible," he said.

To black churchgoers much of what went into the pamphlet and what Woodbey had taught for several years beforehand from California pulpits, was new to them but understandable and made an impressive impact. He compared slavery of the past with wage slavery of the present as the same evil.

At a presidential convention he would summerize statements he had made to churchgoers for years, saying, "In keeping with the tradition of Black Americans since the era of Reconstruction: in 1869, the Colored National Labor Union went on record against exclusion of Chinese immigration." He continued:

I am in favor of throwing the entire world open to the inhabitants of the world. [There was applause.] It would be a curious state of affairs for immigrants or descendents of immigrants from Europe themselves to get control of affairs in this country, and then say to the Oriental immigrants that they should not come here.

Woodbey scoffed at the idea that the entrance of Oriental immigrants would reduce the existing standard of living, arguing that regardless of immigration, it was the "natural tendency of capitalism" to reduce the standard of living of the working class and that if they could not get Oriental labor to do work more cheaply in the United States, manufacturers would export their production to the Oriental countries, where goods could be produced more cheaply than in this country. (Woodbey's prediction was, as American workers later fully realized, to bear fruit.)

As he saw it, socialism was based "upon the Brotherhood of Man," and any stand in opposition to immigration would be "opposed to the very spirit of the Brotherhood of Man."

When at the Socialist party convention delegate Ellis Jones of Ohio presented Woodbey's name in nomination as running-mate to Eugene V. Debs, for the vice presidency of the United States, Jones said, "The Socialist Party is a party that does not recognize race prejudice and in order that we may attest this to the world, I offer the name of Comrade Woodbey of California."

Woodbey's message, essentially, as spread through churches and public appearances in many communities throughout California was "just as once, the elimination of slavery was crucial for the Negro, so today was the elimination of poverty." Socialism would create a society without poverty, a society in which the land, mines, factories, shops, railroads, et cetera, would be owned collectively, and the Negro, "being a part of the public, will have an equal part in all the good things produced by the nation." In this future society, moreover, the Negro will not have to abandon his belief in religion. On the contrary, by providing all with sufficient food to eat and decent places in which to live, socialism would be fulfilling the fundamental ideas set down in the Bible.

Woodbey called for unity of white and black workers, urging them to "lay aside their prejudices and get together for their common good." The socialist movement was the embodiment of this unifying principle.

This leading Negro socialist had been born a slave in Johnson County, Tennessee, on October 5, 1854, and was self-educated, having learned to read after freedom came. He worked in mines and factories and on the streets at whatever supplied food, clothing and shelter, and his life was one of "hard work and hard study carried on together." Woodbey was ordained a Baptist minister at Emporia, Kansas, in 1874. In 1896 he ran for lieutenant governor and Congress in Nebraska. Impressed by Eugene V. Debs, he resigned his pulpit and consecrated his life to the socialist movement, moving in with his mother, who resided in San Diego, and remaining active in California until well after the turn of the century, frequently being arrested and hauled of to jail for soapbox speaking and attempting to sell his pamphlets on the streets. Many of his published treatises were presented as conversations he had with his mother.

It is easy to understand why Jack took this information from Jennie and made it a model and part of his active social crusading life. He too was arrested for speaking from a soapbox under the great oak tree in front of Oakland City Hall about socialism. (After the original oaks were cleared away, a later mayor of Oakland had another huge tree planted there in the memory and honor of the writer, and to this day it is called the Jack London Oak.) Jack London ran for mayor of Oakland on the socialist ticket the week his first daughter, Joan was born. He became an admirer of Eugene V. Debs. Rev. George Woodbey became his friend.

CHAPTER 45

Jack had not felt he could marry with a veil over his ancestry, a clouded heritage. Before the mirror for hours he would scrutinize his face, looking for any possible clue, a hint in the shape of the nose or lips, a sign of mixed race. He searched out an address and wrote letters showing his anguish to a man he never met, Professor Chaney. He asked for confirmation that Chaney had fathered him. Chaney denied him in two letters, the only communication with him that Jack ever had.

Jack knew he could never be prejudiced against anyone because of race, since he could not for sure know his own. Having never been positive, he had all the more reason for sympathy for someone who had been through what Alonzo had gone through, who had his Negro blood discovered in midcareer.

If society—meaning some people—had not set up rules for the different treatment of different races, race would not matter. Jack became more convinced than ever that social change must take place. To have a system to change people, that is what matters. He would not be personally prejudiced in his dealings with others. The closest he came to having the son he desperately wanted was when a young Japanese boy in Jack's later life worked for him. Jack finally presented this boy with a typewriter as a parting gift when he left for college, an education Jack also helped pay for. Jack's first wife bore two daughters, from whom he would later be estranged. Jack's second wife bore a daughter who lived only three days.

Jack did not feel fulfillment in either of his marriages, for what he wanted from a sensual procreation, ultimately, was to father a son. Even as he chose his own death, according to rumors spread by his Bohemian friends, he had considered leaving his second wife, Charmain, for he had met perhaps in Hawaii, and planned to meet again, perhaps in Iceland, some mystery woman he wanted to believe could still become the mother of his unconceived son.

Yet even as he went to his death Jack London was seeking still a closer unity with those two living daughters, bearers, he hoped, of the seed of his genius, inheritors of his creative mind and his writer's destiny. He was writing his daughters to meet him in Oakland. He had subjects for Joan to discuss with him, subjects for whom he needed a confidant. Joan, first child of Jack's marriage to Bess Maddern, this daughter demonstrating her inclination toward writing, could have become for him the chosen inheritor of his secrets. He had written that poignant letter in which he visioned he could talk to her "about race . . ." and other things.

Joan already knew he could not rule out any possibility of blood and race in the genes he himself carried and passed on to her. Joan knew from her father he could not be prejudiced about race, as he could not prove his own parentage. He and she must be prepared to love beyond the boundaries and limitations of race. He had not resolved the content of his physical being.

Jack knew enough of Alonzo's life, Alonzo's shock of discovery about his race, to be prepared that such things happened and know of the effect on the families of those who were not open to the possibilities. This was another very strong reason he wanted his own children to know and love Jennie like another mother, as he did. Black people were his family through his love bond with Alonzo and Jennie. All his life through whatever phase he went, Jack never broke or denied his bond, and his true feelings he knew.

Love is an even stronger bond than blood. Jack's feelings for Jennie compared to his feelings for Flora told him that. Jennie had kept the bond of love alive with her kindness through all Jack's growth and changes of philosophy and search for himself, and she even served as a liaison between father and his daughters to keep their love for each other intact.

CHAPTER 46

There were voices in his head. It was 1903 and Alonzo was dying. He had outlived both Priscilla and Will and his only grandchild, Will's little daughter, Eliza Viola Prentiss, who died March 27, 1894, at three years, five months, eight days. Her mother, Eliza Tingle Prentiss, had been pregnant with the child when she was widowed by Will's death. Will died at age twenty-three from typhus and malarial fever. He was sick from March 1, 1890, to March 18, 1890. He had died at 6:30 P.M. on that date and was buried at Mountain View Cemetery, in those wide, tree-covered green, earthy fields near where Piedmont Avenue in Oakland edges up and meets the tree-green hills. Albert Brown, the undertaker, made the arrangements. Will's doctor had been his neighbor, B. A. Babe, who lived one block away at 1553 13th Street. Will had died at home, at 1415 13th Street. His widow eventually remarried, to a Mr. Holmes. She was still emotionally close to the Prentiss family, as was her cousin, Willie Tingle of Vallejo.

Oh, they mourned the death of that beautiful and vibrant son, and that he had not lived even to see his child, his sweet child that died so young.

And they, Jennie and Alonzo, had mourned Priscilla, who died in their home, in their arms, at 1139 East 15th Street January 8, 1891, at age eighteen years, six months, twenty days, at 6:00 P.M., an evening death almost like Will's, at the hour when, from family custom, the family would gather at table for Jennie's blessing. Priscilla's doctor, too, was a neighbor, A. F. Childs from 580 East 12th Street, and she also was buried at Mountain View Cemetery, on January 11, at 1:00 P.M. On the death certificate the barely educated clerk misspelled her name as Percella Anna Prentice. She died of consumption of the lungs after a lingering two-year illness—Priscilla, their joy.

J. H. Shepard, the husband of Eliza London, had become the Oakland liaison for Civil War veteran pensioners at a salary, after the act of June 27, 1890, to make invalids' pensions possible, and he had helped the invalid John London apply for and receive his pension. Shepard's office and home was at 1068 East 15th Street, one block away from the Prentiss home, and he had helped Alonzo file for his own pension, which was awarded when Alonzo could no longer work, for reasons of rheumatism and old age.

Now Alonzo was eighty-four years, seven months, and fourteen days old, and his doctor, A. H. Dodge, was standing by. Alonzo supposed he would die of chronic nephritis. He saw no mourning yet in Jennie's eyes, only love. He had loved her long and well—Jennie, father unknown, mother a slave born in North Carolina and sold away from her infant; Jennie, born into slavery, freed by the Civil War, Union soldiers, himself. She was thirty-four years old when she had married him in Tennessee. They had gone to Chicago, then San Francisco. It is true, when it is time to die the wonders of life are relived. Fragments of his life continued on in the mind of the dying Alonzo.

Alonzo, far from Tiffin, Ohio, had another family. They had Will, Priscilla, and a daughter born January 12, 1876, stillborn, but Jack came into their arms, fed by Jennie's milk.

Alameda: snowy egrets, long-billed curlews, white herons, clapper rails. The pure light over the estuary—artists dream of that. In Eden were two people so loving? Here the original people brought their beloved dead to a center of encompassing beauty, hallowed it with their passing. Alonzo saw the body as a vessel the spirit had passed through. There was a rhythm of the water. It was very quiet

It was said that prejudiced new people had come there. Someone told people of color they could not swim in the pool. *If we had not left there, would these others have come with their racial prejudice?*

Remember when Jack came back from Livermore, after so long with Flora, the light gone out of his golden complexioned face under the shock of tawny hair like a lion's short mane, and he seemed sad and drab, with a hangdog look, the play and the glory in being a small boy gone out of him. The white boys at school called him a nigger-lover. A house divided.

And I love Jennie, die knowing that.

One of the most striking things about Jennie, to him, was the way she held her head. He thought of a flower held on a strong, erect stem.

Her posture was stately and graceful. She moved with such fluid smoothness that he was hardly aware of her movement, yet he was always aware of her presence. Alonzo could understand how she had survived so well as her own person. She knew how to be unobtrusive. It was as if she had the same capacity to exist he had seen in the instinctive creatures in the woods, the deer and quail and bear, how they blended in to be a part of the environment so that they could not be noticed, an organic instinctive ability to be present without an enemy noting. So she had survived in the South.

There was nothing seductive in her clothing. It was as if she chose to be perfectly plain, to conceal. The high-necked dresses with the long sleeves, long, full skirt, were working apparel that did not accentuate a body strikingly female.

The first time he saw her in marriage he could hardly believe her perfection, as if hers was the original body, after which others could be only failed copies. It was vibrant and primal, as if it had an energy that he would be able to generate with a smoothing of his hand along her skin, like a cat's purr, that supple and elegant body with the sleek head like a flower. *To her creator . . . did I say thank you?*

She saw him through the time he felt limited by white society, by her own spirit prevented him from becoming a carrier of the hate and prejudice that he accused others of holding. Hatred gains nothing for the world. It can go on from generation to generation. It can be caught from others like a disease, spreading from country to country, person to person. Who can be whole enough to say, "It has stopped with me; I will not pass it on"?

We all pass on. Alonzo suddenly could not remember who was living and who was passed on. There seemed to be many from the past crowding his mind.

John London, he thought. *Now there was a friend. Was he still alive?* They had talked together about the war. No one knew or hardly cared anymore what had made the passions flare—the daring war deeds, who was with the volunteers, cavalry, pickets, who had been a copperhead, who all the heroes had been.

Of course, if a person had the prestige of being called Colonel or had been a Captain on either side he'd take that title to the grave. Lots of men, more than possible it seemed, were in their civilian life called Captain or Major. Lieutenant didn't count. Once men vied for that title; people gave it no importance now. Lieutenant Alonzo Prentiss.

News, which once went mouth to mouth across many states, people gave no importance to now, like when in Massachusetts Colonel Shaw had shaken public opinion and aroused hostilities by giving up command of a white regiment to command ex-slaves, one of the first regiments of enlisted Negroes. That was in July 1863, one year and five months after

169

Alonzo was discharged, but seemed like yesterday. Later he heard talk of erecting a statue to the man. Whether this was or would be he could not remember. *Strange, the thoughts that come to mind. And he could not lead or serve, being put into limbo, being neither black nor white.* An old man was dying, it took a long time. Was that his Jennie crying?

Alonzo remembered Jennie had helped him befriend the London family. It was an intrinsic part of her nature that she responded to someone else's need and pain. Since she had the capability of dealing with another's deep sadness, since she knew how to transfuse a better attitude and give strength and gladness, she could go forward into difficult relationships. In this she was a true heroine. Alonzo acknowledged that quality in her.

Jennie was compassionately giving to Flora. But Flora was not pliable. Was Flora capable of emotional growth? Alonzo was vexed to think of Jennie's talents wasted on Flora. When it came to soaking up attention he thought Flora was a bottomless pit. As for John, well he would continue to encourage John in his efforts to get on his feet.

Alonzo felt more and more sorry for poor old John, but Jennie didn't have to fall under Flora's spell. He knew it was her compassion for Jack that drew her. He hoped she had her own clear mind when it came to dealing with Flora. John was dead, he suddenly recalled that, but Flora talked with John.

Flora wanted Jack for manipulative purposes, each time involving money, whatever profit she could get through the child or his presence. It was not only as if she felt he owed her something by coming into the world, because she felt his coming had changed the conditions of her life, but also because she mismanaged her finances and was always needy. Through him she could perhaps get money by seances—his beauty, innocence, and cherubic face and form laid on a table as medium—occult, sinister—her victim. This had affected his nervous system. Eliza, his stepsister, tried to spare him, taking him to sit on the edge of the teacher's platform, to be under her gaze, where the learning was, where he could be happy. Jennie, her milk had saved him; the milk of her human kindness would continue to give him life. She would talk to Flora. She would lend Jack money to get out of the shanty. He would sail away free.

"Follow the drinking gourd," a code, a way to sing of deep feelings and, Alonzo thought, *the singing of spirituals, church songs. The field hands in slavery sang together; the North Star in the Big Dipper guided them north to freedom, home over Jordan, that huge body of water, the ocean over which they had been transported to slavery. Beulah Land, was it Africa or the North?*

There was Queen Victoria standing on the shores of England with her arms wide open as if she were some Statue of Liberty. "Forsake your native land of slavery, and come to me for peaceful love," southern slaves had a song containing

170

those very words. In 1776 there had been a revolution to free America from England, now her friend. But who stood now, arms open wide for me? Alonzo, from the slavery of life "come for peaceful love."

"Is it true, Mama?"

"Priscilla, do you expect me to be an old-enough old woman to have seen what happened in Ireland hundreds of years ago? I expect everyone tells history the way it was told to them, with a little bit of their own imagining thrown in to spice it up.

"You know it yourself, Priscilla, everyone, even in the same family sometimes, has a different point of view. Sometimes Will has one opinion and you another about what happens. Now those English people say one thing and the Irish another, and how can we in another country and hundreds of years later decide between them? Girl, it takes the wisdom of Solomon to figure this world out, like the North and the South had their war each believing in their own rightness. Now they are one country."

Sally said, "Spirits, I should say they surround us every minute, sure and every one a saint, couldn't raise such a brood of children without every one of those saints, Saint Brigid, Saint Patrick . . ."

The battlefield, those that perished. Alonzo remembered his time as a soldier. Repelled by destruction. *God perfected a body, then allowed its brutal destruction.* Duty, the soldiers, instruments of destruction.

The daughter that never drew breath in this world had somehow empowered, set in motion, the process that would nurture Jack, the process that would feed him and the emotions that would love him. One night Alonzo cried, head cradled in Jennie's arms, for that stillborn daughter as if death were penance for real or imagined sin. How that night Jennie had caressed and consoled, whispered love to him, given him her words, until he understood something different about the baby girl they had created together, that baby who gave life to little Jack because she had made it possible for him to have the milk he needed. The baby had given the gift of life, and Alonzo and Jennie had to love not the child they didn't have, but the one they had. If only Alonzo could accept him, believe that there was some reason for Jack to be born and live and for he and Jennie to love him in this way, and that he was their daughter's gift, from a wise pure soul who gave her life. They had to love and accept her gift. *And ever after, oh, what had been done for love of Jack London.*

Jack's Mama Jennie said to love the Chinese after all they have suffered. Well, it showed he had a conscience, that boy, carried away by righteous zeal, impetuous, joining the Fish Patrol. She didn't mean he had to do something like that. But she did believe he would do good, some way.

Now there he was on the soapbox, making speeches under the oak tree, getting arrested as a socialist. Well, Alonzo guessed *that was Woodbey's influence all right.*

Jack had written his first book. He remembered Harriet Beecher Stowe had said she wrote a book to give the children a voice for justice in the world. *Imagine, that young one, Jack, a writer.*

Let it lie, Jack, Alonzo thought. *Professor Chaney has some positive evidence for his defense. Flora did have other relations.* She did belong to the free love group. It was common knowledge. Alonzo knew it himself. *Many things have not and will never be told.*

Alonzo had learned of his own racial background and a long time after that learned of charity, of not being judgmental about race. He had always been open with Jack about why he had lived as a white man after learning his true identity and when he came to San Francisco and why this had been done, about the economics of exploitation of race in the work field. Alonzo tried to impress upon Jack that sometimes it is better not to know the truth about the past, how not knowing what race you are can make a person more tolerant and teach compassion. Alonzo hoped this was something Jack could pass on to his own children.

Mary Foley had told of the priest traveling through vast California early undeveloped territory, living off the land, being invited into hovels whenever there was one. One night in one of the hovels, the priest put his bedroll on the floor of the one room, the husband, his wife and small children slept on a narrow, thin mattress, the only bed, normally shared. The men rose to go out in the morning to the bushes, the woman patting tortillas on her bare thighs for their meal and putting the extra ones for safe keeping under the mattress, her storage place. For supper she had taken out some flattened by her own weight, put a spoonful of beans already several days old into each, chopped on it their only fresh food, a tomato, folded it together, and cooked it in front of their hut on an open fire. Someday there would be a church for them, bread of heaven. Now Jack said there was some plan to feed them all!

Jennie, would it have been different for you if I had gone with you to your church? Alonzo wondered. *Did you know I have the soul of a poet? The same feeling as the poets who wrote the Bible? They could put their thoughts into a cadence of beauty and power. Lucky the man who could express himself with some poetry. Words are a wonder and what a wondrous pleasure to have them come*

easily. I can only feel, not say them, these words I want to express. But I find
words for you in the Proverbs:

"When one finds a worthy wife,
   her value is far beyond pearls,
Her husband, entrusting his heart to her,
   has an unfailing prize.
She brings him good and not evil,
   all the days of her life.

"She reaches out her hands to the poor,
   and extends her arms to the needy.
Charm is deceptive and beauty fleeting,
   the woman who fears the Lord is to be praised,
Give her a reward of her labors,
   and let her works praise her at the city gates."

Jennie, I wanted to live through our children, but Priscilla and Will have
died before me. What meaning has my life had? An obscure life, not that of a
public figure, a life in which I held my own secrets. I tried to be unselfish in the
support I gave you, Jennie, and the children, William, Priscilla, and Jack. But
Jennie had my whole heart.

Alonzo, born May 4, 1819, died December 18, 1903, age eighty-four
years, seven months, and fourteen days. He was buried in the Soldiers
Plot #12, grave 8, Mountain View Cemetery, Oakland.

CHAPTER 47

Jack demonstrated his love for Jennie in many ways: when he bought
her a house, when he contributed fifteen thousand dollars to her church,
when he wrote dedicating inscriptions and love messages by hand in
books that he gave her, copies of books he had written, when he brought
her to his own home in the Piedmont hills after Alonzo's death to care
for his little girls, Joan and Bess.

Jennie lived many places in Oakland. Besides places already named
she lived in 1896 at 1063 26th Avenue, in 1897 at 1327 25th Avenue,
in 1901 at 1130 East 16th Street, in 1903 at 1139 East 15th Street, in
1903 at Jack's Piedmont home, in 1906 at 490 27th Street, in 1918 at a
24 East 10th Street, and in 1921 at 809 East 11th Street.

Jack bought a home for Jennie located at 490 27th Street, in the earthquake year, 1906, when she was seventy-four years of age. For a time Flora, bringing Ida's son, little Johnny, whom Flora had adopted, came, from financial necessity, to live with Jennie. A visitor to the two women describes Flora as having gray hair, bobbed in the current fashion. The visitor stared a little, as it was the first time she had seen a gray-haired woman with bobbed hair, a style of the young flappers and movie stars. Jennie, surprisingly, wore a wig, and this again brought discreet stares. Jennie was described as immaculately dressed in a white starched apron, which she affected by choice. She had grown vain over the years and was meticulous as to appearance.

Flora, thickening and stooping as if she were older than her years, was a few inches under five feet tall and still wearing size 12 child-sized shoes. She was also still inclined to periods of melancholy. She complained to neighbors that Jack, who they knew was generous to her, did not give her enough.

Jennie, five-five, stood cheerful, erect, and proud. Part of her pride was in the love and care that Jack, now a most famous and wealthy writer bestowed on her, which made her an important personage to those who knew this. His care for her extending after his death. He remembered her with an income for life in his last will and testament, signed in 1911.

Jack's devotion is evidenced by the inscriptions in two of the books that he presented to Jennie.

The first was when he was a man of twenty-seven years of age and the other two months before his death at the age of forty. Today these books are the property of the Oakland Public Library.

The first inscription reads thus:

To dear Mammy Prentiss
With best love,
From one who loves you well.
Your son,
Jack
Piedmont, California, May 11, 1903

The second:

Dear Mammy Prentiss:
Well, it took a long time to pay back
what I borrowed from you with which to buy the "Razzle Dazzle."
    But I learned a lot of life when I
sailed the "Razzle Dazzle," and here is
loving you, and always lovingly,

Your white pickaninny
Jack London
Glen Ellen, Calif., September 24, 1916

CHAPTER 48

Four-ninety 27th Street was Jack London's permanent mailing address as long as Jennie lived there, though it was never his residence. He was at home anyplace Jennie lived. After he bought her this house, she always kept one room ready, convenient for him and Charmain to relax in and where Jack could write. Jennie continued to be active in her church, with friends and social activity, and kept the home immaculate. She continued to be "on call" for any who needed her as a nurse among her longtime friends in the church. Visitors were always impressed with her housekeeping and her hospitality.

Elizabeth Fisher Gordon, wife of attorney Walter Gordon, who as graduate of the University at Berkeley became the first black police officer of Berkeley and later a governor of the Virgin Islands and federal judge of the Virgin Islands, met Jack London at the home of Jennie Prentiss on 27th Street, in Oakland. She confirmed this description of Jennie, adding her own statement of Jennie as stately, neat, always wearing an apron, and having a kind face. Mrs. Gordon is one of the many who knew Jack gave Jennie's 27th Street address as his own and as his mailing address whenever it suited his purposes, that he considered her home his own wherever she lived, and that he never ceased to regard her as his foster mother.

When Jennie at last moved out of 490 27th Street, Jack kept the house only a short while; then he sold it.

After Jennie had been in this house quite some time Flora came to stay with her. Jack's daughters, Joan and Bess, spent many days and hours in this house with Jennie and Grandma Flora. If by chance Daddy was there, then they would have some time with him also. Jennie had a great admiration for Joan and Bess, whom she had also helped to raise in their early years. She always got a message to them at their home at 606 Scenic Avenue when their father would be in Oakland so they could come visit. He avoided going to Bess Maddern London's home because of his own guilt and anger and Charmain's jealousy. Flora's attitude complicated the problems. Jennie treated Flora very carefully and with patience. Even though Flora would provoke Jack, she could not be changed.

Although Flora was younger than Jennie, her health was failing quite rapidly. She was becoming a burden on Jennie, who felt compelled because of love of her foster son and her longtime friendship Flora, to serve her. She knew Flora would otherwise be quite alone. The closeness that continued for the two widows under one roof was a strain on Jennie's tact, because Flora brought with her the invisible spirits who had peopled her life, but Jennie wanted to help her and did.

Glen Ellen, California, in the Valley of the Moon, located in Sonoma County, was the site of the Beauty Ranch Jack London created as his writer's paradise. He wanted to bring his young daughters into this Eden, but their mother, and they too, felt that Charmain was a barrier. Flora sided with Bess Maddern London, Jack's first wife. This alienated Charmain and Jack both from Flora. There was no open break, just tension, but Flora was never invited to Beauty Ranch.

Both Charmain and Bess loved and accepted Jennie equally. She was fair to them equally. Charmain took a liking to Jennie, needed her friendship, and naturally would have her with them. Jennie attended picnics and other events on the premises. Jennie was also a link holding father and daughters together. Whereas Bess and Flora could cause strained relations with Jack, Jennie would be entrusted with bringing his daughters into their father's presence and with being mediator in difficult family situations. Eugene Lasartemay, on several visits to Doulton Court in Pleasant Hill, which was the home of Joan and Charles Miller, learned from Joan of the special fondness created in the hearts of all the members of the London family for Jennie. Joan related memories of her kindness and gentleness, her exceptional cleanliness, and her good example. These qualities, and Jennie's ability to express love were held dearly in her heart. Joan loved her father's foster mother.

Joan London became a sensitive writer with the sharp instincts of a reporter, motivated to racial and social justice issues such as the farmworkers' struggle for better living and working conditions in the fields of California. She tried also to understand and do justice to her father's life in biography. In one of her books, *Jack London and His Times*, she wrote: "Jennie Prentiss lived long enough to hold in her arms the grandson of her foster child."

It was on his second visit to Joan London that Eugene Lasartemay caught her unawares with this question: "Joan, the grandson of Mrs. Prentiss's foster son, was that your son?" She looked at him with a smile and said, "Yes, Gene, that was my son, Bart Abbott." She encouraged the research on Jennie Prentiss, believing this documentation of the neglected story of a person who played such a part in the life of her father should be shared with the public. She offered her expertise in writing it in the future, but before that could be, death called her on January 19, 1971.

Joan expressed her love for Jennie even up to a few months before her death. Joan London, at the age of sixty-eight, recalled that as a teenager she was so happy in her visits to Jennie at the 27th Street address. She could remember only two visits with her father at Glen Ellen. He would come to meet her in Oakland. It was her visits to Jennie that kept her closer informed of her dad's life and his activities.

The late Mrs. Esther Jones Lee, grandmother-in-law of Congressman Ron Dellums, was a resident of Oakland and a close acquaintance of Jennie Prentiss. She became interested in this documentation and brought some important facts to the story of a contained but useful life, that of Jennie Prentiss.

These two women, Mrs. Jennie Prentiss and Mrs. Esther Jones Lee, had given invaluable time and energy to church events and helped set the course of many activities at the beginning of the century in the Federated Negro Women's Club of Oakland, shared in by women of all ages. Though they were decades apart in age, they were equal in friendship.

In 1914, at the age of eighty years, Jennie served as midwife when Esther Jones Lee was delivered of her firstborn daughter, Esther. From her closeness to Jennie she could verify information. She was especially close to Jenny when the Prentiss family lived on 10th Street, near 10th Avenue, and were the neighbors of Mr. and Mrs. Alexander Dewson, aunt and uncle of the Dewson children who had been playmates and friends of Jack London, especially Edwin Dewson, with whom Jack was inseparable until Jack went on a ship to the Orient and Edwin Dewson then joined the navy.

CHAPTER 49

When she was eighty-five and living by herself in East Oakland, Jennie's age started taking its toll. Jennie realized this and talked to Mrs. Eliza Shepard, Jack London's stepsister, executrix over Jack's estate, about her desire to live in a rest home.

On Beulah Heights, in the hill area in Oakland where Mills College is now located, was a home for aged and infirm black people. Capt. William T. Shorey, the master mariner, now retired, was a director of the home and this gave Jenny confidence that it would be a good home for her.

After some time of trying to reason with Eliza, who according to Jack London's last will was to see that Jennie was properly housed, to get her to place Jennie in the home, and failing, Jennie negotiated on her own and was accepted as a tenant. To be a tenant of the home, an entry fee of five hundred dollars, plus a small monthly maintenance charge, had to be paid.

Jennie was happy there for only about a year. She was not permitted to help other tenants in the home as she wanted to. There were regulations that prevented that, which dissatisfied Jennie. Her life had been one of service, as a nurse, as a housekeeper, as a churchwoman, visiting the sick and infirm and cheerless. She could not be resigned that this vital part of her life was to be over and wanted to continue her charitable acts and works of mercy wherever she lived.

The now unhappy Jennie put in a call to Mr. Maynard Wilds, the son of John H. Wilds, a longtime friend. John Wilds had been born in slavery. He had come to Oakland with his wife and four children. He became the appointed night watchman and janitor of the Oakland city hall and served for thirty-three years. He was always active in the service to assist the black race to advance. He founded the newspaper *Oakland Sunshine*, and his editions of this paper contained information not only for cultural and educative advancement but for his readers to contend for their rights as American citizens. At this low moment in her life, Jennie felt she needed the encouragement of a crusader for doing good. "Come and get me," she said. She wanted to be where her help would still be appreciated or, at least, permitted. Jennie got into Wilds' buggy and was driven to the home of Maynard Wilds' parents, where she remained until relocated a short distance from the Wilds' home to live with Mrs. Mariah Bridges and her granddaughter, Ruth Bridges, at 809 East 11th Street in Oakland. She was happy there for several months. Then a fire broke out in her room from the coal stove. A neighbor rushed in and threw the stove into the backyard. Luckily the fire was extinguished very quickly, but this was enough excitement for Mrs. Bridges. Arteriosclerosis was setting in fast on Jennie. She was forgetful and could cause an accident. She was her loving and normal self most of the time, but there were times she would act vague, strange, and cross, so Mrs. Bridges elected to use this occasion to have her move from her residence.

Another living place was found a short distance away from the Bridges' home. Jennie lived for a while on East 10th Street. Finally the call went out to those responsible that Jennie had to have all-day care. The decision was that she be committed to the Napa State Hospital. She had outlived all who could take care of her—her children, her husband, and many of her old friends. She was not insane, but senility was causing concern.

Jennie realized what had happened to her, for she had lucid times in which she would talk about the past and her current condition. It grieved her. She lived in her memories of Alonzo, Will, Priscilla, and Jack.

Jennie Prentiss died at the age of ninety years on November 27, 1922.

Charmain London, Jack's widow, ordered the release of Jennie's body and had Eliza Shepard execute the wishes of Jack's will, which concluded by saying: " . . . any expense extraordinary her demise, within reason, shall be borne by my estate."

Her remains were taken from the Treadway Mortuary of Napa, California, to the Hudson Funeral Home in Oakland, to be buried in Mountain View Cemetery. Her husband, Alonzo, is buried there in the soldier's plot and Jennie's remains are buried in a family plot that adjoins the Elk plot, with her daughter, Priscilla Anne, her son, William, and her granddaughter, Eliza Viola Prentiss.

The day of her funeral, November 29, 1922, was a cold, blustery day. In gray light friends gathered at the Butler-Hudson Funeral Home at 8th and Myrtle streets in Oakland. Come to pay their last respects to Jennie were many of the Mothers' Charity Club members, and also in attendance were Eliza Shepard, Bess Maddern London, and her two daughters, Joan and Bess.

The Rev. J. M. Brown in the eulogy made mention of Jennie's services rendered to Jack London and of the love that had borne her through all her relationships. For the peace of her soul he called out praise for "The Mighty, working whereby He is able to subdue all things unto Himself.

"From henceforth, blessed are the dead who die in the Lord: even so, saith the Spirit, for they rest from their labors."

The Rev. Mr. Brown concluded the committal services with an apt quotation:

> " 'Servant of God, well done!
> Thy glorious warfare's past,
> The battle's fought, the race is won,
> And thou art crowned at last.' "

Sorrowing friends at the burial site were Mrs. Bessie Maddern London, Mrs. Eliza Shepard, Joan London, Bess London, members of Mothers' Charity Federated Club Mrs. Davis Sloan, Mrs. Silvester R. Hackett, and Mrs. Esther Jones Lee, and other close friends.

APPENDIX

Following is a talk Eugene Lasartemay gave to the public on many occasions, attended once by Irving Shepard and Joan London. This talk was also later given at the Oakland Free Library on the occasion of the opening of the Jack London Room, 1972. This opening was attended by Bess London (Jack's youngest daughter), Mary Rudge, James Sisson (a Jack London historian), and numerous others were present.

Before I begin my story, I want to call your attention to the fact that one can start as early as 1781 in California history and find black men establishing, building, exploring, mining, buffalo hunting, fur trading, and Christianizing in company with the Mission Padres and early expeditionary groups. Some of these black men were performing slave labor. Others, self-employed by reason of being free, were gleaning a personal living or working to buy the freedom of loved ones still held in chattel bondage.

In 1828, the first known slave, William Warren, is recorded in the annals of California history.

The archives of California history show black men doing things that helped to build our great state and which made an impact on the nation. We cannot let the history of their achievements, which are being brought to light, return to oblivion. A great deal of the black man's eminent history is lost forever; much was unrecorded; but what is in possession must be brought to the knowledge of the inquiring minds.

Now to my story of the contributions of a Negro woman who was an instrument that set a course of history here in Oakland!

Many of you who are present have not had a reading acquaintance with Jack London, the author. But many of you have often mentioned the name Jack London Square. In this square, you have enjoyed a stroll just sightseeing, sat indoors in regal atmosphere of social festivity, danced, wined, and dined. This is the place named for the man of literary note who inspired the city of Oakland to establish the famed and cosmopolitan memorial.

One of Jack London's best-sellers was *The Sea Wolf*. The book was based on the whaling vessel captained by one William T. Shorey, a prominent Negro pioneer of Oakland. William Shorey was a seaman and became the first known black sea captain who navigated to the Alaskan and Arctic waters. Down on the waterfront, Jack gave eager ear to Shorey's tales of the polar north. These tales made most exciting lore. He and Jack talked many times about the masterly skills in handling sea craft.

On August 5, 1907, the city of Oakland named a street in honor of Captain Shorey. It is Shorey Street—located in the extreme end of West Oakland.

Very little of Jack's early life was generally known, or, if known, it was not discussed openly. A brief glance behind his life screen will reveal the causes which determined his emotional traits, shaped his rugged qualities, and decided his destiny.

Jack was born in San Francisco on January 12, 1876. His father was said to be W. H. Chaney, his mother Flora Wellman. Jack's body was frail and undernourished, which added to the pointed rejection by the mother. The mother was unable to furnish sufficient breast milk to feed him. No other type of milk could be digested.

Flora Wellman's doctor was deeply concerned about further injury to Baby Jack's health. At this time, the doctor had another patient who had lost a child. He and Flora Wellman agreed to secure the breast-feeding services of this sorrowing mother. It was at this point in Jack's infancy that Jennie Prentiss made a life-saving entrance.

Mrs. Jennie Prentiss was born in the year 1832 in the state of Tennessee and named Daphna Virginia Parker—just thirty-three years before Abraham Lincoln severed the chains of involuntary servitude in the South.

Jennie had the proud air and bearing of the well-born. She was tall, modestly sedate, and intelligent. These distinguishing traits indicated that she had spent nearly all of her thirty-three years in the "Big House" on the Parker plantation in welcome association with a mistress—gracious but exacting in demands. Jennie had been taught to practice discipline. She had also learned to keep her own counsel. She spoke nothing which would tend to jeopardize her own personal interests or those close to her.

Jennie's very dark complexion was in sharp contrast to the nearly white skin of her husband, Alonzo Prentiss.

It was in Tennessee in 1866 that she was wooed, won, and married by this Alonzo Thomas Prentiss, who was born in 1819 in Ohio. He was a Civil War veteran, having served in Company 1, Ohio Infantry, as first lieutenant in the Forty-ninth Regiment.

Jennie and Alonzo's first child, William G., was born in Nashville in 1867.

The three Prentisses left Tennessee and took up residence in

Chicago, Illinois. Here in 1873, Priscilla Anne was born. As providence would favor, the Prentisses were fortunate to live on property owned by a wealthy and influential Negro citizen by the name of John G. Jones.

In the days following the Gold Rush in California, the virgin West was growing rapidly. Mr. Prentiss's carpentering ability was a convincing assurance that he could succeed there. Hence Mr. Prentiss left Chicago, bringing his family to San Francisco. They settled at 17 Priest Street in the area now known as Nob Hill. Employment doors for Mr. Prentiss were open. He was accepted on his color, or should we say he was accepted because he lacked evidence of his true color. The subject of color was mute with Jennie. The public could think or reason or conclude whatever they chose.

While at the Priest Street address in January 1876, a stillborn daughter was delivered to Jennie and Alonzo Prentiss. In this same month, Jack Chaney came into the world. Doubtless the chartered and resistless course for the human spirit of Jack was to be implanted under the influence of Jennie Prentiss. A spirit which later was to be misunderstood, misinterpreted, and to become a mystery to his close friends and those persons afar off.

As a result of Lieutenant Prentiss's acquaintance with one John London, Flora Wellman, Jack's mother, was introduced. Friendship between the two culminated in marriage. Mr. and Mrs. London with Mr. London's own two daughters, moved to Oakland.

In 1879, little Jack at three years of age was still living in the home of the Prentisses. They too moved to Oakland and for a brief time resided at Fifth and Brush streets, thence to East Oakland at the corner of Dennison and Kennedy streets. This location was near the foot of 23rd Avenue.

At the age of seven, Jack had adopted the surname of London. He was a student at John Swett School, nearly fifteen blocks from his home.

We must recall before the year 1875 attendance at a school for white children was denied to Negroes, Mexicans, Indians, and Orientals. Even following the integration of schools, an aura of racial intolerance still persisted.

Priscilla Anne Prentiss had the responsibility of escorting Jack to and from school until he was old enough to care for himself physically. Children were quick to make stinging remarks about family ties or association with a person of color.

As Jack grew older, he became more sensitive to the racial fanaticism displayed by older men and women, also. He tried to avoid hearing the pupils' giggles, the taunting remarks and insulting names shouted at him. He could not meet the wanton challenge. It was a trial that brought endless despair.

Even in the classroom there were days when he would slip down in his seat. He hoped the teacher would overlook him and not bring his presence to the attention of the pupils. They were unaware that he was fostered and protected by persons of color who loved him dearly.

It is probable that Jack resorted to defensive violence in early life. I learned, however, that he employed a strategy. He took another route to Mama Jennie's home or continued to walk past her house until all children were out of sight. There was no soothing counsel that understanding Mama Jennie could proffer. And for Jack's broken spirit there was no abiding or welding substance.

Mrs. Prentiss was a member of the First African Methodist Episcopal Church which, in early years, was located on 15th Street between Market and West streets. Here Jack was taken to Sunday school and church. In manhood, Jack made a sizable monetary contribution to this church.

The year 1885 came. John London, his wife and two daughters returned to Oakland from another county. They took residence on San Pablo Avenue and 22nd Street.

The Prentisses were living at 825 18th Street, and Jack and Priscilla Anne were attending Cole School.

In this same year, 1885, Jack was in the third grade. He graduated in May 1891 from the ninth grade—a straight A student. Now at fifteen and one-half years of age, Jack was trying to make his own way in the world—hustling to wrest a living by doing anything that would yield a paltry sum. He tried with earnestness to support himself. He sought to be independent, but his struggling efforts brought only small returns. Jack could not derive a livelihood or even seek to exist on the income of his mother and stepfather.

Whenever he was in dire need of some necessity, although small, he knew where there was cash to spare—at Mama Jennie and Papa Alonzo's. Papa Alonzo was earning a good living at the carpenter trade, in addition to receiving a military pension.

"Jack," Mama Jennie was often heard to say, "you know where I keep my money. Take what you need."

True. There was money to spare—money to pay for Jack's first saidlboat—a cash sale of three hundred dollars.

Between 1890 and December 1903, Jennie had buried her son, daughter, and husband. She was all alone. In a year or so, Jennie moved into the household of Jack London's ex-wife, Bess. This home was at 519 31st Street. Jennie began to assume the care of Bess and Joan, Jack's two daughters. For the first time, she was called Mammy by these two little girls.

About this time Jennie learned that Jack had written a book in which

184

he referred to her as "Mammy," the term his daughters used. Jennie was grievously hurt. She confided to Mrs. Esther Jones Lee, her friend, that she had upbraided Jack for the disrespect imposed on her as he had always recognized her as his foster mother.

Jennie Prentiss and Flora Wellman London, Jack's natural mother, became fast friends. They lived close to one another. We find the Prentisses around the year 1896 living at 1063 26th Avenue, the Londons at 1327 25th Avenue. Jack was living at 645 25th Avenue.

On February 19, 1906, Jack closed a deal for the purchase of property at 490 27th Street, Oakland. This property became the home of Jennie and Flora, who had also become a widow. Jack sold this property in 1908, but the two women continued to occupy the home until after Jack's death in 1916.

Jennie left Flora at this house, moving to 924 East 10th Street, around the corner from the home of a Mr. and Mrs. John Wilds, her close friends. In 1920, Jennie moved to 809 East 11th Street. In 1922 she negotiated and purchased quarters in the Home for Aged and Infirm Colored People at Beulah, a site where Mills College is now located. Following a few months of domicile, Jennie became ill. In October 1922, she was committed to Napa State Hospital, where she passed away in one month at the age of ninety.

Jennie Prentiss was buried at Mountain View Cemetery, Oakland, in the Elks' plot beside her son William, daughter Priscilla Anne, and granddaughter Viola. Alonzo Prentiss, the husband, father, and grandfather, lies in the old soldiers' plot, also in Mountain View Cemetery.

Jack London made his last will and testament on May 24, 1911. He did not forget his benefactor. The will read: "To my Old Mammy, Jennie Prentiss, my estate shall pay fifteen dollars each month, also and in addition, my estate shall see that she is suitably housed and shall pay for said housing, also any expense extraordinary accompanying her demise, within reason, shall be borne of my estate."

Jennie Prentiss was a benefactor to Jack London. I feel a half has now been told. The other half will never be known.

Eugene Lasartemay wrote many letters over the years concerning Jennie Prentiss's exclusion from history, in attempts to restore her to public knowledge for her important role in nurturing Jack London as his foster mother, guide, and inspirer. He states, "In 1968 on a photographic field trip with my camera club, we went to Valley of the Moon, the home of Jack London which thousands of people visit annually. This is the home of his second wife, which has been converted into a museum. There on the museum walls the State of California had placed a picture of all the people who were close to Jack London. Among them is even

Oakland's first librarian, Ina Coolbrith—but not Jennie Prentiss."

Eugene Lasartemay challenged the state's resource officer on the omission of Jennie Prentiss, in a letter, and by telephone. The written response said this was a very important question. But the question was not answered. Mr. Lasartemay's letter had stated: "In your museum you show those who were close to Jack London . . . but not Jennie Prentiss and family . . . Why has the State of California failed to search for the facts and inform the public in your splendid museum? . . . For history's sake I hope that you will be instrumental in having thie vital information available for others to enjoy . . . " This was an omission that was never rectified.

In Mr. Lasartemay's possession are other letters such as one he wrote to an Oakland Tribune columnist as to why Jennie Prentiss was omitted in a newspaper story. The response was that "limitations of space," not "the fact that Mrs. Jennie Prentiss was a Negro" accounts for "her being left out of the Jack London story." This response was sent to Mr. Lasartemay dated December 6, 1966.

His long history of research and of writing to others in order to bring to the public information about Jennie Prentiss and her family which otherwise time would erase did not bear the full fruit he had hoped for from his cultivation of her life story with Jack London. Jack's daughter, Joan London, was his comfort and supporter in his efforts from time to time and he still treasures a letter written to him by her on March 12, 1970, in which she encourages his research.

Others of the family who encouraged Eugene Lasartemay were Mr. Irving Shepard, son of Mrs. Eliza London Shepard, the stepsister of Jack London, who attended with Joan London one of the many talks Eugene Lasartemay gave on Jennie Prentiss and Jack London. Irving Shepard also invited Eugene Lasartemay to visit him, and searched for old letters and papers and photographs to be of assistance but most had accidentally burned. While attending with Joan London a talk by Mr. Lasartemay, Mr. Shepard pulled from a coat pocket a cancelled check of the monthly pension Jack London sent to Jennie Prentiss and presented this documentation to Mr. Lasartemay with the words "we thought you should have this!" The check is drawn on The Merchants National Bank of San Francisco, February 27, 1911. Check no. 210, paying to Jennie Prentiss on order $15.00, signed by Jack London.

The title of Mr. Lasartemay's talk was: "Jennie Prentiss—Jack London's Benefactor." The gift of Jack's check to Jennie acknowledged their mutually loving lasting relationship.

THE MERCHANTS NATIONAL BANK No. 240
OF SAN FRANCISCO.

SAN FRANCISCO. FEB 27 1911 191

PAY TO Jennie Prentiss OR ORDER $ 15.00

Fifteen ——————————— DOLLARS

Jack London

24
MAR 3 1911

Front and back of a check given by Jack London to his foster mother, Jennie Prentiss, a
monthly love gift to support and sustain her in her old age.

To dear Mammy Jennie:—

With best
love from one who
loves you well.
Your son,
Jack.

Piedmont, California,
May 11, 1903.

Jack London's inscription in his book given to Jennie Prentiss, now in the Oakland History room of the Oakland Free Library.

Dear (Mammy Jennie:—

Well, it took a long time to pay back what I borrowed from you with which to buy the "Razzle Dazzle." But I learned a lot about life when I sailed the "Razzle Dazzle."

And here is loving you, and always lovingly,

your white pickaninny Jack London,

Glen Ellen, Calif.

Sept. 24, 1916.

Jack London's testimonial to Jennie Prentiss, his foster mother, in her book now in the Oakland History room of the Oakland Free Library.